CHILDHOOD OF THE MAGICIAN

A
Liveright
New
Writer

*In the 1920s Liveright was the first publisher of
William Faulkner, Ernest Hemingway, e.e. cummings,
Eugene O'Neill, Dorothy Parker, Sherwood Anderson,
Hart Crane, Nathanael West, to mention just a few.
Now the new Liveright is once again publishing the
first works of America's most promising young
writers in the Liveright New Writers Series. Its
innovative format provides clothbound quality at
near paperback prices. With this series
Liveright seeks to encourage today's young
writers, provide the best of contemporary writing
for the reading public, and again play a part in
discovering tomorrow's greats.*

NANCY WILLARD

CHILDHOOD OF THE MAGICIAN

LIVERIGHT New York

These stories originally appeared in the following publications: "The Child-hood of the Magician," in the *Quarterly Review of Literature*; "The Hucklebone of a Saint," in *Perspective*, reprinted in *The Lively Anatomy of God* (Eakins Press); "The Doctrine of the Leather-Stocking Jesus," in *Audience*; "Theo's Girl," in the *Massachusetts Review*; "Judgment City & Lonely Town," in the *Chicago Review*; "Going Blind," in the *Massachussetts Review*; and "Sinner, Don't You Waste that Sunday," in the *Chicago Review*.

Liveright
386 Park Avenue South
New York, N.Y. 10016

1.987654321

ISBN 0-87140-571-1

Library of Congress Catalog Card Number 73-82429

MANUFACTURED IN THE UNITED STATES OF AMERICA

*For Eric and James
and my mother and father*

CONTENTS

PART I

CHILDHOOD OF THE MAGICIAN

The Childhood of the Magician

In those days I wanted to be a magician. I was seven and Kirsten was twelve when Father took us for the last time to the party given by the chemistry department for faculty children. In our identical red velvet jumpers, we sat with forty other children in the big lecture hall. Someone had drawn wreathes and Santas on the blackboards and put up a Christmas tree by the demonstration table in front. We nibbled the popcorn balls passed out by old Mrs. Buelo, the department secretary, and waited for the show to begin.

At last the magician appeared. He was a young man with a heavy thatch of blond hair and very thick glasses. His labcoat flapped around him like an enormous nightshirt. Briskly he took his place behind the table and set out an impressive array of beakers, tubes, and calipers. He lit the Bunsen burner under a pot and peered into it anxiously.

The lights over the audience dimmed. The magician picked up a steel pipe, dipped it into the pot, and brought it out again. At the end hung a wad of molton glass, which he turned till light caught it. Then he pressed the pipe to his lips and began to blow. His face grew red, his cheeks swelled. And suddenly I saw a swan on the end of the pipe.

I knew about glassblowing. I'd met the old man who blew the special equipment for the lab. He was pink and bald and had huge cheeks, like an aging squirrel, and he taught my father's students to blow flasks and bulbs and pipettes. After they'd blown enough flasks to please the glassblower, they blew toys to please themselves. A glass flute that played. A glass trumpet with movable valves. Half my mind argued that this wasn't magic. The other half argued that it was, because I knew that if I blew into that pipe, no swan would come forth for me.

"Look!" whispered Kirsten.

After the swan came a bell and a ball and another swan. We all clapped. The young man blew silver into them, bowed, and handed them to some children in the front row. I thought I would die of envy.

"Now he's going to make the star. He made that last year."

He lifted the pipe to his lips. Soon I forget to covet the swans and bells; the blob of glass was leaping out, point by point, until a star glowed at the end of the pipe. Even the grown-ups clapped. I saw myself blowing a whole universe of glass. If I started now, by the time I was twelve I could be a fairly good magician. I asked for a magician set for Christmas and received the Sears Roebuck Deluxe, the most expensive one in the catalogue.

The first thing I learned was that magic depends on natural ability, not on equipment. The Sears Roebuck Deluxe included everything the young magician might require to start him on a brilliant career. A black wand. A moustache. A book of instructions for doing simple tricks with string, pennies, and a drinking glass. These came nestled in a fake alligator bag lined with cardboard, just like the Sears Roebuck Deluxe Play Doctor set. Slots cut into the cardboard held the wand, the moustache, the book, and the plastic drinking glass, so you could carry the set around.

Now the wand was very good for doing the tricks described in the book, but not for doing anything more complicated. You couldn't wave it over a dish of spinach, for example, and sink it into the ground. In vain I waved it over my head, trying to shrink myself just a little, so that I would not be a head taller than everyone else in my class. After a week of practicing magic to no effect, I asked my mother to return the set. She refused.

"You can do magic with it, but not miracles."

"What's a miracle?" I asked, knowing very well what one was.

"Christ turning the water into wine. That's a miracle," said my mother. She knew I knew this already and sealed her mouth into a hard line to signify that the subject was closed.

Christ, the arch-magician. No wand, no fake moustache, just whatever He happened to have lying around—a few loaves of bread, a basket of fishes, a barrel of water—that's all it took to make a good show when you had the talent.

If He did it, could I do it?

I asked Miss Brandenburger, the hunchbacked spinster who taught my Sunday school class in the basement of the Lutheran church. I came early and sleeved her as she was setting out the workbooks and crayons.

"Miss Brandenburger, if I wanted to turn a barrel of water into wine, could I do it?"

She put down the workbooks and looked me in the eye.

"What do you want with a barrel of wine?"

"Nothing. I just want to know if I could do it."

Miss Brandenburger's forehead, pulled tight by the braids pinned across her scalp, twitched into a frown.

"Do you know what happens to people who drink a barrel of wine? They bloat up and die. Does your mother know you want a barrel of wine?"

"I don't want a barrel of wine!" I yelled, and Miss Brandenburger pressed her finger to her thin lips.

I didn't tell her that I hardly knew what wine was. No one in our house drank it, not from moral scruples, but from ignorance. Somebody once brought a bottle of Mogen-David into the house on New Year's Eve, and Mother let Kirsten and me take a teaspoon of it—she held the spoon—as a sort of initiation rite. Then she took one herself and rolled up her eyes like a dead turkey. *I believe I'm drunk,* she exclaimed. She said it whenever anyone served her rum cake at a party. *I can feel it going to my head.* I could very well imagine what a whole barrel of wine would do to her. Or to me.

"Oh, Miss Brandenburger," I bellowed. "I just wanted to learn how to make a miracle."

Miss Brandenburger looked relieved.

"You can't learn to make them," she said in a kinder voice. "It takes faith. But if you have faith, you have only to ask in God's name that this mountain be removed—" she waved histrionically toward the window which faced the flat churchyard, crowded with dandelions and gravestones "—and it shall be removed."

Clearly, faith had it all over wands. The next evening I decided to test my faith. There was no point in trying to move mountains. That seemed awfully presumptuous for a beginner, and besides, there weren't any mountains within three hundred miles of Detroit. I would start with something small. I chose a milk-china hen sitting on a china nest that held my mother's hairpins. I could hear my mother downstairs, unsnapping bridge tables; the ladies would arrive in half an hour. I set the hen at the edge of the dressing table, perched myself on the bed, and whispered, "Move, hen!"

It moved not an inch. I leaned forward and pushed it ever so slightly with my finger, so it would understand.

"Move, hen!"

Suddenly I felt faith filling me up, a full tank of faith. I watched the hen carefully, certain it would move now. I leaned forward again and gave it another little push. Galvanized, it leaped off the edge of the table and plummeted to the floor, where it broke as if preordained into four regular pieces: the hen into two, the nest into two. I stuck the scattered hairpins in a drawer, picked up the pieces of the hen, and flushed them down the toilet. The plumber arrived in the first throng of guests, and two hours later when they went upstairs to find their coats, the toilet was sitting, white and shy like a rabbit, in the middle of the hall.

Two weeks later—it was the first Sunday in May—my mother informed Kirsten and me that a magician was coming to call on us.

"A real one?" I asked eagerly.

"Well, call him a sleight-of-hand artist," cautioned my father. "A lab assistant, actually. Haig Saunders."

"I thought Haig was a student," said my mother. She was

making a large pitcher of lemonade. I wished it were mine alone.

"He *was* a student. He quit to take care of his wife. She got hurt in an accident."

My mother nodded understandingly. "How did you happen to ask him over?"

"Well, now that you mention it, I didn't ask him. He said he wondered if we needed a babysitter."

"But we don't need a babysitter. Kirsten is old enough to sit this year."

"I'm old enough to sit this year," said Kirsten, dumping cubes of ice from the tray into the pitcher.

My father looked bewildered. He was twenty years older than my mother and had always left to her the matter of taking care of us.

"Haig seemed to think if you met him, you'd feel differently," he said. It sounded like an apology.

That afternoon, I watched for a dark-haired man named Haig Saunders to appear on our front walk. He'd taken the first semester of my father's introductory chemistry class, and he lived rent-free above a funeral parlor, where he answered the telephone at night. He made a little money as an amateur magician.

I remember him standing in the front hall, nodding cheerfully at my mother, watching us all slyly, I thought, from behind enormous sunglasses. In his arms he held his wife, Julia, whose straight brown hair hung loose down her back and whose legs dangled like sticks in the trim black slacks she wore. Her face was powdered very white and she quaked all over. Her head nodded like a bell, and her hands shook when she extended them to my parents. She looked so grim and helpless that I knew I shouldn't laugh.

"Her chair is outside," explained Haig. "Julia, meet my professor."

My father nodded, pained.

"May I bring her into the living room?"

He darted in and set her down on one of the easy chairs by the fireplace and ran out to the car. Mother and Father and Kirsten and I stood around and avoided Julia's eyes.

"Don't mind me," she snapped. "I was in a car accident. These things happen to people."

But already Haig was back, unfolding the wheelchair for her. Tenderly he lifted her into it; she grimaced and said nothing, as he straightened up, shuffling his feet together nervously. In his leather jacket and cowboy boots he did not look like the other students I'd met—mild, serious young men, who were brilliant, I knew, but without much style. Jagged lines and old scars welted Haig's face, which was as flamboyantly broken and mended as a stained-glass window. Under his thick black hair, his head came to a point at the top, like a lipstick.

"Well, I suppose you want to see a trick," he said briskly.

Kirsten and I nodded and plumped down on the sofa. And here was the first trick: Father disappeared and so did Mother. Julia sat in her wheelchair, her back turned to us, as if changed to stone. The house fell quiet, the street outside fell quiet, the blackbirds in the blossoming pear trees beyond the open window fell quiet. Kirsten and I sat alone in the universe with a magician who pulled out a little canister labeled "Peanut Brittle," and handed it to me.

"Open it," he commanded.

I opened it and saw nothing.

"It's empty, right?"

He closed the canister and shook it vigorously, hopping first on one foot and then on the other.

"Abracadabra."

And he handed it to Kirsten.

"Open it, *niña*."

Even before she took it from him, I could hear the faint buzzing of things inside being called forth. She lifted the lid and a huge purple snake sprang out and landed on the piano. Kirsten and I screamed, then broke into giggles. Haig, his face deadpan, was already reaching for the next trick.

"I always dress properly when I call on young ladies," he explained, bowing slightly as he flexed his fingers and eased them into the gloves. Suddenly his confidence turned to alarm.

"My flowers! Did I forget my flowers?"

Hastily he pulled off the left glove. Out popped a bouquet of red roses; the glove shriveled away like a dead skin. Now he pulled off the right one. Blue roses for Kirsten, because she had red hair, and red roses for me.

"But of course, real flowers are better than paper ones. I'll bring you real ones next time I come."

The roses disappeared. In their place he offered me a velvet bag which hung on a circle of gold at the end of a rod, the sort of ceremonious container you could use for collection at church.

"Reach into the bag, *niña.*"

I reached in and pulled out a red silk scarf.

"Now, make sure the bag is empty."

I thrashed my hand around inside, then peered into the bag. It was dark and spacious as a stomach.

"Now replace the scarf."

Folding it carefully, I laid it at the bottom. Haig shook the bag hard, closed his eyes, muttered to himself, then thrust the bag at me.

"Can you find the scarf?"

I felt something soft and pulled my hand up fast.

"It's blue!" shouted Kirsten. Blue as a summer sky. A magician, a maker of miracles. Rabbits out of hats. Water into wine. Pebbles into gold. Suddenly Julia gave a little sigh, Father came back into the room, and the spell was broken.

At dinner that night, he told us about Haig Saunders.

"Haig's father disappeared right after Haig was born, so his mother had to bring him up alone. He left Detroit after high school and worked his way across the country toward California. The army rejected him and he went—"

"Why did the army reject him?" demanded Mother.

"His head," explained Father. "They couldn't find a helmet to fit it. You didn't notice his head?"

"Kind of pointed," said Kirsten politely.

"Well, he combs his hair to hide it, but it's very pointed. I never saw a head like it before in my life. Well, when the army turned him down he went to New Mexico and got a job doing the sacred eagle dance in a traveling rodeo."

"What's an eagle dance?" I inquired.

"Why, that's a dance the Indians do to make the rain come. Haig told me how he wore an eagle head over his own head, and an eagle's wings over his arms, and every time he danced he brought down the rain. Which was the whole point of the dance, of course, but bad for the tourist business. He was asked to move on."

My father paused for questions. Like skeptical students, Mother, Kirsten, and I chewed our macaroni and ruminated in silence.

"Well, it's true!" exclaimed Father defensively.

"Nobody's crossing you," said Mother. "Go on."

"All right. After he left Santa Fé he rode broncos and bulls across Nevada and ended up in San Francisco. He lived at the edge of Chinatown and everybody thought he was Chinese. A man from South Dakota who'd lost his money in real estate was starting a Chinese Opera Company, and invited Haig to join."

"Is Haig a Chinese or an Indian?" asked Kirsten.

My father shook his head.

"I don't know what he is."

"How old is he?"

"He told me he's twenty-two."

"And how did he get here?" asked Mother.

"He won five hundred dollars on the horses and decided to go to college."

"Well, I hope you told him we don't need a babysitter. Did you?"

"I forgot," said Father.

Usually my father said nothing during dinner, only turned up the radio if Kirsten or I talked too loudly and he couldn't hear the weather and the news. It was the first time I could remember him speaking to us at the table. That in itself was a miracle.

The following Saturday, Mother and Father were getting ready to leave for a football game, when something exploded in front of the house. Running to the windows, we saw a man in a black leather jacket and boots parking a motorcycle on our sidewalk.

"For pity's sake," cried Mother. "It's the police."

We hurried downstairs, but not fast enough. Haig knocked on the door and opened it and stepped inside.

"Thought you might need me," he said cheerfully. "I had the afternoon off. You want a little ride on 'The Yellow Peril,' Professor?"

"The what?"

" 'The Yellow Peril.' The motorcycle, Professor. Don't worry, I'll be very careful."

Now I knew that getting my father on a motorcycle took magic. Or faith. Or both. Twice, the motorcycle tore past the house. My father hung on hard, as helpless as a soul being carried off to hell. His gray hair stood straight up like fur on a scared cat, his shirt sleeves winged out behind him. Across the street, Mrs. Hanson was shaking her mop out the window. I saw the mop-head drop off, but she didn't, and she kept on shaking the stick until the cycle roared toward us a third time, and Haig drew it to a stop. My father limped across the lawn, a little bowlegged.

"Hot ankles," was all he would say. "Makes your ankles very hot. It's the exhaust."

"Make him promise not to take the girls on that thing," warned my mother.

Haig promised, but we didn't, and we soon found his promises weren't worth a straw. The moment the family car drove out of sight, Haig proposed we ride to Saint Joseph's and visit Julia. He always visited her at mealtimes, he explained, and he felt bad about going alone. Kirsten and I were elated. Haig hoisted first me and then Kirsten onto the back seat of the cycle.

"Ready?"

I opened my mouth to say wait a minute because I wanted to tie my sneaker, and then everything blew away. Words, shoelaces, braids, hair-ribbons, all gone. Huge hot winds tried to lift me from my seat. After a few minutes I opened my eyes and saw within six inches of us, the massive side of a Mayfair Moving Van. Kirsten was squeezing my neck in her arms; I closed my eyes and hung onto Haig's leather jacket till the cycle slowed down, sputtered and stopped, and Haig climbed off.

Before us squatted a huge brick building where hundreds of windows twinkled.

"You ever been to Saint Joseph's before?"

"No," I said.

"Yes," said Kirsten, "When Grandmother died."

Haig took us each by the hand and herded us into the vestibule, past a large chipped statue of the Virgin Mary and a desk where several women sat busily typing. Beyond them, a man in a blue uniform was peering out of an elevator crowded with doctors in long white coats and elderly people carrying plants.

"Wait!" shouted Haig, and he hurled us between the doors, which snapped shut behind us. The other passengers glanced at us distastefully, then averted their eyes.

"Four," said one of the doctors.

"Six," said Haig.

"Eight," came a chorus of other voices.

Lights flashed over the door, which hissed open and expelled the doctors. We rode up two more floors. The lobby was deserted, except for the statue of a monk holding a child and a crucifix. I wanted to touch it, but Haig urged me along. He began to look very sad, not just his face but his whole body. At the end of the hall, we paused in the doorway of a large room full of beds.

"Well," said Haig, "Here we are."

I let my eyes roam over the faces that turned toward the sound of Haig's voice. Old faces, with punched-in smiles. No teeth, not much hair.

"Where's Julia?" asked Kirsten.

"Over there."

She was propped up against a heap of pillows, watching us. Haig's sadness slipped away like dew; he approached her almost shyly.

"Well, old girl, how are you feeling? Brought some friends."

"So I notice. You afraid to come up by yourself?"

I tried to smile brightly at Julia, but found myself staring past her at the odd assortment of bottles and dishes that cluttered her bedside table. Kleenex, two water glasses, three pill bottles, and an untouched meal on a tray.

"You remember the girls," said Haig, shuffling his feet. "I'm keeping an eye on them during the football game. Are you comfortable? Is there anything I can get you?"

"You can get that damn priest to let me alone," said Julia, combing her fingers through her hair. Her hand shook, her hair spilled over her face. "Him I don't need. Tell him anything. Tell him I'm Jewish."

"What does he say?" asked Haig.

"Says I'm being punished for my sins," snapped Julia, glowering.

Haig sighed. He pulled the little table close and the soup slopped over and trickled into the corner of the tray. Julia snorted.

"You're almost as good at spilling things as I am."

"Open," said Haig. He held her chin in his hand and brought the spoon to her mouth, and Julia made hard swallowing sounds.

I wished I could disappear on the spot. A grown woman having to be fed! Kirsten and I made a great show of disinterest and wandered out into the ward. Thirty pairs of eyes gaped at us from faces as blank as dinnerplates. Everyone except Julia wore white nightshirts, which made them look as if they belonged to the hospital. Julia wore a pretty quilted robe and a flowered sweater over it.

"Out of the way, please."

A buxom nurse pushed a wagon past us, loaded with dirty trays and half-eaten lunches.

"Excuse us," said Kirsten.

The nurse smiled and wheeled the wagon toward Julia's bed.

"Are these your children, Mr. Saunders?"

A look of acute pain crossed Haig's face.

"No," said Julia.

"Oh." The nurse stopped smiling. "Don't hurry, Mrs. Saunders. I'll be back for your tray later."

"I'm through," said Julia. "You can take it now."

"Shall I get the wheelchair?" asked Haig. His eyes followed the nurse as she left the room. "A little ride to the end of the corridor. Change of scenery."

Julia curled her lips into a smile.

"Just what I need. A change of scenery."

"Well, if there's nothing I can do for you, I guess we ought to go."

"Sure," agreed Julia. "You've done your rounds for today."

He bent down and kissed her, though she turned her cheek away ever so slightly, and her head bobbed up and down, and her hand, still shaking, tried to wave him away. We rode the elevator down in silence, the only passengers in it. On our way out of the building, Haig stopped and got three bags of pistachios from a vending machine beside the Virgin Mary, and we sat out on the curb in front of the hospital to eat them.

"Julia is in a lot of pain. Don't mind if she seems grouchy," he apologized.

"I don't mind," chirped Kirsten.

"I like her," I lied. "What happened to her?"

"Car accident. She used to be a different person. Look."

He pulled a fat wallet out of his pocket—fat with pictures, not money, and unfolded a whole sequence of pictures, dim and foggy images behind the scratched plastic covers. First, Julia and Haig on a beach, then Julia and Haig in front of a house, then Julia and Haig on the motorcycle, then a fancy card with Haig's picture and the words "Ordinary seaman, coalpasser, wiper, messman" written over it. The picture of Haig hardly flattered him; his eyes were drooping closed and his cropped hair showed the odd shape of his head. A magician's head, pointed like a magician's cap. Julia hadn't changed, but in the pictures her face seemed prettier.

"Where was this one taken?" inquired Kirsten politely, pointing to the beach picture.

"Lake Erie."

"And what's this funny card?" I asked.

"That's from when I worked on the boats."

He tucked the pictures away and we cracked pistachios and said nothing for awhile. The sun warmed my back; I wished I knew how to purr. I could hardly feel sorry for anyone when I felt so comfortable myself. Nevertheless, I felt sorry for Haig. Why should a magician put up with these problems?

"If you can do magic," I said, "why can't you cure Julia?"

Haig chewed very slowly, as if he were shaping his reply on his tongue.

"Too old," he said at last.

"Miss Brandenburger says that if you ask for a mountain to be removed, it will be removed," I assured him. "If you ask it in God's name."

"There's the rub," said Haig. "I don't believe in God."

Kirsten and I could not have been more stunned if he'd disappeared in a puff of smoke.

"Why not?" she asked.

"Never heard much about Him when I was a kid. And it's too late now."

"If you started right away," I suggested, but he lifted his hand to cut me off.

"Nope. God isn't much interested in people like me. The trouble is, if I believed in God, I'd have to ask Him why He let the accident happen in the first place."

I leaned my head against his leather sleeve. He smelled almost as good as my cat. Suddenly he reached over and tweaked my braids.

"Have you removed any mountains lately, *niña*?"

"Not yet," I said, a little stiffly. "But I'm practicing."

"That's good. You keep on practicing."

He patted me on the head, stood up, and threw his empty pistachio bag into the gutter. Hesitantly Kirsten threw hers down, and I threw mine.

"Come on, *niñas*."

"What's *niñas*?" asked Kirsten.

"That's Spanish. That means you're my little girls."

"Oh," said Kirsten. "We're not really yours, though."

Haig smiled mysteriously.

"And maybe I'm not really Haig Saunders."

We stared at him.

"Maybe," he said softly, "I'm really a bear in human shape.

Maybe at night I turn into a bear. Don't you think I look like a bear?"

Silence. I glanced at his arm in its sleeve of leather. His wrist. Very hairy. Bearlike. He lumbered to his feet, hung his arms in front of him like paws, and shuffled his feet. Several cars slowed down, and he stopped dancing.

"I know a good song about a bear. A man meets a bear and tries to push it into his Volkswagen so he can take its picture. And the bear eats up his wife."

He lifted us to our places on the motorcycle and all the way home he sang about the bear. Wrapping my arms around him, I could feel the song vibrating his chest, but could hear nothing. Later Kirsten wondered if we ought to tell Mother that we'd taken a ride on the motorcycle. We decided against it.

Two evenings later, my mother opened the front door to let the cat out and nearly collided with Haig who was standing on the steps. He wore, on his left arm, a glove that nearly covered his elbow. On the glove sat an enormous bird with one yellow eye and a hooked beak.

"How nice to see you," said my mother, glancing at the bird. "But I'm afraid we're not going anywhere tonight."

"That's all right," smiled Haig. "I just came by to see how you were. Corby and I were out taking the air."

Hearing Haig's voice, we all came to the door.

"I didn't know you kept a bird," said Father. "What kind is it? Looks like a hawk."

"It is a hawk. It belongs to a guy over in the forestry lab. I thought the little girls might like to see one up close."

Haig lowered his wrist. Corby and I confronted each other, eyeball to eyeball. He wore a downy coat of mail; the front feathers, white stippled with brown, lapped over each other like links of chain. Dark feathers fell along his back to form a cape. He fixed his eye on me like a mad preacher.

"Very nice," said Kirsten, stepping back. "Do you let him fly around loose?"

"He's got a string on his foot. He's very clever. Watch."

Haig whipped a yoyo out of his back pocket and let it rise

and fall before the bird's eye. I could almost hear the eye clicking on and off like a light switch. Up. Down. On. Off. On. Presently he would pounce. Haig pocketed the yoyo and shook his head.

"He did it better before he lost his eye. He lost it in a fight with an owl."

"We were just about to sit down for dinner," said Mother. "You're welcome to join us." Her voice trailed off as the bird gave a violent twitch. Haig took her arm and escorted her into the dining room.

"What are you having to eat?"

"Roast beef."

"Corby loves roast beef. And I'm starved."

Kirsten set Haig a place next to her, across from mine, and he drew up a chair and helped himself to the peas with his right hand, and held the bird on his left. My mother omitted the blessing.

"A little meat?" asked my father, pointing to a well-done haunch on the biggest platter.

"After you," said Haig warmly.

"I'm a vegetarian, myself."

"Is that so? Well, I'm not. I'd be very pleased if you'd cut me a slice, Professor."

My father had no more idea how to slice meat than how to fly.

"I'll do it," said Mother quickly.

"Cut it up real small, please," said Haig. "I'd hate to set Corby down. He gets upset when he's not on an arm he knows."

"What does he do when he gets upset?"

"He flies around. No string can hold him. And he gets terrible attacks of diarrhea."

Having cut up the beef into small chunks, my mother was now shredding it.

"Is this small enough?"

"That's fine."

Haig took the plate from her, speared a little roast beef on the end of his fork, and tasted it, like the footman checking the king's goblet for poison, then slipped the hawk a sliver. The yellow beak opened and clamped shut like a voracious flower, the feathered throat bulged and went still.

"How's Julia?" asked Kirsten suddenly.

Sighing deeply, Haig helped himself to the mashed potatoes. "She needs an operation."

"That will be expensive," remarked my father.

"And she keeps wanting to put it off. She's scared, poor girl."

"How long has she been paralyzed?" asked Mother.

"Why, she was paralyzed when I married her."

My father stopped eating, dumbfounded.

"I was driving," said Haig quietly. "I couldn't very well *not* marry her after that, could I?"

The hawk began to beat its wings, and Kirsten jumped from the table.

"He's only stretching himself, just like you do," said Haig. "Sit down, *niña.*"

Then he turned to my father.

"Julia really needs me, you know. You may not see it when we're together, but she does need me. I'd like to make a lot of money and take her to the mineral baths in Arkansas. There are still a lot of things we haven't tried that might help."

After dinner, while Mother cleared the table, Haig showed us a new trick he'd learned: a magic ring that disappeared from his finger and turned up in odd corners of the room, under the carpet, in the bookshelves, on top of the lamp. The bird yawned and shut its eye.

"Corby isn't very polite," observed Kirsten, who never yawned when anyone was looking.

Haig shrugged.

"He's seen this trick before."

"Show me how to do it," I begged.

To my surprise, Haig shook his head.

"Then it'd be no fun anymore. None of it. My tricks are pretty simple. But there's a fellow coming to Detroit with the circus next week that's really good. I suppose your dad takes you to the circus a lot," he added in a wistful voice.

"Mother took us once," I said, "a long time ago."

I didn't tell him that I never even got a seat in that circus because somebody lit a firecracker behind the elephants as they were entering the ring, and they stampeded, and all I saw was the inside of a telephone booth where Mother hastily incarcerated Kirsten and me as the panicked crowd fled.

"I'll take you to this circus," said Haig.

"On the motorcycle?" asked Kirsten.

"No, I got a car."

The morning of the circus I woke up and felt cold all over and I knew I was sick. As I dressed myself, I tried to decide what kind of sickness it was—would it go away in the afternoon if I pretended not to notice it? If it didn't, then I might be very sick indeed by afternoon, and I didn't want to get sick at the circus. On the other hand, I did not want to miss the magician.

I went downstairs, held my breath, swallowed my orange juice, and felt a twinge in my guts. I decided I would not give in. Haig arrived at eleven, nearly an hour later than he had promised.

"I was arrested," he announced in the doorway. "On my way over, I was arrested."

"What for?" exclaimed my mother.

"For carrying an unregistered weapon." He waved his clenched fists. "Every time I go to Detroit, it takes me hours; I have to stop at every police station on the way and register my fists."

And he did a little dance step, right there in the front hall.

"Come on, niñas. We don't want to miss the beginning."

We climbed into the car. This time I let Kirsten sit in front next to Haig, and I stretched out on the back seat and fell asleep. When I woke up, the bad feeling hung just out of sight, and I told myself I felt better. I pushed it out of my mind as Haig led us through the crowded lobby of the indoor stadium and bought our tickets.

The show had already started, but the seats were only sparsely filled, and we found three close to the front. A cold wind rustled our program books, my seat left splinters in my thighs, and my head ached, but I watched with terrible patience the trained bears, the clowns, the rope-walkers, the man who made the horses dance, and in between each act, the Master of Ceremonies, sleek as a seal in black velvet. I watched and applauded and waited for the magician. I had almost given up hope when a man whipped through the curtains, bowed, and began pulling doves out of his vest and shaking them out of his sleeves so casually he might have been giving directions.

"That's him," whispered Haig. "That's Meramera."

Behind the magician, two men rolled out a platform on which stood a microphone, a blackboard, and an organ. A young man sat at the organ playing, "You are my sunshine," while the doves vanished in the rafters overhead.

I stared at the magician, not wanting to miss a single movement. I stared so hard that he disintegrated before my eyes. His long-tailed coat of gold broke off from the rest of him like the wings of an exotic butterfly. My eye traveled down his coat to his hands, which distance reduced to a vague movement. I looked at his head, bobbing like a balloon, and could not join it to the coat and hands. I tried to knit the hands, coat, and head into a whole man, but he was like an object seen too closely, and I could not bring all the parts into focus.

The Master of Ceremonies stepped up to the microphone.

"Ladies and gentlemen, the act you have all been waiting for. The man who needs no introduction, the master magician himself, Meramera!"

I leaned forward and clapped madly, but my praise was lost in the general applause.

"We need a volunteer for the first act. Who would like to volunteer? A little simple hypnotism."

Nobody moved. All over the audience, people craned their necks to see who was getting up. The magician and the Master of Ceremonies whispered like conspirators for several minutes, then the Master of Ceremonies returned to the microphone and said in coaxing tones, "Come, come, ladies and gentlemen. Hypnosis is perfectly harmless. Meramera will not allow his subjects to embarrass themselves in any way."

Suddenly an elderly man in a wrinkled raincoat walked

down the aisle to the stage. The Master of Ceremonies retreated and the magician announced for all to hear, "This is the bravest man in the audience."

Everybody laughed.

"Would you give us your name, sir, and tell us where you work?"

The old man leaned up to the microphone.

"My name is Harold Penny. I work at the Lifeline Insurance Company."

"Well, Mr. Penny, I wonder if you would mind writing your name on our blackboard here, so everyone can see it."

In a large but delicate hand, the old man wrote his name.

"Now, Mr. Penny, if you'll step over here, I'm going to put you into a light trance."

To my great disappointment, it happened so quickly that I did not even know what I'd seen. The magician gently pulled the old man away from the microphone, spoke to him for a few moments, and all at once Mr. Penny was standing motionless, gazing straight ahead of him, while the magician told us what a fine subject he'd found. Then he turned back to Mr. Penny, moving the microphone so everyone could hear.

"Mr. Penny, you are six years old. Write your name. Write it big, please, so we can all see it."

Obediently, the old man picked up the chalk and wrote in huge black letters:

HARY PENNY.

A gasp went up from the audience. The overcoat, the bald head, the paunch and wrinkled skin seemed but a disguise for the child hidden inside. An old man, six years old. At that moment I was older than Harry Penny. Yet at the same time I was not even born.

"What grade are you in, Harry?"

"First grade," piped the old man in a small, high voice.

"You are in the first grade. Tell me the names of your classmates."

Slowly, as if facing an invisible row of children, he counted out the names.

"Johnnie Drew, Jack Morrow, Anna Woloski, Richard Fisher—"

Fifteen names. I listened, astonished at the change in him. Though the draft had stopped blowing, I felt very cold.

"What do you like to do best in school, Harry?"

"I like to sing," shrilled the child in the old man.

"And what do you sing?"

"We sing 'London Bridge is Falling Down.' "

And he sang it very thin and soft, all the verses I knew, and several I didn't.

> *What did the robber do to you,*
> *do to you, do to you?*
> *What did the robber do to you,*
> *my fair lady?*

Suddenly, the magician snapped his fingers. The old man awoke, bewildered, to the rattle of applause. He blinked uncertainly at us, at those countless faces blurring into one unnamable substance, but already the magician was shaking his hand.

"Thank you very much, Mr. Penny. You've been a fine subject. Did you know that you were remembering events that happened to you when you were six years old?"

"I was?"

"Yes, indeed. Tell me, Mr. Penny, can you remember the names of your classmates in first grade?"

Mr. Penny scratched his ear.

"Did I remember that?"

"You did. Can you remember them now?"

"No. Nothing." He considered and shook his head sadly. "Nothing."

"Out of the trance, everything is gone," said the magician significantly. And then, "Thank you for being with us, Mr. Penny."

The old man stepped down into the audience. We followed him with our eyes, a little awed by the powers he didn't know he had.

"And now," said the magician, "I am—"

Then the microphone went dead.

"What's happening?" I whispered to Haig.

"He's going to hypnotise the audience."

"I don't want to be hypnotised," cried Kirsten.

"Well, you don't have to be. If you're afraid, put your fingers in your ears."

The lights lowered; the young man sitting patiently at the organ began to play a slow stately tune. The magician's voice broke over our heads in waves, then flowed over us to the farthest corner of the coliseum.

"You are riding in a boat. You are growing sleepy. Close your eyes. Close them. You can hardly stay awake."

Kirsten leaned across Haig's lap and hissed at me.

"Plug your ears!"

I stuck my fingers in my ears, then pulled them out again. How could I be a magician if I couldn't hear the words? I glanced at Haig; he was listening as calmly as if he were watching a movie. The boat swayed, the organ gushed song, and suddenly I disappeared.

It wasn't like falling asleep. It was as if I had simply ceased to be. No time passes, no morning comes; one walks into a forest, lies down, and walks out again a hundred years later. It was a little like being put under when I had my appendix out, only worse, because I had not expected this. I was gone, and then suddenly I was back, looking from a strange shore at the country I'd just left. Beside me stood a young man, two teen-age girls, and an old woman. They seemed as dazed as I was.

Now I saw Haig standing at the edge of the platform. He grabbed my hand and led me back to my seat.

"Come on, *niñas*. We're going home."

As we crossed the lobby and waded through programs and candy wrappers, I burst into tears, not because I wanted to stay but because Haig looked angry, and I did not know what I had done.

"What happened when I was asleep?"

"Why, not so much," said Kirsten. "He told you it was your

third birthday. And you told all the presents you got that year. You weren't nearly as good as some of the other people."

From Kirsten's voice, tinged with envy, I gathered I'd done rather well.

"Is that all?"

"You said you saw a ship in the sky."

"A ship in the sky?"

Where had the magician found that? Once, in summer, I was standing by the garbage pail and I looked up and saw a ship overhead. White and simple, like a cloud, with three smokestacks. I never mentioned it to anyone and forgot about it because I never saw it again. What was lost to me lay open to the magician.

"Maybe we shouldn't tell Mother," said Kirsten, stealing a glance at Haig.

He was galloping ahead, pulling us behind him. I could feel my feet numbing into lead and my stomach shifting.

"I got to stop. Wait a minute," I whispered.

And before Haig could turn to ask what was the matter, I threw up, relieved that the sickness had finally come and that Haig would carry me the rest of the way to the car.

Mother put me to bed and I stayed there for two weeks. I think I would have gotten up sooner, if it hadn't been for the magician. The first night I woke up and remembered the ship and wondered what else his presence in my past had displaced. I always thought of my mind as a huge office, rather like my father's, only round: a room inside a giant tree trunk. Papers everywhere that came alive when I called them, on shelves, in drawers, in baskets and bins, some neatly stacked, some stuck together with old apple-cores and lollipops. Everything I'd ever thought or done. Sins. These could be forgiven, stamped NULL and VOID, but not destroyed. And the magician had seen them all.

I felt utterly naked. Someone had been walking in my mind.

Worse, he had overturned everything in it. What did I do last Tuesday? I couldn't remember. What was the tune that

Kirsten taught me only the week before? Gone. What were the words of the magician I'd risked everything to hear? They hovered just below the surface of my mind. I could not remember a single one.

I used to imagine that at night the office turned into a projection room and the papers turned into reels. I never knew what was being shown each night until I found the room and started to dream. Now my whole past lay in a tangled heap, feeding into the projector, looping up, and unrolling all over the floor. It snapped and broke under my feet as I waded through the room, trying to put everything back together again.

A piece of footage, torn off from one of the reels; I picked it up and held it to the light, and saw myself asleep on a mattress on a floor. Passing it through my fingers, I recognized my grandmother's house. On another mattress lay Kirsten, and on the sofa under the cuckoo clock slept my mother, and then it ended. I held in my hand a fragment of the night before my great-grandmother's funeral. Now I remembered how the mouse crept into my hair and frightened me, so that I woke up all the relatives, but it was not here, and where could I find the rest of that experience? From which reel had this image broken away?

I sent my body out for meals, and locked myself in the room, and began to mend and sort. Everything. Everything. Old sheet-music memorized for piano recitals years ago. Bible verses learned and forgotten. Strange streets where I'd tried to lose myself for the joy of finding myself again. All lost, all found. All saved, every scrap. I filed, arranged, and put things away, stepping carefully over the strands and papers. A smashed coral, a honeycomb; it ordered itself according to no pattern of mine, and I had no idea how to put the pieces together again. I sat down and wept in the wake of the storm, and slowly the room fogged over like a cataract, as if someone had breathed on it in cold weather.

What had wakened me? What day was it? And what room?

My own room. And beside my bed, a radio and a bell. I felt as light as milkweed. I tried to turn the knobs on the radio, but all the strength had left my fingers. I reached for the bell, but could not lift it.

"Mother!"

She came as quickly as if I'd conjured her out of the air.

"Guess who's downstairs," she said brightly.

"Who?"

"Haig Saunders. He's been over every day to see you."

"To see me?"

That revived me at once. Nobody ever called just to see me. My mother went back downstairs and soon I heard heavier footsteps approaching.

He sat on the edge of the bed and filled the sickroom with the smell of outdoors which always clung to his leather jacket.

"I brought you a present," he said.

At the mention of a present, I felt almost well.

"What kind of present?"

"I'm giving you my tricks. You're my heir, as it were."

He pressed the peanut-butter canister, the ring, and the velvet bag into my hand. I wrapped my fingers around the bag.

"But I don't know how to do them."

"My tricks aren't hard to do. Your dad will show you how they work. It takes practice, that's all."

"I'll try," I said.

"That's good. You keep on trying."

"You aren't going to be a magician anymore?"

He sighed and shook his head.

"I never was a real magician. But you're young. You'll do bigger things than pull scarves out of hats."

I began to mistrust his motives.

"What things?" I asked.

"Oh, heal the sick, raise the dead."

"I can't," I whispered, and self-pity engulfed me. "I feel all cracked up inside."

"Hell, I've been cracked lots of times," said Haig. "Most people don't get cracked up enough. They just sleep their lives away and nothing ever happens to them. If you're going to do any real magic, you got to keep moving around."

"Moving around?"

"Sure. You get older and you feel everything sliding away

from you. Well, a magician worth his salt doesn't just sit there and watch it go. He runs after it and brings it back."

His speech had the awful finality of a farewell, and I hardly dared to ask what I wanted to know.

"Are you going away?"

"To Arkansas. With Julia."

"How is she?"

"Not so good. She socked the priest."

"When are you coming back?"

He shrugged, stood up, and shuffled his feet.

"Christmas, maybe. But don't expect me. You know how it is. I'll send you a card if I don't make it back."

"Yes," I said.

I heard him go downstairs, then I heard the motorcycle sputter once, twice, three times before it roared away, leaving behind a huge silence like a gaping hole. The house fell quiet, the street outside fell quiet, the blackbirds in the pear trees fell quiet, as if the whole world were falling asleep and waiting for him to come again.

The Hucklebone of a Saint

In my father's house, moral ambiguity was not allowed. It was considered unhealthy, like soft drinks and candy, not to be kept in the house and to be eaten only with reprimands that kept you from enjoying it. As a result of this stricture, until I was ten, my father and I saw little of each other. We had a nodding acquaintance at meals, during which he listened to the news on the radio and spoke to no one. When I heard his car crunching up the driveway at night, bringing him back from the laboratory where he worked both morning and evening, I knew I should be asleep.

It was my mother who gave me my faith in the black arts, which came to dire fruition in my tenth year. Faith takes root in the insignificant. We would be sitting around the dinner table and I would drop my knife.

"Pick it up, Erica," my father would say. Or perhaps he would say nothing, but I would feel a discomforting frown.

"A man is coming," my mother would add.

Or if I dropped a spoon:

"A child is coming."

I never thought to notice whether or not the prophecies came true. I only remembered that if you dropped a knife, a man would visit the house for certain. Not that day, perhaps, nor the next, but sometime when you did not expect it. When you had even forgotten you dropped the knife.

My father did not recognize the power of a knife to bring a visitor, anymore than he recognized the power of an umbrella opened indoors to bring bad luck. Knowing that differences exist most peacefully under one roof when they are unaware of each other, my mother did not practice her black arts openly before him. If she knocked over the saltcellar while clearing the table, she brushed a small pile of salt aside and waited till he was napping before she threw a pinch of it into the fire. She knew he would ask, just as I asked, and he would be harder to answer:

"Why?"

"Judas spilled salt at the Last Supper. And look what happened to him."

I had seen da Vinci's "Last Supper" hanging like an enormous postcard in the Sunday School parlor of the Lutheran Church, and I resolved to look for the salt.

"See for yourself. It's lying on the table by Judas' hand, just like it's lying on our table now."

"But just because Judas had bad luck, why should I have it?"

"Just because."

Not because one man, this particular man had had it, certainly. The more I thought about it, the more I knew I could not inherit Judas' bad luck the way you inherit the color of your eyes and the shape of your face. Rather, in spilling the salt he had somehow stumbled upon a law. Others had probably discovered it before him. But it took the Crucifixion and Potter's Field before its validity was recognized.

It occurred to me that there must be many such laws I did not know. It had never worried me before. I knew it was my father's business to find out the laws which kept the world running. When he took me to the laboratory with him, I saw that it was full of things whose secrets he was wresting.

"What are those pretty stones?"

"Those are minerals."

"Why do you keep them in that funny box?"

"Because they're radioactive."

It was his pleasure to open the laws that lay hidden in things and make them clear, so clear that I could touch them with my hands whenever I picked up the models of molecular structures he kept in a little glass case on his desk. What he found was beautiful and utterly irrelevant to the way I lived my life. The world would go on turning whether my father or anyone else's father found out why. To discover the law of gravity, for example, was only to name what you already knew. It didn't change a thing.

The uselessness of my father's laws made them easier to learn than my mother's. He had marvelous instruments to extend the range of the senses and reach into the very cells of being. And when you found one law, you found others contingent on it. Whereas the laws in my mother's world were utterly capricious. You stepped on a crack and if your mother's back broke, you knew you'd found the reason. There were no conclusions, only an infinite number of particular cases.

And knowing the laws that worked in particular cases did not free you from the fear of breaking them. It only committed you more deeply to a power that gave you nothing in return for your obedience, except the vague feeling that you were somehow maintaining the status quo.

As soon as I acknowledged the existence of my mother's laws, life became immensely more complicated. Since each law was a particular event, the smallest events suggested themselves as a possible means of discovery. Riding my bicycle, for example, I would innocently imagine that if the stoplight turned red before I reached it, something bad would happen. If it didn't, things would stay the same. Nothing good would happen, but nothing bad would, either. Once I had decided it might be so, the game became real. The stoplight had the power to direct the traffic of my future. I began to avoid stoplights.

Other events acquired a similar authority which had to be countered with rituals and taboos. Certain dresses brought bad luck and hung unworn in the closet. Tuesdays meant low marks on spelling quizzes and mistakes in mathematics.

The most discouraging part of the whole business was that it was so much easier to bring bad luck on oneself than good luck. It was so much easier to break a mirror and live in the shadow of impending misfortune than to count a hundred white horses and wish for happiness.

As the games I invented mysteriously turned into statutes, I believed that I was maintaining the even keel of our joys until one day I came home from school to find two suitcases in the front hall. Grandmother had left her husband and decided to live with us.

She was to live out her life in our guest room, which quickly took on the color and smell of her life. It was a cold room, shut off from the house, with a pink satin bolster on the bed and doilies on the dressing table and a clean blotter on the desk; one of those anonymous rooms often slept in and rarely lived in, like a room in a hotel. Now the bolster gave way to a dozen eiderdowns. The radiators clanked and pounded; the room was kept at eighty degrees. My grandmother went about in heavy underclothes and sweaters and seldom left her quarters for more tepid parts of the house.

Further, its innocent spaces were suddenly thronged with medicine bottles of all kinds: lecithin, calcium, supplementary organic pills, Kaopectate, and Hexylresorcinol. There were also cases of vitamins, each regulating some function of the body and therefore necessary—Grandmother believed—to its survival. In her suitcase, which I observed was never wholly unpacked, she kept a reserve supply of everything.

On the wall over the bed hung a Chinese painting of a mountain. This she disliked, though she never asked us to take it down.

"Mountains! What good are mountains? You can't farm land like that."

Her chief amusement was going to church. She listened to the sermon with great attentiveness but could never remember a word of it afterward. She enjoyed the music and the feeling of being united with so many people for the good of their souls, which she had been taught was the only good.

She passed her days with what I considered an unbearable monotony. In the morning my mother brought up her oatmeal and orange juice on a tray. Grandmother sat at the dressing table and ate in front of the mirror, while my mother combed her long white hair into two braids and pinned them crosswise on her head. Then my mother went down to the cellar to hang up the wash—for it was early April when my grandmother came, and too cold to hang clothes outside—always listening for the sound of the old woman's voice.

"Daughter?"

"I'm right here."

Assured she was not alone, Grandmother would set about arranging the accoutrements of her life—that is, the contents of the suitcase. In addition to her impressive collection of medicines, she kept extra sets of heavy underwear and rolls of toilet paper which she sometimes unwound and wadded into her garters like an amulet to ward off attacks of nervous diarrhea.

It seemed to me that she was pursuing a secret journey, the destination of which constantly evaded her. Sometimes she would come to lunch wearing her hat and her big sealskin coat, inquiring about bus schedules, hinting that she had not been well-treated. My mother's response was always the same.

"There are no buses today. It's a holiday."

"Ah, then, I'll have to wait."

Then she would mention her responsibilities at the house in Coronna which she had so recently left and where my mother had grown up. Men were coming to pick the cherries in the orchard; she had to look sharp that they did not cheat on the hours. Grandfather was waiting for her; who would fix his dinner? She would explain it to us with pathetic urgency.

My mother maintained the illusion through a round of outings which never got the woman to her destination but only postponed the total collapse of her reason.

Grandmother's favorite escort on these outings was her brother Oskar. He was seventy-one, seven years younger than my grandmother. To me he was ageless, a spry, dapper little man who always wore two-toned Oxfords and a black and yellow vest, giving him the look of a frail and friendly bee. He was retired, not from any single occupation, but from a great variety of them, including brief stints as homesteader, circus barker, undertaker's assistant, and shortstop for an obscure ball team in

Minnesota. He had once had a wife and child, both of whom were dead, and I remember neither.

Sometimes he wrote poems—jingles, he called them—on the placemats he got every noon at Howard Johnson's, surfaces as suggestive to him as marble to Michelangelo, their floral borders and bright colors concealing clusters of language. Slipping a finely folded jingle into my hand, he would greet me with a mock bow, his shoes twinkling.

"Ah, Miss Callard," he would say.

"Oh, Bowser, how I've missed you."

That was in honor of the candies he kept in his pockets, Callard and Bowser's Plain Jane Toffees, or Lady Fingers, or Licorice. If he had no candy, then I knew he was bringing a game, a cardtrick, perhaps, or a Cracker-Jack toy. My mother justified his passion for Cracker Jacks by saying they reminded him of baseball, but I could see well enough how he broke into smiles of satisfaction when the toy appeared at the bottom of the box. Of all his presents he said, with a mixture of shame and pride, "It's nothing; I got it for pennies."

He would drive Grandmother around town to parade, as he called it, in my father's car. Sometimes I went along, sitting alone in the back seat.

"You want to take the wheel, my girl?" he suggested, turning solemnly to his sister.

Grandmother looked at him with horror.

"You used to do very well. I remember how we had the only car in Deep River, and how you used to make me get out at every corner and look in all directions to see if another one was coming."

Her early scruples eventually overcame her, for when my mother was fourteen, Grandmother drove the car into the garage and forgot to take it out again. No one else in the family had a license, so there it remained while my grandmother thought of more and more reasons for walking to this place and that, until it was understood that the car was now part of the house, as immovable as the walls and the floor.

On Sundays, my great-uncle came for breakfast, bringing with him a small flute of his own carving. He never went with us to church but waited at the house to join us for dinner, after which he retired to the sun room for a nap. He slept with his eyes open for about an hour and then I would hear him talking to the flute, as if he had no idea of gaining my audience.

"There was an organ in the house where we grew up. All the German farmhouses had them. Your grandmother used to sit in the parlor and play it by the hour."

"Where is it now?" I had always wanted to play an organ but thought that all organs were indissolubly joined to churches.

Oskar shook his head.

"The spitzwinks took it."

It was the German farmers in Iowa who told Oskar about the spitzwinks. Sometimes the crops failed because of rain, sometimes because of drought. And sometimes they failed for no reason at all. Then the farmers said, "Ah, the spitzwinks have done it." The spitzwinks made holes in your best stockings and chipped the cups and saucers that you used every day. They were the reason that plants marked "annuals" on the box at the market would not return in the spring.

"But why didn't great-Grandpa lock up the organ so the spitzwinks wouldn't steal it? Didn't he know there'd be other children?"

"He never thought of it."

The spitzwinks, I thought, were a sort of game, with no more substance than a figure of speech. But as weeks turned into months and Grandmother stayed on, I soon saw them as a name for forces which enmeshed her in propitiatory rituals far more suffocating than my own.

When she was dressed for bed and had drunk the hot milk that my mother brought her, she closed her door and began the long process of barricading it. Lying in my bed I could hear the moving of furniture, the heaviest pieces in the house and a chilling testimony of my grandmother's strength. A long slow scraping across the floor was the chest of drawers. Then came the slow bump of the dressing table with the oval mirror. That did not move so easily because the castors had disappeared. And finally I heard a persistent scuffling sound, as if my grandmother were waging a battle with the forces of darkness. In half an hour the sounds ceased but the light still shone under her door; she was awake.

"Margaret, did you lock the front door?"

That was my mother, who always sounded like somebody else when anyone called her by her first name.

"Yes!" My father was already asleep; he left to my mother the responsibility of answering.

For a few minutes it would be still. Then I heard the furniture moving again, the chest of drawers, the dressing table, the chair. This time, it was being forced away from the door. When the door opened, Grandmother's voice sounded near. She had stepped into the hall.

"I say, did you lock the front door?"

"Yes, of course!"

"I think I'll just go down and try it."

Like the soul of an extinct bird she glided swiftly down the stairs, her two braids springing out over her ears just as they fell when she took out the pins. She rattled the knob of the front door for us all to hear.

"Good. I just wanted to be sure."

Then her own door would slam, as if she had reached her room in a single bound. And presently the moving of furniture would begin again.

Night after night I acknowledged the danger that lay in such defenses. Clearly my grandmother's rituals only brought her closer to the fears she wished to avoid. Mine were still part of the games that a child plays, when by an act of the imagination he wills his own life into what has none, for the sake of companionship. If my grandmother's rituals were a game, then it must be a game that she played in deadly earnest, the stakes to be paid with her own life. Whenever I recognized this, I had the uncomfortable feeling that we were becoming more and more alike.

What linked us was a discovery that the faith we had gathered from generations of Sundays was no match for this greater faith in the reality of darkness. Where did it come from? We had not invited it. Who put it into my heart that the darkness under the bed gathered itself into invisible hands, waiting to snatch my feet when I groped my way back from the bathroom at night?

How was it that my mother, my father, and Uncle Oskar stepped quietly into their beds with no knowledge of this danger and therefore no fear? How could you lose your freedom without knowing who had taken it? If my faith in the darkness could not be broken, then it was not faith as I knew it but a love for all that could not be named and a secret desire that it never should be.

Because of this love my mother wore her best dress wrong side out to my cousin's wedding for fear of bringing bad luck on the heads of the newly wedded pair. Because of this love she knocked on wood whenever she spoke of my achievements in school and asserted half-jokingly—but only half—that Thomas Dewey had lost the presidential election because he had a horseshoe hanging upside down over his door and all his luck drained out. She had grown up in a neighboring town and seen for herself the quiet gnawing emblem of his doom which, if heeded, might have changed the course of nations.

By day, Grandmother's diversions alternated between drives, church, and Abby's beauty parlor. The beauty parlor and the church stood kitty corner from each other, on a block named by persecuted German immigrants who wanted their children to grow up on Liberty Street. The slow but ceaseless arrival of new settlers gave it such a vivid restlessness that even now I think of it not as a place but as a way of being alive.

The excitement began early in the morning when men in white overalls streaked with blood hauled carcasses from trucks to the back of the butcher shop. But when its doors opened for business, the very memory of blood had been quenched. Sausages were hung high on the ceiling, tucked out of sight like poor relations, to be asked for by name but not displayed. On shelves that ran the length of the shop you found cocoa from Holland in delftware jars, flatbread from Norway and flowered tins of gumdrops from Paris.

Abby had her beauty shop above the butcher's, and it was there that I met Mary Ellen. She was two years older than I and had the job of answering the telephone and unwrapping the little pieces of cotton which Abby tucked into the hairnets of her customers to protect their ears from the sirocco blasts of the dryer. She also kept the glass atomizers filled with the heavy scented lacquer, which "set" the finger-waves so that hair came out dry and rippling as dunes of sand.

In exchange for these favors, Abby allowed her to read the movie magazines she kept by the dryers. Mary Ellen devoured the legends of her favorites as faithfully as she attended Mass. The stars were her secular saints, their changeless identities to be consulted in the minute crises of daily life. She borrowed a gesture from one, a hairstyle from another; all, I thought, to no effect. There was a faint aura of dirt about everything she wore, like a shading sketched on the original color, and as she washed the pins and curlers, customers would stare at her fingernails in amazement. For she did not believe in cleaning them; she simply bit the dirty portion away, peeling it with great fastidiousness like a delicate fruit.

In warm weather we walked to a vacant lot behind a funeral parlor, where we could play undisturbed. The only other building on it was a warehouse full of coffins. Squeezing among them like bankers checking their safes, we would collect the number of different kinds, the way you collect out-of-state license plates or the number of white horses you pass when you are traveling. Most of the coffins were dark and plain. We decided it was lucky to find a baby's coffin, because we found them so seldom. A few of the large ones were scrolled, and we watched for these, too, though their luck was considered less potent. At the end of the day we remembered how many we had found.

Or rather *I* remembered how many we had found. I had come to believe that the luck things carried augmented like interest only if I kept my books straight, never forgetting how much I had saved. When the total number of white horses, license plates, loads of hay, baby coffins, and other spectacles deemed lucky by us grew too large to keep in my head, I wrote the sums down in a little notebook, with the conviction that it was both useless and necessary to some final reckoning of my fate.

By this time the last platoon of Abby's customers would be touching their brittle curls as they emerged from under the dryers. Grandmother never sat under the dryer, as it threw her into a panic and she would roll her eyes about like a horse being pushed into a van. With her hair pinned in wet braids across her head, she turned the pages of the movie magazines, clucking at the wages of sin until my mother emerged with her hair pitilessly knotted into ringlets.

"It's so hard to find someone who can do my hair plain the way I like it," she would say.

Abby's hairdos were utterly without style. She believed in durability rather than immediate effect. She made pincurls so tight that they kept their kink for days and only ceased to remind you of sheep's wool or Fiji chieftains a week later. On her walls hung photographs showing a wide variety of styles, but no matter which one you ordered you always came out looking the same. This attracted a host of elderly ladies whose conservative taste could not be met in the salons uptown, where ratting and backcombing were the fashion.

Although I knew Abby had been a widow oftener than some wives have been mothers, I could not imagine her in love. She was a stocky figure, in her white smock, with sparse brown hair and thick glasses, and as she tipped your head into the sink and scrubbed your scalp, she sang at the top of her voice:

> When you're smiling,
> When you're smiling,
> The whole world smiles with you.

And while she sang, always a little breathless from reaching and scrubbing, she talked and talked and her bosom heaved like a full sail over your face. Neither I nor my mother knew any of the people she talked about, except as we might feel we knew the characters in a radio serial—Pearl, Maria, Charley, and all the others whose foibles she expounded to us according to her mood.

"He's gone to see that widow lady downstairs, that's what. He lies around on her bed all day and she feeds him white albacore tuna. It's nothing but grub what he's after, a heartless beast, no feelings at all."

Not for a long time did I learn that many of the names I associated with people actually belonged to cats. Abby fed all the stray cats that came to her door and demanded in exchange a scrupulous fidelity. If one stayed away for two days, or a week, she railed against him like a forsaken lover.

With Grandmother, however, she never spoke of cats. Every conversation was an exchange of ailments and remedies, Grandmother defending her drugstore prescriptions and Abby speaking for her teas. Among her rinses she kept a packet of alba camomile, the label of which showed a man coming out of a forest and handing a spray of blossoms to a little girl. To me, that alone argued for its magical properties.

"Someday you'll be drinking a good dose of henna if you're not careful, keeping it all mixed up like that," warned my mother.

But Abby's cupboard contained a greater wonder than alba camomile tea. It was locked away in a small chest behind the bleaches and dyes. Sometimes, when all her customers were safely tucked under the dryers and time lay heavy on her hands, she would bring it out for Mary Ellen and me to look at.

"It's the hucklebone of a saint," explained Abby.

I did not dare to ask what a hucklebone was and decided that it was the place on your elbow that tingled when you accidentally bumped it against a table or chair. I have since learned that it is the anklebone.

The tiny splinter of bone lay pressed between two discs of glass in the middle of a brass sun from which crude rays emanated. Abby's grandfather, a connoisseur of the marvelous, had bought it in the catacombs outside Rome from a priest who took him through by the light of a serpent twisted around his staff. At Cologne he had kissed the skulls of the Magi and the nail driven into Christ's right foot; at Trèves he had touched part of the thigh of the Virgin Agatha and seen the devil carrying the soul of his grandmother in a wheelbarrow. He had walked on the holy stair of Saint John Lateran and wagered for a tooth of Saint Peter. He lost the wager, but the same day he was miraculously healed of a lifetime of headaches by combing his hair with the comb of a saint.

"Which saint?" asked Mary Ellen.

"I don't know. What does it matter?"

I liked the saints, faded as they were in the liturgies of my church. I liked them because they attended so patiently to the smallest human catastrophes. If you lost something you went to Saint Anthony. If you wanted a husband you went to Saint Nicholas. Even thieves found a comforter, among the ranks of the blessed, who would not turn a deaf ear to their problems.

I had need for such a comforter. Since my grandmother's arrival my dependence on the dark powers had grown steadily worse. I had come to believe that certain words released the forces of evil, being part of that vast body of laws of which spilling salt was only a tiny amendment. All my life, words had come to me wrapped in feelings that had nothing to do with their meanings and everything to do with the way my hand felt when I printed them. But now they lost all connection with the things they named and took on the opacity of a magic formula. Not being able to say *tree* didn't mean that trees were evil. It only meant that saying the name released forces beyond your control.

Perfect obedience led, clearly, to perfect silence, and the slow death of all my delights. You cannot serve two masters. Or rather, you can, but the moment will come when you must choose between them.

We were crossing the lot on our way to the coffins when suddenly Mary Ellen stamped her foot and cried,

"Lucky Strike!"

"What?"

"I stepped on a new one. See?"

So I stepped on it also.

"Lucky Strike."

She shook her head.

"You can say it if you want to, but it isn't as good as if you'd found your own. It counts less. And don't EVER step on a Pall Mall."

I felt a whole new mesh of complications engulf me.

"Let's not count cigarette packs. It's too hard."

I wanted her to tell me that in the scheme of things, Lucky Strikes and Pall Malls did not matter. Instead, she only looked at me in astonishment.

"Too HARD?"

"I can't remember so many things." I was beginning to feel irritable. "Why do we have to count things all the time? You keep track of license plates, you keep track of everything."

"It's only a game," she said in puzzled tones.

"Well, it isn't a game to me!" I bellowed.

The door of the funeral parlor opened and a man stepped out and cleared his throat. We scuttled across the lot to the street and began walking quickly past the houses toward downtown.

"A lot of people in there," whispered Mary Ellen, looking back over her shoulder. "You want to watch?"

"I don't want to watch anything any more! I'm tired of counting. All those things, I *have* to count them. I don't know why but I have to count them. And I don't want to. My head is so crowded with junk already that sometimes I feel like it's going to explode."

"Then why don't you quit?"

"I don't know!" My voice had risen to a shout. An old woman sitting on her front porch stared at us. "It's like there was some other person inside of me making me do it. Every time I want to quit there's that other person who won't let me."

Mary Ellen nodded.

"Somebody has put a hex on you, maybe," she suggested.

"Maybe," I agreed.

"If it happened to *me* I'd just go straight to Father Hekkel and he would make it all right."

The notion of involving a stranger alarmed me at once. Now that I'd dragged the thing into broad daylight it sounded foolish even to my own ears.

"Since you aren't in our church, maybe Father Hekkel wouldn't work. We better try and find somebody else."

"What about Abby?"

We were lucky. The only customer was white-haired Miss Briggs who worked in a dry goods store and looked like some-body's memory of a piano teacher. Miss Briggs was hunched under the dryer reading a confession magazine with the front cover folded back, and Abby was sweeping up the hair clippings that lay around the chairs into a feather pile.

Mary Ellen walked in and came right to the point.

"Erica has a devil in her."

"Lord-a-mighty!" cried Abby, nearly dropping the broom. "What makes you think so?"

And now I turned the light on my dark voices, and told her everything, all my rituals from beginning to end, spewing them out like a bitter and humiliating confession. White horses and spilled salt and words that went cold on my tongue. The number of steps to the bedroom door and the long leap in the dark.

Abby listened gravely, glancing now and then at Miss Briggs who sat insulated by the hot rushing air like a silent and skinny warrior.

"Well," she said at last. "Well, well. A devil. Yes, indeed."

She did not seem to understand what we wanted of her, so Mary Ellen explained.

"We came to you because we thought you could call him out."

"Ah," said Abby, as calmly as if we'd asked her the time of day. "Well, I don't know the words for it. Go get that little black book over by the telephone."

Mary Ellen brought the book and Abby thumbed through it slowly. At last her finger paused on a page.

"Here are the words for the exorcizing of the devil."

She peered over her glasses, first at Mary Ellen and then at me. "A matter not to be taken lightly."

"No, of course not," I said, feeling myself in the presence of a great physician who would now perform a miraculous cure.

"If you're absolutely certain it's the devil, we ought to have the priest do this."

"I'd rather you did it, Abby."

Abby looked very pleased.

"Well then, you two stand behind that table."

Suddenly inspired, she went to the cupboard and took out the reliquary.

"There's nothing holier than the hucklebone of a saint."

She set it in the middle of the dressing table so that the mirror caught it from behind. Then she pushed Mary Ellen and me together, joining our hands on the relic as for a marriage, and laying the book open before her, she began to read in a loud voice.

I exorcise, thee, most vile spirit, the very embodiment of our enemy, the entire specter, the whole legion, in the name of Jesus Christ, to get out and flee from this creature of God. He himself commands thee, who has ordered thee cast down from the heights of heaven to the depths of the earth. He commands thee, He who commands the sea, the winds, and the tempests. Hear, therefore and fear, O Satan, enemy of the faith, foe to the human race, producer of death, thief of life, destroyer of justice, root of evils, kindler of vices, procurer of sorrows. Why dost thou stand and resist, when thou knowest that Christ the Lord will destroy thy strength?

Under my grasp, the hucklebone warmed. It had acquired for me a life of its own wholly different from its first life, just as it was Abby who read, and yet not Abby, but someone much older. Ancient, even. Not for Abby the beauty operator would the spirit of darkness depart, but Abby the magician's daughter, daughter of Eve, descendant of saint-seekers and wanderers of holy places.

Her voice was rolling like thunder as she turned the page:

Now therefore depart. Depart, thou seducer. He expels thee, from whose eye nothing is secret. He expels thee to whose power all things are subject. He excludes thee, who has prepared for thee and thy angels everlasting hell; out of whose mouth the sharp sword will go, He who shall come to judge the quick and the dead and the world by fire.

"Too hot! Too hot!" shouted a voice, and we all yelled, and I thought I saw the devil in the mirror and shouted to Abby, but then he shriveled into Miss Briggs making signs that she wanted to come out, forgetting, as the deaf do, that others can hear.

There was a snapping of hairpins as Abby pushed the dryer back and Miss Briggs emerged, as dazed as if she had awakened from a long sleep. Her hair lay against her scalp in crusted waves like cake frosting.

"What a funny color," observed Mary Ellen. "I believe your hair's darker than it was."

Miss Briggs sat down at the mirror and Abby took off the net and shook the pins loose. Nobody said a word for several minutes. Then Miss Briggs spoke up.

"It looks green," she whispered hoarsely. "Does it look green to you?"

Abby bent low for closer inspection, but you could have answered her just as well from across the room.

"It does have a sort of greenish cast. Sometimes a person can be allergic to the cream rinse."

"I never was before," said Miss Briggs, her face working.

Abby shook her head.

"I don't think a light rinse will cover it. You wouldn't want anything stronger than a rinse, would you?"

"Oh my, no. Just something to cover up the green."

"I could make it darker. Black, for example."

"Black!"

"It's better than green."

The silence prickled with voices. Why, Edith Briggs, what have you done to yourself? Would you believe it, running after the young men at *her* age?

Abby stuffed some change into my hand.

"Run downstairs and get two teas and some honey rolls."

Coming back, we met Miss Briggs talking to herself on the stairs with her hair hanging black around her face in big rollers, like spaniel ears. Abby was nowhere in sight.

When I got home, a palpable emptiness had invaded the house. Out of the dining room, with a rustling like blown curtains, stepped Oskar. He had been sitting alone in the falling light.

"They're all out looking for your grandmother," he said brokenly. "She's run away. Slipped out of the house while your ma was hanging up clothes."

"She couldn't have got very far," I said. "She has no money."

"No. But she's a strong woman."

She was found about five blocks from the house, headed, she believed, for the bus station. It had started to rain and the drops glistened on her big sealskin coat and her white hair. Mother hurried her upstairs and I heard the commotion—bath water running and heaters being turned on—that always arose when I came home from school with wet feet.

"She'll catch cold, you wait and see," said Oskar, sorrowfully.

She could not go outside now but lay in her bed, swathed in sweaters, while the radiators pounded in her room and the lights burned all night long. On the fourth day after her flight she decided to get up. She seemed to have gathered strength from her illness instead of losing it.

"I'll take her to market with me on Saturday," suggested my father. "Better to take her out than to have her run off again."

Market days were minor feast-days in our family. We bought honey and vegetables to last us for the week and sometimes such curiosities as acorn pipes and peacock feathers. Oskar and I would hold mock duels with our feathers all week till they broke.

It was unseasonably brisk for May. The egg-seller was warming her feet at a tiny stove and the honey-vendor had incarcerated himself in a little hut with a plastic window, behind which he waited as if for you to confess your sins. Grandmother walked among flats of pansies and beamed. For the first time that I could remember, she did not notice the cold.

She did not get up for church on Sunday, but lay whispering quietly in bed, unaware even of the presence of the doctor, whose attentions would have been a welcome diversion in her hardier days.

"For pneumonia at her age, there's not much hope. You should take her to the hospital all the same; the oxygen facilities there will prolong her life a little."

"I want to have no regrets," said my mother. "It's so dreadful to have regrets afterward."

My grandmother was put into a private room with nurses round the clock and a little cot near her bed for my mother, who told us how awful it would be to wake up at such a time and not know anybody.

But on Tuesday she was dead.

My mother came home from the hospital, her eyes ringed

with blue. Neighbors brought in food, and casseroles—mostly chicken—began to accumulate in the kitchen. Suddenly plans for the funeral absorbed her with a thousand tedious details which ramified and consumed her grief. When Oskar stopped by our house that evening, she ran up to him, eager and awkward, like a little girl.

"I don't know how I'm going to manage. Oskar, if you'd only stay. You could sleep on the sofa."

"Wouldn't it be easier to put me in Grandmother's room? I'd be out of the way."

My mother looked flustered.

"Do you think you'd be *comfortable* in there?"

I knew from her voice that she thought nobody could ever be comfortable there now.

"Well, well, we'll see," said Oskar.

His valise in the middle of the floor announced his decision. Keeping a wary eye on the open door, my mother stripped the bed with a studied casualness. Never had I heard her move so quietly, as if she were afraid of awakening the air itself. Suddenly the door slammed and she let out a shriek of terror.

Oskar rushed in.

"Let me do it," he said.

And I heard him plumping the pillows and humming tenderly to himself, straightening the bed, it seemed, for the woman who had recently left it.

Darkness fell so gently that nobody remembered to turn the lights on. We did not sit down for supper, but picked at the casseroles spread out in the kitchen as for a church potluck. Oskar and my father, balancing paper plates on their knees, sat in the sun parlor, remembering death.

First Oskar remembered that the only extant photograph of his grandfather showed him in his coffin because Aunt Betty argued that a picture of him dead was better than no picture at all, and if you had the eyeballs touched in you could imagine him sitting in a first-class railway carriage.

Then my father remembered the funeral of a young girl he attended during a diphtheria epidemic, in which the mourners stood across the street and the coffin was tipped forward at the window by the girl's mother at a signal from the minister, who shouted his sermon from the front porch within hearing of both parties.

And then, in low voices, like children after the lights have been put down, they mused on the motions of the body after death. How hair and nails continue to grow and how the dead sit up in the furnace and their bones crack.

"You won't catch me being cremated," said Oskar. "When I'm down, I want to stay down."

At ten o'clock my father started the movement to bed. Last one up will be the first one dead—

I bit my tongue, remembering my newly won freedom, waited till the others had gone on ahead and then ascended the stairs. In my room I undressed quickly and started to jump into bed—

There is no one under the bed who will grab your feet.

I walked to the edge of the bed with slow and measured stride. Let the hands come if they dare. The body snatchers.

And then my mother's voice called out,

"Oskar, are you sure you won't be afraid in there?"

"Afraid?" His voice was filled with mild amazement. "Why should I be afraid? I loved the woman!"

His door closed, but I heard him moving around, and a light under the crack spilled faintly into the hall. Presently he opened the door. The radiators were pounding. Mother had turned up the heat for Grandmother.

I got out of bed and stood in the doorway of my room and saw him, isolated in a little shell of light, as if I were looking at him through a mailing tube. He was sitting at the dressing table where Grandmother ate her breakfast, and he was writing calmly and steadily. I decided for no reason that he was writing a poem. On the back of a placemat, perhaps, or a menu, the surfaces which he preferred to write on above all else.

He did not see me. His back was turned and the light touched the thin places in his waistcoat with a soft shine. His habit of keeping his shoes on until the moment he stepped into bed gave him an air of expectancy at this hour; he would arise soon and go out for a visit, or perhaps someone was coming to visit him. Suddenly I believed that if he turned out his light, every light in the world would go out. Then there would be no more left of him than the hucklebone of a saint.

When the sun came up his light disappeared. I was awakened by the sound of shoes dropping, and I dozed intermittently until I heard him shuffling quietly downstairs. There was a brief clatter in the kitchen and then the smell of coffee. I pulled on my clothes and went after him, trying to remember if my grandmother was already dead, if they had buried her yet, or if they would bury her today, but the only person I could find was Oskar. He poured me half a cup of coffee and filled the other half with milk.

"Do you want to take a little walk to the park?" he suggested. "Before anyone else gets up?"

We walked slowly past the teeter-totters and sat down in the swing, though the seats were wet with dew. My uncle glided back and forth, trying to keep his swing even with mine, swinging without a word, as though the morning had turned him young again and he knew no more what had happened to Grandmother than I did.

The Doctrine of the Leather-Stocking Jesus

On the day before Easter, in my father's garage, just before supper, I drew a chalk circle around Galen Malory, and said,

"Now I am going to change you into a donkey."

"Don't," pleaded Galen.

He was five, three years younger than I, and the second youngest of eight children. His father had worked for forty years on the assembly line of the biggest furniture factory in Grand Rapids and was given, on retiring, a large dining-room table with two unmatching chairs. On holidays Mr. Malory sat at one end and Mrs. Malory sat at the other, and in between stood the children on either side, holding their plates to their mouths. The rest of the time, they ate on TV-tables all over the house.

"Now you will turn all furry and grow terrible ears," I said, smoothing my skirt. "Hee haw."

"If I turn into a donkey," shouted Galen, "my mother won't ever let me come here again."

"Too late," I howled, rolling my eyes up into my head. "I don't know how to undo it."

Suddenly, Mrs. Malory rang her cowbell and all over the block children leaped over hedges and fences and fell out of trees.

"I have to go," said Galen. "See you."

As he ran out of the garage he bumped his big furry nose on the rake leaning against the door. He stopped, reached up and touched his floppy ears, and burst into tears.

Out of the sight of God-fearing folk, we sat together on the compost pile where three garages met, and we wept together. I stared at Galen's ears, large as telephone receivers, and at his big hairy lips and his small hands browsing over all this in bewilderment.

His hands. His hands?

I looked again. I had not turned him into a donkey. I had only given him a donkey's head.

And I thought briefly and sorrowfully of all the false gifts I'd given him, the candy canes I hung on his mother's peonies, left there, I told him, by angels.

"Dear God," I bellowed, addressing the one power I did believe in, "Please change Galen back."

"Somebody's coming," whispered Galen, terrified. "I think it's my father."

An old man in a brown overcoat and curled-up shoes was crossing the snow-patched field, poking the ground with a pointed stick. He was spearing bunches of dead leaves and tucking them into a white laundry-bag.

"That's not your father," I said, "and he doesn't even see us."

But who could fail to see us? The old man skinned the leaves off his stick like a shish kebab, put them in his pack, and sat down half a yard from us, nearly on top of the hole where a little green snake once stuck her tongue out at me. He pulled a sandwich out of his pocket and ate it slowly, and I saw he had dozens of pockets, all bulging, and sometimes the bulges twitched. We watched him wipe his hands on his coat, stand up, and turn toward us.

"Once a thing is created," said the old man, "it cannot be destroyed. You cannot, therefore, get rid of the donkey's head. You must give it to somebody else."

"Who?" asked Galen.

"Me," said the old man.

"I asked God to get rid of it," I said.

"I *am* God," said the old man. "See if you can change me into a donkey."

The smell of crushed apples and incense filled the garage

when God stood in the center of the chalk circle and my voice weasled forth, small and nervous.

"Now I am going to change you into a donkey."

And because it was God and not Galen, I sang the rhyme that expert skip-ropers save for jumping fifty times without tripping:

> *Now we go round the sun,*
> *now we go round the stars.*
> *Every Sunday afternoon:*
> *one, two, three—*

Then I saw God stroking the tip of His velvet nose with one hand. His eyes, on either side of His long head, smiled at Galen's freckled face.

"After all, it is not so dreadful to be mistaken for an ass. Didn't Balaam's ass see My angel before his master did? Wasn't it the ass who sang in the stable the night My son was born? And what man has ever looked upon My face?"

"We have," said Galen.

"You looked upon my God-mask," said God. "Only the eyes are real."

He stepped out of the circle, opened His bag of leaves, and peeped inside.

"What are you going to do with all those leaves?" I asked him.

"I save them," said God. "I never throw anything away."

The leaves whirled around as if a cyclone carried them, as God pulled the drawstring tight.

And suddenly He was gone.

And now I smelled the reek of oil where my father parked his Buick each night, and an airplane rumbled overhead, and Galen was jumping the hedge into the Malorys' yard, and Etta called me for dinner.

And, conscious of some great loss which I did not understand, I went.

My mother and my sister Kirsten had already left for church to fix the flowers for tomorrow's service. Etta, the babysitter, and I ate macaroni and cheese at the kitchen table, out of the way of the apples waiting to be peeled, the yams and the onions, the cranberries and avocados, and the ham which Etta had studded with cloves.

I wanted to tell Etta all that had happened, but when the words finally came, they were not the words I intended.

"Do you know what Reverend Peel's collar is made of?"

"Linen," said Etta.

"Indian scalps," I told her. "Do you know what chocolate is made of?"

"It comes from a tree," said Etta.

"It's dried blood," I said.

"Who told you that rubbish?" she demanded.

"Timothy Bean."

"A nine-year-old boy who would shave off his own eyebrows don't know nothing worth knowing," snorted Etta.

Etta gathered up our dishes and rinsed them in the sink.

"Can we go over and see the Malorys' new baby?" I asked.

When we arrived, Mrs. Malory and five of her daughters had already gone to church to make bread for the Easter breakfast. The Malory kitchen smelled of gingerbread, but nobody offered me any. It was so warm that the windows were weeping steam. The corrugated legs of a chicken peeked out over the rim of a discreetly covered pot. Etta comfied herself in the Morris chair by the stove, mopping her face with her apron as she crocheted enormous snowflakes which would someday be a bedspread. Helen Malory, who was nineteen, plump, lightly mustached, and frizzy-haired, sat in the rocker nestling her baby brother in her arms. She was newly engaged to a mailman. Thank God! said my mother when she heard it. Helen's got so many towels and sheets in that hope chest down cellar, she can't even close it.

Today Helen had given Galen a whole roll of shelf-paper and some crayons and now he and I were lying under the table, drawing. Because tomorrow was Easter, I drew the church: the carved angels that blossom on the ends of the rafters, the processional banners on either side of the altar, the candles everywhere.

Galen drew Nuisance, the golden retriever who at that moment slept beside the warm stove. The dog's head would not come out right, nor the legs either, so he drew Nuisance wearing a bucket and walking behind a little hill.

Tenderly, Helen tested the baby's bottle on her wrist and touched the nipple to its mouth. The baby squinted and pawed the air and milk sprayed down its cheeks. The lace gown it would wear tomorrow for its baptism at the eleven-o'clock service shimmered in a box on the kitchen table. Etta was allowed to touch it before Helen put it safely away on top of the china cabinet.

"What are you giving him?" inquired Etta.

"Scalded calves' milk," said Helen.

"You could add a little honey. That won't hurt none. John the Baptist ate honey in the desert and he grew up strong as an ox." As Etta spoke, she peered at the baby knowingly over her glasses. "Is that a scratch on his nose?"

"He scratched himself in the night. His nails are so small I don't dare cut 'em," explained Helen.

"If it was mine," said Etta, "I'd bite 'em off. 'Course I'd never bite anyone else's baby," she added quickly.

A white star gathered slowly at the end of Etta's crochet hook. Comfort and mercy dropped upon me in good smells that filled the kitchen. I was in heaven. I was lying in a giant cookie jar. Cuckoo, cuckoo, shouted the bird in the living-room clock. On its fifth cry, the grandfather clock in the hall started bonging away, nine times.

"Galen, take your thumb out of your mouth," said Helen sharply.

Galen took it out and examined the yellow blister on the joint.

"I had a niece who sucked her thumb," observed Etta. "Her mother tried everything. When she got married, her husband said, 'I'll break her of it.' She finally quit when she lost her teeth."

"Better to suck your thumb than smoke," said Etta.

"Why?" I asked.

"It's wicked," said Helen.

"It'll stunt your growth," said Etta. "I had an uncle who smoked young. He never grew more'n three feet tall."

Deep in a shaggy dream, Nuisance growled and thumped his stubby tail.

"I think I'll latch the screen," said Helen, and she stood up fast. "Caleb Suarez told Penny if she wouldn't go out with him tonight, he'd come and break down the door. But I do love the fresh air."

"You want to go upstairs and see Penny's stuff?" whispered Galen.

"Sure," I whispered back.

I was more comfortable in the same room with Penny's stuff than with Penny. Penny was sixteen and religious, but like every other girl in the high school, including my sister Kirsten, she dreamed of Caleb and would dream of him long after she was married to someone else. Whenever she looked at her mother, she would burst into tears, and her mother would shout, "So sleep with him! Go ahead! But let me tell you, you can't get away from your upbringing. You'll feel guilty all your life. It's a sacred act, you don't just do it with any boy that comes along."

Caleb had black hair, all ducktailed and pompadoured, blue eyes, a handsome face, and a withered arm—the scar of infantile paralysis, my mother explained. His father was one-quarter American Indian and owned the Golden Cue Pool Parlor and came, when Caleb was six, from Sioux City to find his relatives in Northville. There were no relatives, and as far as anyone could see, there was no wife.

Caleb spent his days at the Fire Department, reading and waiting for fires, and his nights drinking at the Paradise Bar.

"He's read all the books in the library; now he's starting the second time around," said Mr. Malory, shaking his head at such folly. "I will say one thing for him, though. I've never seen him drunk."

Galen turned on the light in the room Penny shared with Helen. Over a dressing table littered with bottles hung a big framed picture of Jesus, surrounded by photographs of brides clipped from the newspapers.

"That's Penny's," said Galen bravely, pointing to the picture. His voice was too loud for the room, as if he were shouting before a shrine. "We gotta go now."

"Did you tell anyone about God?" I asked.

"I wanted to, but I couldn't," said Galen.

"Me neither."

Down the hall, Helen was putting the baby to bed. Suddenly it cried furiously, and Galen and I hurried back to the kitchen. Seeing us, Nuisance lifted his head, and his rabies tags jingled like harness bells.

"Here, Nuisance," I called.

"His real name is Winthrop," said Galen. "He has a pedigree. If he had the rest of his tail, he'd be worth a lot of money."

Nuisance loped after me into the dark dining room, his nails clicking on the bare floor. China gleamed on the sideboard like the eyes of mice.

"Galen, get me a piece of chalk."

"If you change Nuisance into a donkey," said Galen weakly, "my mother will never let me play with you again. That's my dad's best hunting dog."

But he brought the chalk.

"Sit, Nuisance," I commanded.

Nuisance rolled over. I drew the circle around him and stepped back.

"Out of my way, Galen."

Galen did not need to be told twice. I fixed my eye on the golden shape of Nuisance, motionless, save for the stump of tail which wagged.

"Now I am going to change you into a donkey," I whispered.

And because it was Nuisance and not Galen, I sang to him:

> Nuisance go round the sun,
> Nuisance go round the stars.
> Every Sunday afternoon:
>   one, two, three—

The sweetness of apples and incense hovered around us again. But nothing happened.

Then suddenly Nuisance jumped three feet into the air and, barking wildly, charged across the kitchen and crashed through the screen door. Etta shrieked and Helen came running.

"Is it Caleb?" she yelled.

"Nuisance broke down the door," shouted Etta. "You better lock him up good."

Galen burst into tears, and Helen sank to her knees beside him.

"There, there, honey lamb. No one's going to hurt you. Helen will lock the doors and windows." She held his head against her neck. "And I'll let you play with my Old Maid cards." Galen's shoulders stopped shaking. "And I'll even let you touch my new lampshade."

"Can I go down cellar and see your chest?" Galen said in a sodden voice.

Flicking the switch by the cellar door and taking each of us by the hand, Helen led us down the steps, dimly lit, past a clothesline sagging with diapers, to a big brass-bound chest.

"Can I open it?" snuffled Galen.

"Go ahead," said Helen.

So Galen lifted the lid very slowly. It was like a thing from dreams, this box, big as a coffin, full of bedspreads and blankets and dishes. This is the way I would like to keep my whole past, I thought, folded away where I could take out last year's Christmas or my first birthday and play dress-up whenever I liked. Resting carefully on top of a platter painted with turkeys, the lampshade waited. It needed a light to show clearly the man and woman walking in a garden painted on the front.

"I got it for seventy-five cents at a rummage sale," Helen announced proudly. "It's not paper, either. It's real satin, and all clean."

"Too bad it's purple," I said thoughtlessly, and then, seeing I'd hurt her, I added, "but I like the two people in the garden."

"What comes after the garden?" asked Galen, pointing to the edge of the picture.

"Nothing. Don't poke at it," said Helen crossly.

And she herded us upstairs.

Etta had gotten control of herself and was crocheting as if

nothing had happened, but her face looked like bleached flour. The lower half of the screen door was hanging out, torn in two—I touched it, awestruck. Helen went to the sink and started snapping the stems off the beans heaped on the drainboard.

"Etta," I said, and I felt my tongue thicken in my mouth, "Did you ever see God's face?"

"Nobody has ever seen God's face," said Etta. "Only His hinder parts."

Helen touched her buttocks absentmindedly.

"His what?" said Galen.

"His hinderparts," repeated Etta. "Nobody will ever see His face till the last day."

Etta knew the Bible better than any of us, but she didn't know I gave God the head of an ass.

"How do you know which day is the last day?" asked Galen.

"When all the signs have come to pass, that will be the last day," said Etta, mysteriously. "Oh, they won't all come at once. They'll be spread out over the centuries, for a thousand years in the Lord's sight are but as yesterday when they are past."

"Something's burning," exclaimed Helen. She peeked into the soup pot, pushed the chicken legs down, clapped on the lid like a jailer, and turned off the stove. Then she said to Etta, a little sadly, "All those things are mighty hard to understand—"

A crash outside cut her off. For an instant none of us moved.

"The coon is rummaging through the garbage pail again," Helen squeaked. "He comes pretty near every night."

We all exhaled.

"Go on about the signs," I urged Etta.

Etta smoothed a finished snowflake across the back of her hand.

"When my grandfather was a little boy, he saw the darkening of the sky. That's one of the signs. The cows came home and the chickens went to roost just like it was night. And stars fell out of the sky. People thought they would get burnt up, and some folks killed theirselves."

"Is this a ghost story?" asked Galen nervously.

Etta scowled at him over the top of her glasses.

"I'm telling you what's in the Bible."

She opened her purse and pulled out a small book bound in white paper. "It's the new translation, and it only costs twenty-three cents. You could own three of 'em if you wanted to. And it's got pictures. See—"

"Who's that wild man?" demanded Galen.

"Where? Where?" cried Helen.

"There."

He pointed to the picture of a hairy man dressed in skins waving a big stick.

"That's John the Baptist," explained Etta. "But I believe this one is my favorite. It's from Revelation."

Over a crested wave, the red sun and the black moon bobbed like apples, and fish floated belly up among the spars of sunken ships.

"And every living soul in the sea shall die," said Etta.

"Fish don't have souls," said Helen.

Etta frowned.

"But that was the title of our lesson last week! What could it mean, then?"

"Don't fish have souls?" I asked, surprised.

"Of course not," answered Helen. "Only people go to heaven."

"What happens to the animals?" I hardly dared ask her.

"They turn back into earth."

"All of them?"

"All of them."

And my lovely spotted cat who loved nothing better than to nap by the stove in winter, would she too lie down in darkness? But I knew there was no point in asking about special cases if the rule applied to all. No doubt God didn't want puppies chewing up His golden slippers and peeing on His marble floors. I felt like crying, I could not imagine a world without animals. Even if I had none around me by day, I would need them at night. For whenever I could not sleep my mother would say, count sheep. I counted, one, two, three, four, and waited for the sheep to appear. But it was always buffalo that came to be counted, shaggy yet delicate, as if sketched on the walls of a cave.

They floated out of the wall by my bed, crossed the dark without looking back at me, and passed silently into the mirror over my dressing table.

Suddenly I thought: if God does not mind wearing an ass's head, then why doesn't He let the whole animal into heaven?

"Not a one will get there, because they have no souls," said Helen.

"Do you think Nuisance will come back?" asked Galen.

Helen sighed.

"Dogs always come back."

"Tell some more signs," I said.

"In the last days," continued Etta, "God will send His star, just like He did when Christ was born. It will look like a big hand coming closer and closer. And then God will appear, not just to a few people in Sweden or Japan, but to everybody at once, like lightning."

Somebody tapped on the window over the sink, and a man's face lurched past, like a cracked moon.

"It's Caleb!" screeched Helen. "Don't let him in!"

We all rushed to close the kitchen door, but Helen rubbed the latch on the screen the wrong way, and in walked Caleb with his hands up, empty whiskey bottles on all his fingers.

"I've come to pick up Penny."

"Penny is at church," said Helen, her voice shaking.

"Church? Well, I'll wait for her."

"Suit yourself," sniffed Helen. "When my father comes home, you'll get it."

"Me and your old man are going hunting together next Sunday. Doves are thick this year."

"You shoot doves!" cried Etta. "Dreadful!"

Caleb shook the bottles off his fingers, one by one, and lined them up against the stove. Then he pulled off his sheepskin coat and threw it on the floor. Then he kicked off his boots. I could see skin peeking through his black socks like stars.

"Tell your dad to keep his bottles at home," said Caleb. "Tell him I saw ten empties running up Mulberry Street like a pack of dogs."

He drew up a kitchen stool and sat down.

"You can wait here till doomsday," snorted Helen. "No girl will look at a man who can't make a decent wage for himself."

Caleb smiled. He'd seen plenty of girls looking.

"I make a decent wage. I got my own place now, too. A little cabin behind Mount Kisco. No water except for a stream. No electricity. No cops." And then he added as if it had just occurred to him, "Why doesn't Penny want to go out with me?"

"Because you're no good," Helen said vehemently. "What woman wants to sit up with a man on Mount Kisco? A woman likes to be comfortable."

"Penny said that?" asked Caleb, surprised.

"Mother said it," admitted Helen.

I knew it was all over now with Mrs. Malory. Caleb's revenges were swift. When a Mercedes nosed his old Ford out of a parking place, Caleb came back to let all of the air out of the tires and stole the hubcaps. He sent snakes to those who spoke ill of him; Reverend Peel's wife received one in a teakettle, sent anonymously, which slithered out of the spout the first time she filled it with water.

"What do you do on Mount Kisco?" I asked him.

"I watch for forest fires and make shoes."

"Shoes?" exclaimed Etta. "Who taught you how?"

"I taught me. When I've learned everything there is to know about leather, I'm going out to the West Coast to make me a fortune."

A thin wail brought Helen to her feet.

"The baby wants his bottle," she said brusquely, and hurried out.

"If you ever need a sitter," Caleb called after her, "I'm available."

Etta snorted, but Caleb paid no attention and turned instead to Galen.

"I've got a little present here for Penny."

And he bent down and began searching through the pockets of the coat he'd thrown on the floor. A couple of quarters spun out on the linoleum. A keyring with a medal on it plunked at his feet.

"What's that?" I asked.

"That's Jude, Saint of the Impossible," he answered, pocketing it and still searching.

"But you ain't Catholic, are you?" said Etta.

"No, I'm not Catholic. I got it from a buddy in the army."

"Do you believe in God?" persisted Etta.

Caleb shrugged. "When I was an altarboy in Sioux City, I wanted to be a preacher."

"You! A preacher!" shouted Etta, turning red. "The way you drink!"

"Christ drank," said Caleb quietly.

"And running around with women!"

"Christ ran around with a lot of women."

Etta was speechless. She wanted to walk out on him, but she could not take her eyes off what looked like a couple of leather bandages he was unrolling across his knees. Black leather, painted with flowers, the toes tooled with leaves, the cuffs studded with nails and, unmistakably, silver garters at the top.

"What beautiful boots," I told him.

"These are stockings," he corrected me.

"Leather stockings?" exclaimed Etta, astonished. "I never heard of leather stockings."

"Well, now you have," smiled Caleb.

He picked one up and stroked it like a cat, then laid it across the kitchen table. For the first time I noticed he used only one arm. I nudged Galen and whispered: see, one arm.

"How did you hurt your arm?" asked Galen loudly.

I saw Etta close her eyes.

"Jumping down Niagara Falls when I was young."

Etta opened them again.

"How old are you?" I asked.

"Twenty-three."

This saddened me. Anybody over nineteen was, in my mind, old enough to be my grandmother. As Caleb was leaving, we heard Helen tiptoeing down the stairs. Waving to us, he called over his shoulder.

"I'm going to church, ladies. And if Penny is with anybody else except her mother and her sisters, I'll cut him in two."

The privet hedge was wet with dew. I hoped no slugs would drop on us as Etta pushed our way through.

My mother, barefoot, in her bathrobe, let us in.

"It's nearly midnight! Where have you been?" she hissed.

But instead of scolding Etta, she scolded me. "If you want to get up for the sunrise service," said Mother, "You'd better go to bed instantly. You and Kirsten are sleeping on cots in the kitchen. Your aunt and uncle are here. Etta, I made up the sofa-bed for you. It's too late for a cab."

"My nightgown is in my room," I whispered.

"Never mind your nightgown," said my mother. "Uncle Oskar's asleep in there. You can sleep in your underpants. And if you smell the ham burning, wake me up. I've got it on low."

Kirsten was sleeping in the middle of the room with a pillow slip over her head, which she started wearing the night a bee crawled into her hair. Though I lay perfectly still, I could not fall asleep. The buffalo did not come to be counted, and the enamel pots hanging on the walls watched me like a dozen moons.

I heard my cat scratching faintly at the front door.

I got up and opened it, and somebody pulled me outside. But outside was inside; all around me, torches sputtered and popped, clothes smelt of pitch, and my spotted cat was no cat at all, but a girl in a pied gown who scampered away down the aisle that opened at my feet.

The church looked fuller than I'd ever seen it. In front of the altar, Reverend Peel, by the light of the acolyte's torch, was censing the people with a sausage in his left hand and a pot of smoking shoes in his right. He had wreathed his bald head in poppies, turned his vestments wrong side out, and thrown away his glasses.

Kyrie eleison kyrie eleison

shouted the choir from the balcony over my head. And the people shouted back,

Hee haw! Hee haw! Hee haw!

Helen was walking, with measured tread, down the center

aisle, holding the baby wrapped in a rabbit skin. Diamonds blazed on her hair and on her eyelashes and on her white gown.

The King is coming, whispered Mother into my ear. The King is coming from a far country to bless the baby.

Everyone turned.

A donkey was walking sedately down the aisle, its ears crowned with ivy, its legs sleek in black leather stockings, a scepter locked between enormous teeth. The moon sprang out of its left ear, the sun out of its right.

Riding before it on a black goat, Caleb, splendid in white buckskins, strewed grapes for the donkey's hooves to crush into wine. And loping along behind came Nuisance, ribboned with penny whistles piping by themselves.

Now a shout went up from every throat. And in that instant I knew this was no donkey, but a magician disguised as a donkey, and one far more powerful than I. Slowly the beast turned around, showing its handsome black stockings. It stepped up to the altar and laid aside the scepter. Helen held up the baby and it touched the holy water to eyes, lips, and ears.

When it finally spoke I knew the King had always been speaking, only I had not had the ears to hear. It did not ask Helen to abjure the devil and all his works, yet I knew it was not the devil. It did not promise salvation, yet I was sure it had come to save us.

"And some there be," said the donkey, speaking very quietly, "who have no memorial; who are perished, as though they had never been."

Over our heads, the carved rafters remembered their names: oak, ash, maple, and pine. They put out bark and leaves, and the angels carved there were no more. The scepter shrank to a hazelwand, but the beast did not notice.

"But these were merciful men," it continued, "whose righteousness has not been forgotten."

The glass in the windows blew away, sparkling like a million grains of sand. The pews rolled up into logs, grass grew between my toes, I could not see who stood beside me and I could no longer remember my own name.

But the donkey's voice breathed over me like wind across a

field: "Their seed shall remain forever. Their bodies are buried in peace, but their name lives forevermore."

Then, not three feet away from me, Etta turned over on the sofa-bed and sighed deeply.

The morning air raised gooseflesh all over me as I awakened, and I knew it would be cold on Steeple Hill when we gathered at the cemetery for the sunrise service.

Up on Steeple Hill, where all our people lay buried, a wind bowed the bare trees and sent the clouds scudding like foam as we waited for Reverend Peel to open the gates to the cemetery.

Most of the fathers, including mine, were home in bed.

Over the heads of the women and children, the gold cross swayed in the pastor's hands. The acolyte lifted the Easter banner high as a sail; its embroidered lamb sank and swelled, all heartbeat and pulse in the wind.

"Where is the sun?" I asked my mother.

"Behind the clouds."

"But how do you know, if you can't see it?"

"Because it's light outside."

Kirsten fiddled with the little silver cross she wore only on Sundays. She had a new pink coat, and I caught myself wondering how long before she'd outgrow it and I could have it.

His vestments blowing like laundry, Reverend Peel threw open the gates at last, and we marched in singing.

> *Holy, holy, holy! Lord God Almighty!*
> *Early in the morning our song shall rise to Thee!*

Are the dead surprised? Do they look at us, do they look at me? Does an old woman see her features in mine, does an old man see in Kirsten his young wife who died so long before he did? Do they sit in their graves as we sit in our pews, are we the service they wait for?

We walked two by two, singing bravely against the wind.

> *Though the darkness hide Thee*

How lovely it was there in the morning! Patches of snow gleamed in the shade of the headstones, but everywhere else the grass showed damp and green, though it had lain there the whole winter.

An American Childhood or,
How I Made Two Dollars on the Stock Market

When I was a kid I had plenty to eat, plenty to wear, and no money. Not that I had money and used it unwisely. Rather, I never had any at all. Other kids got allowances, which they saved for comics and Christmas presents. Whenever I asked my mother for an allowance (for it was she who managed the dispensation of the money my father gave her), she would say, "What do you want an allowance for? Haven't you got everything you want? How much do you need? What do you want to buy?"

Unlike other children, my sister and I had no plants to water, papers to burn, wastebaskets to empty, snow to shovel, or leaves to rake. My mother could iron a shirt by the time she was seven and for her children she wanted nothing less than the golden age: *no occupation, all men idle, all.* Living off her love and the fat of the land.

But surely, even in the golden age, there were times when you wanted money. *How much do you need? What do you want to buy?* You couldn't go up to your mother and say, *I need ten dollars to buy you a new nightgown,* or *I want five dollars to buy you a pair of slippers.* Why these presents? Because I knew that the things my mother really wanted cost money. A new toaster. A musical fountain for the center of the dining-room table. A black swan. (She never got the swan.) Sometimes I made Mother's Day presents in Sunday School, but I couldn't possibly make a toaster or even a pair of slippers that carried the sheen and status of a store-bought pair.

By the time I knew I was poor, my sister, just turning twelve, was beginning to receive money instead of Girl Scout stationery for her birthday. Five dollars in a card from Aunt Trixie and Uncle Nat who were well-off. Ten dollars from Uncle Win in Alaska who was rich. Kirsten saved diligently and could afford to buy socks and ties for Father, and gloves and lapel pins for Mother. *Real* presents, I thought enviously, because you could count their weight in silver, and other hands made them; you couldn't possibly make them at home.

I was poor in the middle of World War II, when everyone around me was saving like mad. Bacon grease. Tin cans, which my father jumped on after dinner, to flatten them out before stacking them under the sink. Milkweed-down for life preservers. Tinfoil from chewing gum—except you couldn't buy chewing gum and nobody wrapped it in tinfoil any more. In school we saved defense stamps (bought by Mother for Kirsten and me); first period we sat around licking them into our savings books. The teacher had a poster which showed Mickey Mouse in the cockpit of an American fighter plane, making the V for victory with his white-gloved cartoon fingers. Bath-water—if I let the tub fill up, my mother warned me of more stringent economies than mine:

"The King of England is only allowed six inches of water for his bath."

I never knew how my mother was privy to this information, but who was I to outspend the King of England? Whenever I turned on the radio, I heard it again: *save, save, save.* Vital war materials. So conscientious was my mother, that when a radio announcer once promised to describe a nutritious food—available free at most markets because it was wastefully thrown out even while thousands starved—she tuned in the next day and listened attentively to a recipe for stewed cauliflower husks. She unraveled her old sweaters and reknit the yarn into squares for the afghan that her bridge club was making to warm the frozen feet of soldiers in France.

I saved bacon grease, tinfoil, milkweed-down, bathwater, defense stamps, everything but money. And I felt the agony of Christmas and birthdays more keenly than my sister, for even before the relatives gave her money on holidays, she made nice presents in school. She made rafia keyrings and crocheted potholders, mock Indian wallets out of birchbark, and apples stuffed with cloves for sachets, presents that anyone would be pleased to own.

I made nothing in school that could conceivably be given as a present. The endless murals of George Washington and Columbus stayed in the classroom. The bean-sprouts and sweetpotato vines which we grew in science would make a sorry gift to open on Christmas morning. Every year till I was twelve I looked through the magazine my mother ordered in my name: *The Bluebird*. The inside back cover sometimes showed an ad for shoes with bedsprings built on the bottom that would let you leap over fences; I coveted them for years. Two weeks before Christmas, I'd lug all the back issues out of the closet and scan the section headed "things to make." When I was seven, I made —on the advice of the editors—the present recommended for mothers: a lovely nut-bowl out of a dried grapefruit rind. A diagram showed how to peel out the inside, stuff it with newspaper, and let it dry hard as wood. I followed the instructions to the letter, and marched up to Grandfather's tiny room on the third floor, and hid my rind nut-bowl under the radiator.

Grandfather's room easily held everything he owned. He owned nothing and kept nothing for long. Three years earlier, Grandmother had walked out on him and moved in with us, and he had lived on alone in the old house in Coronna. When Grandmother died he decided to visit his daughters, first Minnie and then my mother. He came one Christmas and stayed for good. He allowed himself two indulgences: books and tobacco. My mother bought him his tobacco and he borrowed his books from the Public Library. He never bought books, because whatever amused or interested him, he kept safely banked away in his head. All these stories, poems, people, and places furnished him good company. When he thought he was alone in the house, he recited Poe at the top of his voice:

> *She was a child and I was a child,*
> *In this kingdom by the sea.*

which sometimes turned into:

> *When you were a tadpole and I was a frog,*

because the riddle of evolution gently nagged him, like a conscience he could not appease.

I used to argue this riddle with him for hours, or rather, I used to discuss it, for no one ever argued with so mild a man as Grandfather. A pale, small man, he sat on the edge of his bed, and in his long underwear—which he wore summer and winter— he looked as frail as if he were bent out of pipecleaners. Mother had put a silver bell on the table by his bed, in case he should want something, but he never rang it. I would fold myself up in his easy chair and lop one leg over the arm, and he'd tell me about the time his father had seen William Jennings Bryan on a streetcar in Pennsylvania and heard him rail against the cross of gold. Even in my mother's day, Grandfather assured me, the evolution course in college was considered faintly sinful.

"Tell me about the fire department." For evolution opened the gate to all other topics; that's where you had to start.

"Why, we had a pole to ride down, and sometimes I drove the horses. First time I drove 'em, they galloped clean past the fire—a good ten blocks; we had to turn around and 'start over."

My mother told me a different story: how her father was so brave that he never had to polish the truck, and how he read all the books in the Des Moines Public Library and met my grandmother, who was working as a hostess in a lunchroom. At home in Coronna he kept chickens and bees. He was always very fond of bees, and could walk among them and gather honey without the beekeeper's black hood, because they loved him, and bees never sting those they love.

"If the bees get a new master, he has to come out and introduce himself proper to them. Else they won't make any honey."

"Tell me about the fire department."

"Why, I remember one day I was riding on the truck and a

rat fell into my boot, and I rode half a mile with him nibbling at my toes."

And now he was content to live his life in one room, where his mind sparkled like a star lodged under our eaves. I'm poor enough to see angels, he would tell me with a smile. Haven't seen one yet, but I'm waiting. Right down there among the pear trees I might see one. You got to apply yourself to it, he'd say and spit out the wad of tobacco he'd been holding in his mouth.

My mother disliked his tobacco-chewing, but he would not give it up. Kirsten and I once begged him to enter a tobacco-spitting contest in the County Fair. Out of modesty he declined, but when we saw a young man beat out an old woman who had painted her gums with snuff, Grandfather muttered, "I could've beat *him* easy." When he wasn't chewing he smoked cigars, and once late at night, as he dozed in bed, a live ash set his rug on fire. Rather than raise the household, he stamped it out himself and neatly snipped off the burned part. My mother, bringing his breakfast up the next morning, stared at it for several minutes, without knowing why. And then she said:

"I believe that rug has gotten smaller."

"I believe it has," said Grandfather.

When she emptied the wastebasket, she discovered the evidence and immediately sent away for the Jackson Portable Fire Escape—as advertised in the Sunday magazine section of the *Detroit Free Press.* A month later, there arrived an entanglement of ropes and knots, which lay heaped on the floor in Grandfather's room like a huge platter of unkempt spaghetti. Descending it down the side of our house would have done credit to Harold Lloyd. After two days, Grandfather pushed it into the closet and shut the door on it.

In the summer, he was lonely for his bees. Mother considered putting a hive in the attic across from his room and extending a hose out the window, through which the bees could come and go, till the bee-seller informed her she would be violating an ordinance of the Board of Health. So Grandfather comforted himself by going downstairs every morning and stroking the milkman's horse. She wore blinders and stood patiently in front of each house, undisturbed by the clanking of empty bottles behind her in the truck. And Grandfather would return as pleased as if he'd visited an old friend—one of his fire department horses, big and graceless and comfortable.

It was to Grandfather's room I brought my grapefruit rind, stuffed with newspaper, and swore him to secrecy when I hid it under the radiator. For him, the problem of buying Christmas and birthday presents didn't exist. He had no money of his own, and everyone knew it. Furthermore, at his age he'd already bought a good many. When you get old, people didn't expect it of you; you received, and if you gave at all, you gave yourself all year round, as Grandfather did. When my mother came up to call me for dinner—carrying Grandfather's on a tray—I would exchange wise looks with him, for we knew my nut-bowl was growing gold as the sun and hard as a silver dollar, and I would lacquer it till it shone like a Chinese tea-box, as the instructions advised. Nobody else would give her anything like it.

This, as things turned out, was perfectly true. Two days before Christmas, I took the bowl out of hiding, a brittle, sallow shell of the rind I'd so carefully peeled and stuffed and dried.

"Done to a turn," said Grandfather, politely. "Are you going to paint it, or leave it *au naturel?*"

But nobody in the house had varnish and I had no money to buy any. So with a few misgivings I wrapped my nut-bowl and set it under the tree. I shall never forget my mother's expression when she opened it. She had just received a chenille bathrobe from my father, deep blue and furry, and the aunts, uncles, and other guests were passing it from hand to hand, petting it. Then Aunt Nellie, wearing a Santa Claus face-mask, handed my mother a strange round package, like a large pincushion. I recognized the Happy Birthday wrapping paper and my heart sank. Mine was the only present that didn't come in a box.

"I wonder," said my mother, "what *this* could be. Erica has been working on this for weeks."

The outer wrappings fell away, and then the toilet paper with which I'd swaddled the gift inside. And then she lifted out my bowl. Her head jutted forward, her eyebrows shot up, and she said nervously,

"Oh."

And then,

"How lovely!"

"It's a nut-bowl," I said, ready to weep. For when she set it among her other presents, I saw how it had withered.

That year my sister gave her a pair of purple gloves and I gave her a grapefruit rind as hard and wrinkled as a shrunken head. And what separated the largesse of one from the failure of another was money.

My father had an elderly sister, Aunt Carrie, whom I especially loved because she alone of all my acquaintances seemed to share my predicament. She was stout, unmarried and taught piano in a large old house which bore the sign: *Willard Institute of Music.* Not only did she have no money, but she was crippled as well, and moved about slowly, leaning on a cane. She ordered her presents entirely from descriptions in catalogues or asked her friends to choose them at church bazaars. Every year she gave Kirsten and me dresses that never fit us, and she gave my father handbooks of chemistry that he himself could have written; vast simplifications of the courses he taught at the university. To my mother, she once gave a ceramic cowhead, accompanied by a brochure explaining that it was a reproduction of the figurehead on an Etruscan harp.

My grandfather had no money, but he had no need of it, whereas Aunt Carrie supported herself in a style both elegant and shabby. Indeed, looking at my father's family, I could almost believe I'd inherited my insolvency. My father had invested the legacy given him when he entered Harvard and lost it in wildfire mining stocks. His younger sister married a man from a fine old Boston family who earned so little as a broker that they could scarcely pay their rent, and so they lived like paupers among fine linens, Chinese screens, Dresden candelabra, and silver samovars. Their surname was Coronet, and the little crown they printed on everything, from stationary to sealing wax, suggested that they might be titled and impoverished aristocrats. My mother's people had emigrated from Germany and fallen briefly on hard times only because they'd left all their wealth behind them. But my father's people, having missed the May-flower, caught the next ship out, which meant they'd had at least three hundred years to settle their financial problems. Unless you saw it as an inherited weakness, there was no other way to explain their insolvency.

Aunt Carrie received the family silver and all her sister's treasures, and she sold them without compunction until my father helped her to pay the taxes and the upkeep on her huge house in Battle Creek. I thought it a splendid house to live in. The bedrooms were as big as the inside of a church and each had its own tiled fireplace and mantelpiece carved with unicorns und griffins. Boxes of firewood stood outside them. The floors were patterned in stars and flowers of different kinds of wood; you could amuse yourself stepping from flower to flower, avoiding the stars, or stepping on the stars and avoiding the flowers. Two turrets decorated the banisters at the foot of the stairs, behind which a large oval stained-glass window showed, over an appropriate inscription from Solomon, the lilies of the field that neither toil nor spin.

With all this space and ornament, my aunt lived as if she had none, for she rented her upstairs rooms and used the downstairs rooms for practice studios. Everywhere you looked, even in the hallways, you saw small parlor organs and upright pianos, very old, but always perfectly tuned, for my aunt could not bear an off-key piano. At Christmas, when she played "Silent Night" for us, she sometimes flatted the E throughout and considered the discord a great musical joke.

For Kirsten and me, she composed duets. Kirsten always played the melody and I lumbered through the bass on the grand piano in her living room. I had learned that when you were small, you never got to play the melody.

Once, my aunt gave us a duet book with a sheet of stamps in the back showing famous paintings of musicians in muted sepia. As you learned the piece, you pasted the stamp beside it. I liked best the picture of Mozart playing the piano in his nightgown. He is about three years old and has crept up to the attic to practice, and his family has rushed in and discovered him. That's how I saw myself. During all those years of playing the bass I would learn the melody in secret, and one day I would play it better than any of them.

Aunt Carrie—my mother often said—was a lady of the old school. That meant she kept hairpins in the lap of a china harlequin reclining on her dressing table and had good taste, which was not subject to the whims of fashion. Every winter I looked forward to seeing her put on the fur stole which ended in the paws and heads of miniature foxes, the way I looked forward to seeing my favorite Christmas decorations. From a silver chain around her neck dangled a red stone, clear as Burgundy, about the size and shape of a chicken's heart. On her wrist she wore a plain oval band of soft gold, which Kirsten and I called her Easter-egg bracelet. She kept, among the music books by the piano, a few etiquette books, which—assuming she subscribed to their tenets—made me understand why my aunt had never married. They told you all the things you couldn't do, which included just about everything.

The nose should never be fondled before company, or, in fact, touched at any time, unless absolutely necessary. The nose, like other organs, augments in size by handling, so we recommend every person to keep his own fingers, as well as those of his friends or enemies, away from it.

A lady of the old school foresaw all the awkward situations outlined in Dick's *Society Letter-Writer for Ladies on All Subjects and Occasions Incident to Life in Good Society.* She could write a Letter Congratulating a Friend upon Finding a Lost Child: "God bless Essié." She could write an Answer to a Letter of Condolence on the Loss of a Limb: "Hoping to see you soon, maimed as I am." There were various suggestions for proposals of marriage that warned gentlemen not to sit on the grass with a lady unless the lady invited him. My aunt's only kiss, as far as anyone knew (for she seemed very honest on this point), came from the purser of the *Queen Elizabeth,* which carried her to London when, long ago, she gave concerts all over Europe.

Every year we visited her for Thanksgiving. Kirsten and I slept on a sofa in the front hall, under a yellowing tapestry of minueting ladies attended by the young Mozart, which fanned over our heads whenever the front door blew open. In the morning, waiting for adults to wake up, I kept my eyes on two harpies carved on the arch that led to the living room and waited for them to move. Beyond them hung a large oil painting of a coal shovel and a bag of chicken feed, framed heavily in gold. Kirsten and I would get out of bed and sit on the peacock damask loveseat next to the whatnot stand, and we would look at—but not touch—the crystal stallion bookends, the vinegar cruets, and the china milkmaid whose skirts rang when Aunt Carrie picked her up.

Because my aunt was too crippled to entertain extra guests, and her icebox was no higher than a dwarf's, we always took Thanksgiving dinner at the Mercycrest Sanatorium. We were the only family I knew who chose to spend Thanksgiving in a hospital. The choice was my father's. He followed a strict vegetarian diet and the Sanatorium outlawed meat, serving instead a curious line of meat substitutes: Proto-Bites, Soya-Chicken, Sesame Hamburgers. My sister and I never saw another child on the premises.

And the premises were ponderous. Black squirrels brought from Africa ran over the broad lawns, shaded with hickory trees and chestnuts and oaks. We filled our pockets with fallen chestnuts and peeled off the spiked armor to find the warm brown planet underneath, which Grandfather could make into pipes and jack o'lanterns.

In the parlor, a huddle of old men and women, as white and delicate as toadstools, waited for the dining room to open. Heavy Oriental rugs sucked up our footsteps. Nobody ever lit the fireplace. One end of a long table was heaped with back copies of *Prevention, Garden and Home,* and *The Christian Science Monitor.* A terrarium and an exhibit of stuffed birds—perched on a bough under a glass dome—stood at the other. In the vestibule, darkened by heavy woodwork, we hung our coats on antlers that sprang from the wall and we waited for the grandfather clock, which told lunar time as well as earth time, to ring us into dinner.

On every table bloomed an elaborate bouquet of yellow mums, the kind of arrangements you see at funerals or in sickrooms. Among the blossoms a sign hung like a blight: *Do not come to the table in your pajamas.* An elderly woman who looked more like a nurse than a waitress handed us our menus, which were tucked into blue folders the size of desk blotters. Each had its own silver turkey fastened on the painted snowdrift like a vigilante's badge.

"This is your Thanksgiving turkey!"

My sister's face fell, and did I only imagine that Aunt Carrie shared her disappointment? For when the Soybean Chicken arrived, she attacked it as if she'd been dreaming of it all year. But when the meal ended, I understood why she came here without a murmur: my father picked up the bill. And afterward, at her house, there would be a hurried whispered discussion between them, and he would loan her a little money. And we would sit down in the dark rich house, under the painting of the coal shovel and listen to Aunt Carrie play; my Aunt Carrie, brilliant and elegant, and poor as a snail, and quite dependent on my father.

It occurred to me that unless I nipped my insolvency in the bud, I might end up like Aunt Carrie.

Method #1: How to make money with a telescope.

When I was six and my sister was nine, we suffered together the anguish of buying our father a birthday present. There isn't much you can make for fathers; socks, neckties, and cufflinks must be bought. And we had no money.

How did other children make money? Mother once told me how she set up a little stand and sold lemonade for a penny a glass. But sugar was rationed now, and what would it profit us to sell lemonade and go without sugar for a month? An Indian girl I used to play with every summer in Iowa made twenty dollars exhibiting her grandfather, who had turned senile after being plucked from his reservation and now lived in a tepee in the middle of the dining room. The house was a suburban Cape Cod with wall-to-wall carpeting all over the downstairs, and he used to sit in the door of the tepee staring out of the picture window. It cost a quarter to confront him inside.

There was nothing particularly remarkable about *my*

grandfather, or at least, nothing that showed. One of my father's students, a Chinese girl who sometimes babysat with Kirsten and me, told us stories of how her mother bound her feet until she was seven, and how her grandmother's feet measured only three inches long. Having neither an Indian grandfather nor a Chinese grandmother, we settled upon a cardboard telescope that Father gave Kirsten for her seventh birthday. Whatever you saw through the glass dissolved in the hundreds of scratches that covered the surface. I had often aimed it at the moon, but even when the moon was full, I couldn't find it in the telescope. Nevertheless, Kirsten printed a little sign which she hung around my neck: TELESCOPE. A PENNY A LOOK. She gave me the tin cup that Mother kept by the washing machine for scooping out powdered soap, and sent me to pound the streets.

It was the first day of June, and the morning air was drenched with honeysuckle. Walking slowly under the arms of maples and elms, I scanned the street for customers. When I turned the corner into the next block, I spotted Professor Meyer, an aged physics professor who taught at the university and knew my father. One night he'd called to warn us that someone had found a bomb in the chemistry building where my father's best student, a Japanese boy, happened to be working late. My father rushed down to the lab and escorted him out.

When the old man saw me, he tipped his Homburg and smiled. I squinted at him shrewdly; he was reading the sign. He was stopping in front of me. He was going to give me a penny.

"A telescope! Well, well. What can you see?"

"The moon," I lied. "And the northern lights."

I forgot that in the middle of a sunny day he could hardly have seen the moon with the naked eye. And I'd seen the northern lights only once, when my father, wrapped in nothing but an old shower curtain, woke us all up and herded us out into the summer night to watch the lights blowing like dust across the sky.

Professor Meyer bent down and picked up the telescope, which was still fastened to my neck, and craned up at the sky.

"Ah!"

His breath smelled of garlic, his teeth were yellow, dandruff flaked his elegant gray sideburns, and hairs stuck out of his nose. I shuddered.

"The Pleiades!" shouted Professor Meyer. "The rings of Saturn! The Man in the Moon!"

He moved the telescope intently across the sky, then straightened up, and nodded solemnly at me.

"Well, that's certainly worth a penny."

Into my palm he pressed a Canadian penny. I had not seen one before and rushed home at once. I was elated; selling was easy. My sister was dancing up and down in the driveway.

"Look!" I shouted, waving my fist. "A rare coin!"

She seized it, examined the face of King George, and dropped the coin in the pocket of her shorts.

"What'd he say?"

"Said he saw the Pleiades. The rings of Saturn. The Man in the Moon."

"He did? Let me see."

I unyoked myself from the telescope and we took turns looking, but saw nothing—not even the maple leaves overhead that sometimes cast shadows like stars. We kept on looking until Mother called us for lunch. Ravenously hungry, I hurried to the kitchen, pulled myself up to the table, and started tucking my napkin into my T-shirt, when Mother said sharply,

"What in the world is that thing around your neck?"

I glanced down, trying to look as if I hadn't noticed it before.

"We wanted to earn some money."

"You went down the street with that sign on? Did you meet anybody?"

"Professor Meyer," I whispered. "He gave me a penny."

"Well, you'll just have to give it right back."

Silence.

"Can we mail it?" asked Kirsten. "I don't want to meet him."

"You can walk over and drop it in his mailbox."

She printed an apology on a sheet of Girl Scout Stationery, and glued the penny to the page. I was crushed, not only at the loss of our earnings but because we had to give up the Canadian penny. Couldn't we give him another one? My sister shook her head; if you were going to refund his money, you had to refund the same coin, not somebody else's.

For a long time afterward, I kept peering through the telescope, fiddling with it, hoping that I might see the Man in the Moon looking at me through his telescope—if he had one—and waving back.

Method #2: How to turn your teeth into money and how to make that money work for you.

Two days later, I lost a tooth. Joyfully I popped it under my pillow and the next morning found the dime. I considered pulling out all my teeth, which would net me about three dollars, but then what would I have left to sell?

Well, I had ten cents. So I walked down to Rathbone's "Men's Shop," where my father never set foot, but where my mother always bought gifts for him and for my uncles. Everyone knew us there. The heavy glass door wheezed shut behind me and I found myself surrounded by the hushed elegance of the rich.

There were acres of briefcases, forests of brass umbrella-stands, and a whole fleet of model ships for the well-appointed desk. I feasted my eyes on the silver cufflinks that looked like slide rules and the tie clips set with opals and abalone. The clothes brushes, cunningly shaped like hedgehogs. The alligator belts. The leather albums tooled in gold.

"How's your dad?"

I looked up at a tall smiling man whose handkerchief was folded to a point over the top of his pocket, like a paper hat.

"Fine," I said.

"Anything we can do for you? Socks? A shirt?"

"A handkerchief," I said desperately. I knew no sizes. I also knew that everything around me cost a good deal more than ten cents.

"For your dad, huh?"

"Yes."

The man opened a drawer behind him and drew out a flat box. He laid it on the counter and ceremoniously opened the lid on a handkerchief, held in by a ribbon of silk. The label, a golden shamrock, said *Irish Linen.* I felt my confidence shatter.

"How much have you got with you?" he asked in a kindly voice.

"Ten cents," I answered.

"Why," exclaimed the man, "that happens to be exactly the price of this handkerchief."

Such good fortune never happened to me again.

Method #3: How to make money by using your head.

My father and my uncles saved money by putting it in the bank. My mother and my aunts saved money by going to a sale and buying some article they didn't need. The money saved was the difference between the markdown and the full price. In either case, it took capital. And I hated to go bargain-hunting with my mother. For a good bargain, you generally had to queue up. For shoes, butter, nylons, tires, and sugar, you sometimes had to stand a very long time, knowing the supply was limited and that there might be nothing left by the time you arrived at the front of the line.

During the war the women in our family learned that the race belongs to the swift and the battle to the strong. My father had lost his last chance to buy Kirsten a bicycle because he hesitated. As he was walking it off the floor into the elevator, the store manager barred the way and announced that from this hour forward no more bicycles were being sold and there would be no more until after the war. After that my father succumbed briefly to the psychology of the women, and would stand in any line, whether he knew the object for it or not. One cold winter's day, he hopped into one that reached half a block, thinking he might pick up an extra pair of shoes or a pound of butter. An hour later, he found himself at the head of a line for Playtex girdles. That cured him.

Panic-buying was so common that one cut-rate department store made a regular game out of it. If my mother ever bought clothes there, she carefully snipped out the labels. Nevertheless, she faithfully attended the two-minute sales. A clerk walked around the store waving a flag which she would put down by a counter of goods on which everything was either rationed or half price. When she blew her whistle, all the shoppers ran, grabbing whatever they could carry away in two minutes.

It was at such a sale that my mother's sister, Minnie, obtained a remarkable wig. Remarkable, because she found it on a table of pocketbooks and the cut-rate department store did not stock wigs. My aunt had gone to buy nylons, seen the woman with the flag approaching the pocketbooks, and rushed in. All the pocketbooks eluded her, but when she emerged from the fray, she found herself holding a wig, the only wig in the store. It was unmarked. The girl at the cash register charged her five dollars, as it looked shopworn.

This was a bargain indeed, for Aunt Minnie was the only woman I knew who had a bald spot. She said she'd inherited it from Grandfather, who had no hair at all. But Grandfather was old, and old people got bald. My mother said that young people only lost their hair under dire circumstances. A student of my father's had a cavity filled at the student dental clinic and two weeks later all his hair fell out—including his eyebrows and eyelashes—and none of it ever grew back in again. His name, unfortunately, was Harry. Then there was Abigail Blake, the undertaker's daughter, who was a year older than Kirsten, and who wore satin dresses to school, cut—we supposed—out of shrouds. She'd lost all her hair at an early age because of a mysterious disease and she wore a wig made especially for her, said to have cost a thousand dollars.

Aunt Minnie had no mysterious disease that anyone knew of, and she had never set foot in the student dental clinic. Divorced four times, but not without hopes for better times, she taught seventh grade, drove an ancient Studebaker coupe, and worried about her falling hair. She greatly feared bats and wore a turban to bed that vibrated her scalp. Once a week she soaked her hair in tar soap and retired with a paper bag over her head which gave her an oddly ceremonial look the next morning, like the Pope in his miter. She stemmed the falling tide, but her hairs did not multiply. She used to say, half jokingly, that pretty soon you could count them on the fingers of one hand.

And now, like a gift from an unknown benefactor, this wig entered her life. A shrill blonde wig, knotted into Shirley Temple curls. She was as pleased as if she'd picked it out herself.

At that time, Aunt Minnie lived two blocks away from us. She had a cleaning woman, whose visits twice a week I dreaded, because she brought her two children along to play with me. Tony Bessimar was six, noisy, and harmless. Wilhelmina was eight like me, only dark-haired and skinny, and mean as a camel. If you waited for the bus with her, she'd talk pleasantly enough till it arrived, then she'd shove you into the street, shouting,

"Go catch the bus! Go catch the bus!"

If you played chopsticks on the piano with her, she'd cheerfully offer to take the bass, but when you came to the repeat, she'd push your head down on the keys and close the cover over it. And she smelled like pee.

We invented games and ran through them like candy. We played for a brief period on the swing-set my father put up for Kirsten and me, but he had forgotten to anchor it, and it jumped around so much that Wilhelmina complained it gave her nightmares. Every night she saw herself swinging over the top bar and sticking up there.

Then we played air-raid in Aunt Minnie's garage. We all loved air-raid practices in school, as only children who have never known war on their own soil can. The siren meant you got to sit in the basement, giggling among the pipes and furnaces. If you hadn't done your homework, there was always the chance that the siren might break up the class before you could be called on. One day a tiny girl named Rosalind Warwick appeared in school. She was from London, our teacher explained, and had been in real air-raids, and we must all be very patient with her. She came to my birthday party holding the hand of her nurse and couldn't play any of the games because she was afraid to let go. Rosalind Warwick had long red hair and high-topped shoes which her nurse buttoned with a hook. I thought she was beautiful. The first time she heard a plane fly over the school, she hid under her desk, and after that I didn't play air-raid any more.

So why did I endure Wilhelmina Bessimar and her brother Tony?

Because I was in love with her cousin, Jimmy Trotwood, who delivered groceries for his father's store, until on his eighteenth birthday, he enlisted in the air force. He had such a round, babyish face that he grew a moustache to make himself look older, and then shaved it off when Mr. Trotwood's customers complained their delivery boy looked like Hitler. Sometimes when Jimmy carried our groceries into the kitchen and put the milk and meat into the icebox, he'd see me peeping at him around the door, and he'd say,

"How about a spin around the block?"

He sat high in the seat of the truck and Kirsten and I stood beside him, feeling the wind rush through the open doorways on both sides and watching the familiar landscape grow strange to us, cut by the doorway into long panels, like a series of mirrors. Stacks of wooden delivery boxes rattled together behind us. When we came home again, I'd tell Grandfather about the ride and how I was going to marry Jimmy Trotwood when I grew up.

"What do you see in Jimmy Trotwood?" he teased.

I didn't know. It had something to do with the white shirts he wore and the way he rolled his sleeves up to the elbow.

"Maybe he's got another girl over at the high school."

"Maybe," I agreed. "But it's me he's going to marry."

"Well, how can you marry him unless you can make him stop growing long enough for you to catch up with him?"

When my father read in the newspaper that Jimmy Trotwood's B-29 had been shot down over France (and his remains shipped home in a box, added Wilhelmina), I was shocked, but not sad. Nothing is easier to love than a dead hero. Now he would be eighteen forever. All during the war I collected pictures of B-29s and listened eagerly whenever I heard the radio newscaster mention them.

I loved Jimmy Trotwood, dead or alive, and therefore I was the only person who had a reason to endure Wilhelmina, though that reason had nothing to do with Wilhelmina herself. She belonged to none of the girls' cliques at school, and Wilhelmina desperately wanted followers. She dreamed of being invited to join the club of six wealthy girls who called themselves the Gay Giddy Gigglers and wore gold lavalières with GGG inscribed on them. The lavilières were provided free by Emil Ragusa, a jeweler, whose daughter presided over the GGG girls. Wilhelmina had neither wealth nor father nor friends. One warm spring day, when she knew her mother was safely installed at Aunt Minnie's, Wilhelmina said,

"Let's start a club."

"What kind of club?"

"Any kind," said Wilhelmina.

Tony, who always lagged, kicking pebbles, about four yards behind so as not to be identified with us, gave a shriek of joy.

"Can I be in it?"

"We don't have a club house," I objected.

"I know where we can get one."

"Where?"

"Follow me."

I followed her past all the houses till the sidewalks ended and the raw muddy fields began. Soon we were slogging along the highway to Detroit. My mother had forbidden me to walk there. The road burned the soles of my feet through my sneakers, but the shoulder was muddy, and Tony kept stopping to pick up the butterfly wings that littered our path. Trucks whizzed by us. We passed a small pasture of sheep and then arrived at a bleak Quonset hut which called itself "Smythe's Furnishings." Its corrugated roof glittered in the sun.

Barrels and signs cluttered the road across from Smythe's Furnishings. A man slouched down in a khaki truck was keeping an eye on thirty boys who seemed to be digging up the pavement.

"What's POW?" asked Tony, kicking his sister.

"Where?"

"On that truck."

"POW," said Wilhelmina. "It says POW!"

And she punched me in the stomach. The boys looked no older than Jimmy Trotwood and had sandy hair like his and round faces. They stared at us in silence as we trudged up the muddy path to Smythe's Furnishings. The building was sealed shut, windowless, and studded with padlocks.

"We're here," said Wilhelmina, hurrying around the back. The gazes of the man in the truck and the boys on the road made us both nervous. "Look!"

Scattered over the field lay hundreds of boxes. Boxes so big you could keep a washing machine inside, or a stove. Small boxes, for carrying cats. Middle-sized boxes, big enough to sleep in. Tony kicked at the biggest one, trying to smash it.

"You kick that box once more and you can't join our club," bellowed Wilhelmina. "We're gonna take that box back for our clubhouse."

I didn't want to sit under a box with Wilhelmina Bessimar who smelled, and Tony, who was always kicking things. And I didn't want to lug it home.

"Let's each have our own box," I said. "It'll be more exclusive that way."

We picked out three and carried them home on our heads and set them up in Aunt Minnie's backyard. We could call ourselves the Boxer's Club, Wilhelmina decided, and at all our meetings we would sit under our boxes and talk.

"And you can't come out till I say so," she added.

"When's the first meeting?" I inquired.

"Right now. Get under your boxes."

Mine was hot and dark as a closet. It trapped my own voice inside, like a creature being preserved.

"Hello!" I began politely.

Nobody heard me. I heard nobody, either. There passed a few minutes of clumsy silence. Then suddenly Wilhelmina shouted for all the world to hear,

"Erica wears a wig!"

"What?" I cried.

"Erica wears a wig!" she sang. "Erica wears a wig!"

"That's a lie."

"Your aunt wears one. She told my mother so."

"Well, I don't wear one."

"I'm going to tell everybody in school."

I jumped out of my box and she jumped out of hers.

"Feel!" I yelled. "Feel my hair."

"What's going on?" said Tony's voice.

Wilhelmina gave my hair a great tug and burst into gleeful whoops. She tugged as if she wanted to pull it out; my hair was curly, and much prettier—my mother said—than Wilhelmina's. From then on, whenever I saw her, she'd whisper, "Let's see if you're wearing your wig today?" and she'd pull my hair. I thanked the good Lord that it was firmly rooted in my own head and wondered how Aunt Minnie could ever stand the shame of owning a wig.

If Aunt Minnie didn't make such odd demands on her cleaning women, I thought, no one would ever have to know about her wig. Aunt Minnie never settled for a woman who only swept and scrubbed. The women she found were jills of all trades; while the kitchen floor was drying, they'd mend your underwear, or stitch you a new dress, or bake bread, or play hymns on your piano. Mrs. Bessimar washed hair. She arrived with her mops, a box of curlers, a metal hairdryer so massive you could have jousted in it, and after she'd scrubbed the downstairs, she'd wash my aunt's hair in the kitchen sink. She'd once owned a place uptown, but lost her license when a hairdryer snapped off its stem and fell on one of the customers, trapping her inside like a clapper in a bell.

Mrs. Bessimar had told my aunt that the inside of her wig looked dirty, somehow, like a soiled collar. Aunt Minnie decided to have it washed. Knowing the state of my finances, she telephoned one day and asked to speak to me.

Nobody ever telephoned and asked to speak to me. Elated, I seized the receiver.

"Hello?"

"It's me, Minnie. How'd you like to make a dollar?"

"A dollar!" I shrieked. "What do I have to do?"

"Just let Mrs. Bessimar wash my wig on your head."

I was speechless with astonishment.

"When?"

"This afternoon."

My mother got on the extension and listened, as Aunt Minnie explained why she couldn't have it washed on her own head. She had dislocated a vertebra while trying to bite a loose cuticle off her big toe in the bathtub, and now she couldn't lean her head back for a month.

As soon as I agreed to do it, I worried that Wilhelmina would see me, and I would have endured all those weeks of allowing her to pull my hair for nothing. I called Aunt Minnie and made it clear that this was to be a very private affair. I would go only in the evening. Wilhelmina couldn't come. And all the shades had to be drawn.

At eight o'clock on a Friday night, I let Aunt Minnie drop me off at her house on her way to the movies. She gave me a dollar, which I wadded into the toe of my sneaker. Mrs. Bessimar was waiting for me in the kitchen, as nervous as if she were about to perform an abortion. She kept an unlit cigarette clamped between her teeth; I found out later she'd had a mild heart attack and given up smoking. She was the only woman I'd ever seen who could talk with her mouth shut, like a ventriloquist. Because she hated to stay alone, she had brought her friend Mrs. Toby, the wife of the janitor at the high school. When I entered the kitchen, Mrs. Toby was applying a henna rinse to her hair that made it stick straight out; from the back she looked like a whisk broom. Mrs. Bessimar sat me down in a chair with my back to the sink, swathed me in a plastic tablecloth, and took the wig out of its shopping bag.

"Most wigs have carrying cases," she observed, as she ran it under the faucet. Then she mashed it on my head and pulled the sides down over my ears. I shivered. It was like wearing a cap of icy pulp.

Mrs. Toby turned around and leaned forward. She had tied a huge apron under her chin.

"I never saw any real hair of that color."

"They never look natural," said Mrs. Bessimar.

She squirted shampoo out of the bottle and hit me in the forehead. Soap dribbled down into my eyes. Hastily she dabbed it away.

"You were real sweet to come and help your aunt out," she said. "It's such a trial, having a stuck back."

"Minnie got her back stuck?" exclaimed Mrs. Toby.

"In the bathtub. She can hardly move. There's nothing worse than a stuck back."

"No, a stuck jaw's twice as bad. Belinda Dorsey was singing in church and she got her jaw stuck during the benediction. Went around with her mouth hanging open for a week, things flying into it, flies, gnats, oh, it was terrible."

Suddenly I heard a familiar yell. Somebody was kicking pebbles against the window over my head.

"And you can't come out till I say so!" shouted the voice.

"You brought Wilhelmina!" I roared. "You told Aunt Minnie you'd leave her at home!"

"Why, what's the matter? We got all the shades down, don't we? I told her she's not to come in here."

"She doesn't mind anybody. My mother says so."

Mrs. Bessimar narrowed her eyes.

"She minds me. She gets her nose punched if she don't."

But now I was quaking like a sick bird.

"This water too cold, honey? Wigs has got to be washed in cold water, or they shrink up."

I shook my head and tried to divert myself by counting the number of objects in Aunt Minnie's kitchen. I noticed that she had criss-cross masking tape all over her windows, in case of air attack. I counted two jars of black-strap molasses, a tin of wheat germ, and another tin of soybean flour on the shelf under the cupboard. The cupboard was closed; I would have to estimate the number of plates and cups. It was like counting beans in a jar. I couldn't turn my head to count anymore; Mrs. Bessimar's hands gripped it like a vice. I could feel my ears filling up with soap.

Mrs. Toby scraped the last of the henna from the bowl, sloshed it over her head, stood up, and started walking around the kitchen.

"Your aunt does a lot of canning," she observed, peering into a cupboard behind me. "My stars! She's got at least fifty jars of pickled asparagus!"

"They're from her students," I explained. "She gets a lot of presents from her students."

The truth was, after every holiday, she'd bring them over to see if my mother knew anyone who could use a one-armed doll wearing an enormous knitted skirt—to protect the top of your piano, the child told her—or a set of hand-crocheted fuschia doilies, or a dead cactus, or a bag of diabetic cookies that tasted like dog-biscuits.

"You kick that box once more and I'm gonna smack you!" shrieked Wilhelmina's voice. It set the windowpane vibrating.

"I declare, you're nervous as a flea," said Mrs. Bessimar. "Didn't I tell you she's not coming in here?"

She rubbed more gently now, and I felt myself go all sleepy. Mrs. Bessimar started telling Mrs. Toby that she thought all the Germans who lived on Liberty Street should be routed out of town. She'd heard rumors of secret meetings at the Schiller Inn, where people gathered long after curfew to sing *Deutschland, über alles.* And Mrs. Toby told Mrs. Bessimar about her daughter. Ah, the troubles that a daughter can lay on your old age!

"I told her, 'Trudy Ann, just because you like roller skating doesn't mean it's right to be married on 'em. I know that Timmy skates, but what about Reverend Peel? Is it fair to ask *him* to risk life and limb?' "

"Terrible," agreed Mrs. Bessimar.

"Every night she goes to the skating rink. 'Well, it's your own business,' I told her, 'if you want to spend half your life at the roller-skating rink while other people are working for the war effort. You could get a good job in the munitions plant. Even Veronica Lake is working in a munitions plant now,' I told her. And I showed her the picture from the Sunday paper. And I told her right out that I don't think a roller-skating rink is at all a proper place to be married in."

"When does she want to get married?"

"When Timmy gets his leave. She wanted to get married over the telephone, but I talked her out of that one. 'Ma,' she said, 'I'd rather get married over the telephone than never get married at all.' "

I dozed as their voices hummed over me like telegraph

wires. Far away, a siren wailed. About five minutes later it stopped and we heard a pounding on the door. I was terrified.

"Kill that light!" shouted a man's voice.

"It's the warden!" hissed Mrs. Bessimar and leaped for the string that snapped the ceiling light off. Sitting in the dark, we heard him clumping away down the driveway. Mrs. Bessimar started rubbing my scalp again, as if nothing had happened. At least, it felt like my scalp. All I could hear was the squish squish that her hands made.

Mrs. Toby sighed deeply.

"The last time we had a blackout, it lasted nearly an hour. Why do they always come just when you're in the middle of something?"

Silence. Squish, squish.

"Think I ought to wash it out now?" asked Mrs. Toby's voice.

"Think you better," said Mrs. Bessimar's voice. "That henna takes fast. We may be here for ages. You sit up, Erica."

I could hear Mrs. Toby, as she felt her way over to the sink. Something clanged on the floor behind her. A dish broke. Sneaking up behind me, she lunged for the faucet. Water sprayed out and froze the back of my neck.

"Sorry," she said. "Now where did I leave those towels?"

"On the rack. Mind the table."

There was a heavy scraping sound as Mrs. Toby felt her way back and groped across the kitchen.

"What's the matter?"

"Stepped in a bucket."

"Lean back, Erica. I got to rinse out the soap."

She covered my face with her soapy hand.

"I said to lean back."

I leaned back stiffly, expecting the plants that my aunt kept on the sill over the sink to drop and crush my skull. Water hissed hot over my face and seeped through my hair.

"That'll do. Now you can go under the dryer."

She peeled the tablecloth off me, and gripping my shoulders, she propelled me slowly through the dark. I stretched out my hand and rammed my fingers against a metal rim.

"Ah, there it is! You just slip underneath. I'm gonna give you the dial so you can turn it down if it feels too hot."

She eased me inside, pulled the helmet down over my ears, and dropped a rubber switch the size of a melon into my hand. The wind roared around my ears. I imagined I was walking through a dust storm and waited for Jimmy Trotwood to come and find me. Then all my imaginings dried like the dew. I neither heard the all-clear sound nor saw Mrs. Bessimar turn the light on. Suddenly I looked up and saw her shaking me and felt her harsh grip on my shoulders.

"Where's Wilhelmina?"

"Minnie took her home. I think you fell asleep. Come on out, honey."

I crawled out, half paralyzed.

"Not bad," said Mrs. Bessimar, staring at my head as I plopped down into the chair by the sink. Mrs. Toby snorted.

"What do you mean 'not bad'? She looks like Harpo Marx."

"Well, it hasn't been styled yet."

Mrs. Bessimar plunged her comb into the wig that now felt glued to my scalp. At the first tug, she brought up a large tuft of hair.

"My God," cried Mrs. Toby. "You're killing her!"

Mrs. Bessimar stopped combing.

"That's peculiar," she said, and a puzzled frown settled on her face.

She combed more gently, using short hacking strokes. I saw clots of curls floating around me. Mrs. Toby began to sneeze.

"Is that her scalp showing through?" she exclaimed.

Mrs. Bessimar lifted her comb once more.

"Don't!" I cried. For though nothing hurt me, I believed it was my hair that hung like milkweed silk between the toaster and the stove.

But now Mrs. Bessimar pitted herself against me with all her strength.

"I *got* to get it combed," she shouted.

We watched in silence as the room filled up with hair, drifting lazily as if on the many surfaces of an invisible fountain. At the end of five minutes I was wearing a flesh-colored skull cap.

"For pity's sake," said Mrs. Bessimar. "Where'd your aunt get this wig?"

"At Kittelweed's," I whispered.

"You tell your aunt it ain't worth a dead Indian."

Method #4: How to make money by turning yourself into a magnet.

My sister and I had a knack for finding anything free. Every month we leafed through my mother's *Better Homes & Gardens* and *Ladies' Home Journal* and clipped out coupons for free information, and samples that promised a salesman wouldn't call. We got an endless stream of baby-food samples, fabric samples, flower seeds, plastic nipples, recipes, and descriptions of everything from floor plans to douche bags. If Mother kept us home from school because of sickness, we listened attentively for free offers advertised between the daytime radio serials, "Ma Perkins," "Portia Faces Life," "Lorenzo Jones," and "Mary Armstrong, Backstage Wife."

My father subscribed to science magazines which contained neither offers nor stories, and a spiritualist magazine which contained both, and made you feel rather sinful after you put it down, as if you'd taken part in a Black Mass. I made an effort to remember the stories; they beat anything I'd ever heard anyone tell in camp after the counsellor turned off the lights. I especially looked forward to telling the story of a man who loses his sight during the war and wears plastic eyeballs. He goes to a faith-healer in Madison Square Garden who prays over him, and the man feels it's only fair to warn her about his plastic eyeballs, but she's into it now, so he keeps quiet, and God Almighty! Suddenly he sees faces, hands, walls—the world! The pictures showed a blindfolded man riding a bicycle along the edge of the Grand Canyon; yes, he'd pluck out his eyeballs and read any book that was given to him. In the back of that issue, an ad promised a cure for nearsightedness ("throw your glasses away!") and my father sent for the cure, which turned out to be an eye-patch and a chart of letters. Every evening for a month I wore the eye-patch and tried to read the letters, but when I showed no improvement, he abandoned it.

The magazine also ran interviews with people who had seen flying saucers. My father longed to see a flying saucer and when the newspaper reported some, sighted about fifty miles from Detroit, he wanted to go and try his luck. He was as faithful as a pilgrim to astronomical events and once traveled a day and a night to see an eclipse of the sun visible only from Niagara Falls. He spoke to me of seeing Halley's comet, as a prophet might speak of seeing God; with reverence, delight, and regret at the passing of a vision.

"It'll be around again in 1985. I won't be here to see it, but you will."

At the same time, when he took Kirsten and Grandfather and me to watch Fourth-of-July fireworks in the park, my father saw explosions where Grandfather saw angels.

"Look at those beautiful red and white stars!"

"Strontium and magnesium," said my father.

And he added, as the Roman candles exploded into greenish blue flowers,

"With some compound of copper."

Then a golden chandelier blazed over our heads and we watched its fingers fade into yellow smoke.

"Sodium," said my father, as pleased as if he'd set it off himself. As a graduate student he had determined the atomic weight of lithium, and he knew from having stood deep in the heart of matter that all magic is illusion.

Knowing the limits of the material world, he craved an experience which would contradict them. A ghost. A miraculous cure. A loved one returned from the dead. The advertisements in the magazine which printed such stories suggested that even the most ignorant man could hook up with the spiritual powers that really controlled things, if he had faith. The scientist ciphers and serves matter; the magician commands and serves himself.

I pored over the ads uneasily. There were ads for touchstones and fortune-telling fish, for Tarot cards, genuine Carnelian scarabs, and Voodoo dolls in ten symbolic colors (they came with an instruction manual) which were imported from Haiti. There were love-amulets and meditation-jewels wrapped in purple velvet pouches, courses in the wisdom of the ancients, and crystal balls, "unconditionally guaranteed, suitable for all occult work: an outstanding value for the beginning practitioner." There were cures for bedwetting, stammering, and fainting, there were blessed handkerchiefs prayed over by a woman who accepted specific requests. For a fee, Madame Jupiter would read your horoscope, and the witch doctor Ugo Ugo would solve your problems and heal your parakeet or cat or dog by mail.

It was in such a magazine that I saw an ad that leaped off the page at me and spoke to my condition.

"Rid yourself of money problems forever! Why labor and toil? Let our Wizard record make you a magnet for money."

Kirsten read it over carefully. You could send for the record at ·no charge and keep it for a ten-day trial period. If your life didn't take a turn for the better, you could return the record without further obligation. If you kept the record, you sent five dollars. This was risky, as a five-dollar debt would have demolished us financially. We persuaded Grandfather that our situation was urgent and printed his name on the coupon.

Two weeks later it arrived. My mother signed for the package and carried it up to Grandfather.

"Dad, did you order something from the Goldmine Record Company?"

Grandfather winked at her.

"A little surprise," he said.

"What is it?"

"Why, if I tell you, it won't be a surprise."

"Well, who is it for?"

He put his finger to his lips and smiled. While Mother was getting dressed to go downtown, I carried the portable victrola to his room. Kirsten was already unwrapping the record. The jacket showed a man with a hole in his head and coins strung on rays of light, streaming out of the hole. She started the machine and dropped the needle on the record, and we both lay down on the floor and pressed our ears to the speaker. First we heard a long prelude of harps and violins, and then a man's voice, which seemed to ooze from the depths of the motor.

Money is the staff of life. The desire for money is as instinctive as the flower's desire for water and sunlight. Man's desire for money is an expression of his instinct to survive.

The violins pumped to a crescendo, then eased away like twilight.

I desire all the wealth I am capable of receiving, and I know I can attain my desire. Because my desire for wealth is one and the same with my desire to survive, I shall use my will to procure this wealth.

"Close your eyes," whispered Kirsten.

I closed them. The last thing I saw was Grandfather shaking his head.

I see that through the power of my will, wealth is attracted to me. My will commands and money is drawn into the field of its power.

I felt power gushing through my veins. I poked Kirsten.

"Do you feel power gushing through your veins?"

"Kind of."

The voice droned on.

I make a picture in my mind of the amount I wish to attract, for all created things have their beginning in the mind.

A ten-dollar bill sprang up like a tree. Why stop there? A whole field of ten-dollar bills.

The picture shows me the money responding to my will.

Tomorrow. But that was too soon, maybe. And who was going to give me ten dollars? I visualized myself finding it outside the house. Would my mother let me keep it?

The picture shows me myself, holding the amount I wish to attract. The money has responded to my desire through the beautiful mystery of my will——

Suddenly Grandfather lifted the needle. Kirsten and I sat

up. My mother was calling to us that she had missed her bus and wasn't going downtown after all. Grandfather shook his head again.

"I don't think it's right at all," he said.

"What's wrong with it?" asked Kirsten.

"I don't know how to tell you, but it just isn't right. It's not healthy."

"I feel fine," I said.

"It is easier for a camel to go through the eye of a needle," said Grandfather, "than for a rich man to enter into the kingdom of God."

That night I took the portable to my room; Kirsten would have it the next night. Five days each and we could return the record. I lay down and listened to both sides all the way through, then started it from the beginning once more. Halfway through the second side, I fell asleep. I was awakened not by the record but by a commotion in the hall.

"It's a man's voice! I've heard it for the last fifteen minutes."

"I told you, my radio is off."

"Dad says it's not in his room."

And then my father's voice:

"It's coming from Erica's."

And then my mother's again:

"Call the police!"

I sprang out of bed and pushed the victrola under it. As I jumped back in I heard a cracking sound. When they opened my door, I feigned great sleepiness. Grandfather never gave me away. Kirsten mailed the Goldmine Record Company the five dollars Aunt Trixie had sent her for her birthday. We were no richer than before. I threw the pieces of the record into a trashcan down the street so that my mother would not find them.

Method #5: How to bribe God.

My father's spiritualist magazine suggested one last resort. If I couldn't earn the money, I could pray for it. Grandfather had often told me that faith moved mountains. And to judge from the stories in that magazine, it moved a good deal else: "The Effect of Prayer on Plants," "How Five Nuns Prayed their Way to 20-20 Vision."

The following Sunday, during silent prayer at church, I prayed for wealth. I made it very easy for God; I put my prayer in the form of a pleasant proposition. If I behaved well from now on, that is, if I stopped biting my nails, losing my temper, picking my nose, throwing my clothes on the floor, and talking back, God could send me the money. It was up to Him how He wanted to send it. And every night I would remind Him of our bargain.

Whether I had God or the devil to thank, I never knew. But a week later, my fortunes turned. I found five dollars on the pavement as I was walking to school. Not only was I allowed to keep it, but my father decided to start a bank account for me. It would encourage me to save, he told me. I needed no encouragement. Five dollars. And I had my own bankbook. I hid my bankbook in my notebook in school, and during lunch, I hurried over to check on my earnings. The teller accepted the book, disappeared for several minutes, then handed it back to me without batting an eye. I sat down in a big leather chair near the loan desk to admire the sum and felt my eyes nearly pop out of my head. Instead of five dollars, my account read:

$$\$65.00$$

For several minutes I debated whether to tell anyone about this windfall. It was a superb example of the efficacy of prayer. At dinner, I announced my new wealth and made a shattering discovery.

It wasn't from God. It was my father's mistake. He had gone to deposit sixty dollars in my mother's checking account and grabbed the wrong bankbook. But then God intervened. My mother decided to keep the money in my account. Money toward your college education, she said. And it'll encourage you to save.

She told the story to Aunt Trixie and Uncle Nat the next weekend when they stopped by for Sunday dinner. My mother's brother was a broker. He and his wife lived in a large house in the fashionable quarter of Metamora. Uncle Nat was a slender, athletic man who hunted on weekends and ordered his double-breasted suits from a brace of tailors in New York. He carried a Dartmouth cane that had a dog's head with blown-glass eyes carved in ivory on the top and the date of his graduation engraved on its silver collar. When he sat opposite my aunt in the big chairs by our fireplace, the two of them looked as solid and symmetrical as andirons. Uncle Nat listened to the story of my finances and chuckled.

"Well, well, you've got sixty-five dollars. That's not much to go to college on."

"No," I agreed, "But I'll earn more."

"You should let your money work for you." He leaned forward and clasped his hands. "Why don't you invest it? Seventy dollars would buy you one share of Metro Plastics. And that share would grow, split, and earn dividends for you."

I misunderstood him to say that I could buy one chair of plastic, which would somehow multiply, like the enchanted broom of the sorcerer's apprentice. A company made these chairs, and if they ever caught on, more would come forth from the side of the chair I'd bought for seventy dollars, and I'd be rich.

My father thought it a grand idea and offered to chip in five dollars to make up the sum for one share.

"Is it a safe company?" asked my mother. "You know, Erica, you can lose your money in stocks." She was no doubt remembering the legacy my father had lost.

I considered the possibility of losing it all. I trusted my uncle. I said yes, and signed my sixty-five dollars over to him. I then thanked God for my good fortune, stopped biting my nails, started picking up my clothes, and wondered, as the weeks passed, how my chairs were doing. If my uncle happened to telephone my father about matters of business, I hurried to the extension.

"How are my chairs doing?"

"Fine. Just fine."

Then—I think it was about two months later—he called to invite my parents to see the slides he had taken in Florida. At the risk of being called unpatriotic, he and Aunt Trixie had decided to travel during his summer vacation, though civilians were asked to restrict their travel, and the trains were full of soldiers.

"How are my chairs?"

"Fine," said Uncle Nat, but not as cheerfully as before.

Four days later, on a Thursday afternoon, my uncle came to see us. When I arrived home from school, Mother and Father and Uncle Nat were waiting for me in the living room. I sensed a solemn occasion. Uncle Nat stared into the empty fireplace. Everyone looked away from me.

"You remember you gave me seventy dollars for one share in Metro Plastics."

I remembered.

"Which we hoped would grow into several shares."

He coughed.

"Well, sometimes the companies do badly, and then the shares aren't worth anything. Not just your share, but the shares bought by everyone who has invested in the company."

"Where's my seventy dollars?"

"The company used it. But they weren't very wise. They've folded up, so to speak. Crashed, you might say. And when a company folds up, all the shares are wiped out."

I saw a nameless lunatic smashing the chairs, yanking off the backs, legs, and arms, stamping on them, burning them up.

"We told you it could turn out badly," said my mother. "You remember, Erica?"

"I remember."

"I'm terribly sorry. There was a little dividend, however."

And my uncle handed me a brand-new two-dollar bill. I had never seen one before.

"They're bad luck," said my mother.

"Only if you think so," said my uncle.

"Thank you," I said.

In a state of shock, I marched straight up to Grandfather's room and burst through the door.

"Uncle Nat lost all my money except a two-dollar bill. And Mother says a two-dollar bill is bad luck."

"Lost all your money?" gasped Grandfather.

I explained it to him as well as I could, but suddenly I had the odd feeling he already knew.

"Well," he said, "that's the trouble with money."

"What trouble?"

"You can lose it so fast."

"But I prayed for it."

"The Lord giveth and the Lord taketh away."

Outside the open window, a warm rain began to fall, even as the sun shone. When Grandfather saw this, he smiled.

"Rain and sun. The devil is beating his wife."

I twitched the two-dollar bill between my fingers.

"What'll I do with it if it's bad luck?"

"You can bury it. See if anything comes up."

"Oh, Grandfather!"

"You could bury it and start all over again."

I buried it under the maple tree in the front yard, not too deep because I didn't want to dig up the dead cat. I suddenly felt very clean, clean enough to see angels. The morning after my loss, I awoke to the sound of sirens and firecrackers. Japan had surrendered, crushed by a powerful new bomb. I did not know then that the world I lived in would never be the same again because of it. All over the city the firehouses were blowing their whistles. I was very poor and very unlucky, but there was a new day coming, and with the march of distant drums rumbling in my ears, I ran the twenty blocks downtown to catch the last of the victory parade.

PART II

THEO'S GIRL

Theo's Girl

She woke up suddenly, with the feeling that she had overslept an exam. Someone was throwing stones at her window. She peered at the luminous dials of the clock; the hands said four. If I can get outside without turning on the lights, she thought, I won't wake anybody up.

But there was her mother, standing at the foot of the stairs.

"It's a mighty funny time to be going out with him," she observed. "Did you sleep in those clothes?"

"I just lay down in them. I didn't want to miss him."

"Sit down and eat. I got oatmeal made and everything. You want to ask Theo to come in?"

She couldn't get up earlier than her mother, try as she might. There was always that oatmeal waiting for you, no matter how quiet you were.

"I don't have time. He'll be late."

Her mother made a motion as if to throw it all in the sink, and Erica repented.

"Save it for me," she said. "Save it till we get back."

Theo was in the truck, drumming his fingers on the side-view mirror, and she squeezed in beside him. The back, empty now—its double doors clearly visible—resembled a sepulcher.

"Did you wake your mother?"

"Nope. She's still in bed."

"She didn't think it was funny? Like we were eloping?"

"No. She knows I wouldn't do a thing like that."

It sounded hollow, it hung in the air like a defeat. She should have been capable of it. As they drove out of the city and turned onto the superhighway, Theo stretched in his seat and leaned forward, resting his elbows on the wheel.

"Well, this is another job I'm going to lose. I've been late the last three times. It takes an hour to get to Detroit, another hour to bring the bagels back, and there's a line of people outside Sol's store by eight."

"You overslept."

"Clock didn't go off. The cat slept on the plunger."

They rumbled along quietly; she was falling asleep.

"Hey, wake up! Did I tell you about my new job?"

"Another job?"

"Yeah. At the undertaker's. There's a German family in town, wants me to make a death mask of the uncle."

"Aren't you studying for your exams at all?"

He gave a grand wave of his hand.

"I got all my sculpture projects in. All I have is French."

She leaned her head against the window, trying to keep awake. For days she had imagined the two of them, rolling softly, secretly, into the morning, and here she was, hardly able to realize it. The broad backs of the Ford factories glittered past, the river and the island flashed at them once and disappeared. When she opened her eyes, the heat of the city laid its weight on her, and the bakers were already running back and forth, red-faced, stuffing the last bags of bagels into the back of the truck.

"You goon! Some company you were!" laughed Theo.

But it was the trip home she loved best anyway, she decided, when the bagels filled the whole cab with a smell of onions and fresh dough. Theo reached behind and feeling the top of the bags, helped himself to a bagel, broke it, and handed her half. In silence they watched the sky lighten and the trees grow friendly again as the dark lumps of leaves opened to lacy green. The truck turned into her street; no one was stirring.

"I'll pick you up later if you want to come with me."

"Where?"

"To the undertaker's."

She lingered outside, one foot propped in the open door.
"If you want me to, I will. My Aunt Minnie's supposed to come today."

"She's still working to get you baptized, huh?"

"No."

"You know, if you let her do that to you, we're through."

"I know," said Erica.

"Well, what for, then?"

She had half a mind not to tell him, but she was no good at keeping secrets.

"She's taking us to Hannah's. Now can't you guess?"

"Say it."

"A wedding dress. Hannah's making it."

"Jesus!" He shook his head and smiled broadly. "You really mean it, don't you?"

She nodded seriously.

"I'll wear my *Croix de guerre* that I won in France."

"You've never been to France," said Erica.

Theo pulled a look of broad astonishment.

"Would I lie to you?"

"Mother says you've never been there or won any cross."

"My blue heron," said Theo, reaching over to stroke the hair which swung over her face when she put her head down. "If I can just get you out of here before you start listening to your mother."

Her mother was waiting in the doorway, holding her pink wrapper closed, watching them with that wistful smile she got sometimes.

"I kept it warm for you."

There were moments when Erica wanted to kiss her mother, like just then, but she would have felt funny doing it. Neither of them was very demonstrative. They went into the kitchen, and Erica got herself a dish and skimmed the crust off the oatmeal. Her mother beamed.

"You used to do that when you were a little girl."

She walked around the kitchen, talking, while her mother handed her things: orange juice, prunes, toast, always enough for a battalion. It was a mutual nervous mannerism, her mother handing her things, Erica taking them, putting them down here and there, talking while her mother beamed.

Far overhead, a cracked voice burst into "What a Friend We Have in Jesus."

"I forgot to tell you—Minnie came in last night," said her mother.

Every weekend she came, ostensibly to get her new Ford fixed. There seemed to be no Ford repairman in Detroit. On Sundays she drove back to attend church. When the semester ended, she would move into Kirsten's old room for long periods altogether. Kirsten rarely came home to visit since she'd married and moved to San Francisco.

"Minnie's taking us to Hannah's. But she's got to study."

"Study?"

"They're doing the new math in the fourth grade, and she says it's difficult. You got to learn it to teach it. She's got a new electric organ, she says. And a scalp vibrator."

Instead of a husband, said Theo somewhere in the back of her mind, and she shuddered. But Minnie had had husbands enough. Four. Two insurance men, a floor walker, and—the first one—an engineer. Erica could not imagine what it felt like to have run through so many. A different life with each one—did they fall away like so many winters? But when you repent of your sins, all that is changed and forgiven, said Minnie. Changed and forgiven. You are a new person in Christ. A new person.

And the husbands, thought Erica. Had they been baptized away, the hurts and losses drowned somewhere forever?

"I ate almost all the oatmeal," she said. "I'm sorry."

"Never mind. I can make some more."

Thump, thump. She picked up her orange juice and wandered into the living room. Her father peered up from the floor where he lay on his back, slowly raising his legs and letting them down again. Usually he was up before any of them. Once, on a dark winter morning, she had thought it was a burglar.

"We had a good time, Daddy."

"Eh?" His legs paused in mid-air, and he lifted his head. His gray hair snapped with electricity from the rug.

"I said, we had fun."

"Where were you?"

"Theo took me to pick up the bagels."

"To pick up what?" He had probably never seen a bagel, let alone eaten one. "He still got that old car of his?"

"No," said Erica. "It quit running. He abandoned it."

"Lord," said her father. He lowered his head and closed his eyes. Then he opened them again suddenly, as if something had bitten him.

"Minnie driving you to Hannah's?"

"Yes."

They never spoke much. It wasn't just the gap of generations, though; she didn't know what it was. Now that he was retired she felt she ought to speak to him more, but she didn't know what to say. All he could remember about Theo was that he had a broken car. Sometimes he asked if Theo had gotten the left headlight fixed yet, so it didn't shine into second-story windows when he drove at night.

The voice upstairs gave way to a chorus. Erica heard hymns jogging closer, as from a wayward procession; then they clicked into silence. She went into the dining room and Minnie looked up brightly. Her hair, newly tinted auburn, had an odd shiny look, as if it were cased in plastic.

"If I can just hear a good sermon," she observed, "it makes my day. It's such a blessing to me, this program. I'll be ready to go as soon as I find my teeth. I always throw them out, in the night. It's my bridge, with the two front ones on it."

And then, as she pierced her grapefruit into sections with the wrong end of her spoon: "Why do old people look so bad without them? I look at my kids in school; they lose them and they look cute."

In their identical pink wrappers, her mother and Minnie really did look like sisters, though Minnie was thinner and better preserved. Except she always *looks* preserved, thought Erica, and she felt herself getting depressed, as if some blight had touched her. She let her mother bring her a cup of coffee and tried to be cheerful.

"How old is Hannah now?" she asked.

Her mother considered.

"She must be in her eighties. Imagine, living all alone on that farm, with nothing but sewing to support herself!"

"She has a brother, though," remarked Minnie.

"Divorced."

"No, that was the other brother," Minnie corrected her. "Jonathan went into a bakery and made real good. And when he started, he drove the wagon for twenty dollars a month."

"She's got a half-sister who lives in town."

"She must have married well."

"No, she didn't. She taught piano all her life. I got a letter from her husband after she died, so I wouldn't send anymore Christmas cards."

There was a long silence, during which they all avoided looking at one another. Then Minnie said slyly, humming under her breath,

"Is this your wedding dress Hannah is making?"

Erica had her mouth open to speak, but her mother got there first.

"It's just some white sewing. It could be a very nice graduation dress."

"I thought you told me it was satin."

"Lots of dresses are made out of satin these days."

"*White* satin?"

"Someday I could get married," said Erica in a small voice.

"*If* she decides to get married," added her mother. "There's lots of other things she could do. Paint, for example."

"You have to be terribly careful when you marry. They say you never know anyone till you're married to them," said Minnie. "Oh, I turned down some good ones, all right."

"Remember Irving Tubbs? I'd say you'd have made it best with him."

"Too late now," shrugged Minnie, without bitterness.

But already Erica had that sinking feeling again. They always seemed to be picking on her—not directly, of course, but in conversations she felt were performed for her benefit. My blue heron, I'm not your father, Theo would say. You don't want a father, you want a husband.

She thought of his little room over the laundromat; she had painted mermaids in the shower for him and had lettered his favorite epigram on a sign which he kept over his desk: ENERGY IS ETERNAL DELIGHT.

Sometimes they would lie down on the bed together and listen to the flute player in the coffeeshop next door one floor down, he wholly relaxed, she with one foot on the floor. For running.

That's how it is with you, he'd say angrily. Always one foot on the floor. Who do you think is going to come in, anyway? Your mother?

Did you lock the door? She'd whisper, agonized.

I locked the door, yes. Maybe your mother can go through locked doors?

"Immersion," Minnie was saying. "What have you got to lose? If the Bible says that you shall be saved through water and the spirit, why take the risk?"

"I'd feel a little odd about it," her mother answered. "If it's so good, why don't the Lutherans have it?"

Minnie shook her head. "Billy Graham preaches it. I'd arrange for a very private service."

"And you wouldn't tell anybody?"

"Not a soul."

Still her mother hesitated.

"Could I wear a bathing cap?"

"Did Christ wear a bathing cap?" asked Minnie severely.

Suddenly Erica felt ill. Why don't you say it, she thought angrily; he's an atheist, a confirmed atheist. It never bothered her until they talked about immersion, and then only in a sort of superstitious way because she felt she might be missing out on something—a heavenly reward she wasn't sure she deserved but might, by some fluke, get anyhow. It was that feeling of something left undone that bothered her most. Prudence—the seventh deadly virtue, Theo called it—and sometimes she felt that Theo was more religious than all of them put together. But art is not a religion, said Minnie. All the painting and sculpture in the world won't gain you the kingdom.

Erica had, somewhere, a paper napkin on which he had

written, "Someday I will show you all the kingdoms of *my* world." They were sitting in the German restaurant downtown, which was always so full at noon that they could hardly hear one another.

What kingdoms? she asked him then.

My blue heron, he said. My little Eurydike.

And a few days later he took her to see his city, which he was starting to build on the empty lot behind the laundromat.

It was a city to be made entirely of junk, he told her. Already she could see it rising into shape as they walked between the walls made of washing machines, fire hydrants, clocks, mirrors, and fenders; between the towers made of wagons and marbles, bicycles and animal skulls, wired and cemented together: all the paraphernalia of human life.

And it shall be fifty cubits long to the east, Theo intoned, and fifty cubits to the west. And there shall be an hundred furnaces beneath the foundations, and an hundred mirrors to catch the sun. And over the flagpole, a garbage can.

Where did you get the parking meter?

I took it from my room, said Theo. Didn't you see it in my room? I used to time my eggs by it, when I had a hotplate.

He sat down on a large bed, painted silver. He had stuck paper flowers in the springs. Around it the walls glittered with bedpans, coffee pots and false teeth.

I have a hundred and five sets of false teeth, he declared solemnly. And a medallion of William Blake. You've got to learn how much is worth saving in this world.

Later they were crossing the alley behind Woolworth's on the way home from the nine o'clock show, and they both saw it: a pair of legs sticking out of a trash can.

Jesus! Somebody's fallen in!

The feet were hollow, the legs straight. Pushing aside broken boxes and excelsior, they set them upright.

Too bad it's only the bottom half, said Theo. Who'd throw out a thing like that?

Are you going to keep it? asked Erica.

Put it in the city, he answered. Grow beans on it, or roses. All my life I had to look at saints and flamingoes in my mother's garden. Nobody ever had a pair of legs like these. You take his feet.

As they emerged from the alley, a black car pulled up across the street.

Just keep walking, said Theo. And follow me.

He was humming happily to himself. He turned the corner with easy nonchalance and broke into a gallop. Erica, holding the feet, felt herself pelting after him.

You want to rest? he said at last.

They had stopped in front of the drugstore; a balding man in a pharmacist's white jacket was rolling up the awnings. The neon lights in the window winked out, leaving them in the blue mercurial haze of the street lamps. The streets were empty. They set the legs down on the pavement and seated themselves on the curb. In spite of the warm air of summer almost here, Erica felt a great weariness flood her like a chill. Theo reached over to touch her hair when she lowered her head.

Will you come and live in my city?

They arrived at Hannah's early in the afternoon. Hannah, on hearing the car, had come out to meet them and was standing by the pump in her long blue print dress. Behind her, the house, low-slung and weathered nearly black, crouched in the shadow of several freshly painted barns. She seemed to have been born ancient; Erica could not remember a time when her thin hair, tucked under the green eyeshade, was not already white.

"Afternoon," said Hannah, shyly.

As they stepped up to her, she kissed them one by one, a dry musty kiss on the cheek. The pincushion she wore at her lapel pricked Erica's face.

Hannah led the way through the kitchen. The low ceiling made Erica want to stoop. There was a wooden sink, deeply stained, and an enamel bucket with a chipped rim beside it. On a pedestal near the front door, a large Christmas cactus trailed its branches in all directions.

"A hundred years old," said Hannah proudly, "and it

bloomed this year. I called the paper about it, but Mrs. Schultz had already called them about *her* cactus, and they wasn't interested in two of 'em."

"But you aren't a hundred years old," exclaimed Erica.

"It come with the house, I think. Oh, I could have had a sign out in front about the house, but Jonathan was never much on publicity."

They went into the living room for the fittings. Boxes of cards and buttons spilled over the wicker sofa onto a piano which served as a shelf for photographs and birthday cards and was by this time nearly inaccessible; the keyboard looked permenently shut. On the sewing machine, with its faint traces of elegant scrolls, a cat lifted its head and blinked at them, then stretched itself back to sleep again.

For some reason the signs of faith were less depressing here than they might have been at home, thought Erica, forgiving Hannah the ceramic plaque, JESUS NEVER FAILS and the sign lettered in silver paint, GOD GRANT ME THE SERENITY TO ACCEPT THINGS I CANNOT CHANGE. On the walls, the sepia faces of an earlier generation looked out from absurd gilt frames. They were always stiff, her father told her, because the pictures were time-exposures and you had to wear a clamp on your neck inside the collar, that kept you from moving.

Suddenly she saw it, hanging on a coat-rack shining out over the faded coats brought in for mending and the shapeless dresses of old women.

"You want to try on the white sewing first?" asked Hannah, noticing her gaze. "It's just basted."

Her mother started to hum.

"I got some stuff for you to do, when you're done with that," she said. And Erica saw her studying the pictures on the wall, pausing before a confirmation certificate, lettered in German, showing in faded tints the parables and deeds of Christ. Stuck on the frame was a tiny star-shaped pin, from which several bars fell in ladder-fashion: five years, ten years, fifteen years.

"You never miss a day of church, do you, Hannah?" said her mother. "I'll bet nobody's got a record like you do."

"Raise your arms," said Hannah, and Erica felt the sudden

cool weight of satin falling over her body. "Only one man had a better record than mine; he got the twenty-five-year bar, but the last year they had to bring him in on a stretcher."

She stood with her arms out while Hannah pinned and clucked to herself. Her hands were warm and light, almost like mice walking on her flesh, thought Erica. Minnie cleared a place for herself on the sofa and stretched out, running her eye over the dresses on the coat-rack.

"That's a handsome black one," she said. "Who's that for?"

"Me," said Hannah, "to be buried in. Thought I might as well get some wear out of it."

"Remember how Grandma had a dress she kept in her drawer to be buried in? White wool, it was."

"Fits pretty good," said Hannah. "Now, try on this over-slip."

She shook it over Erica's head—light, vaporous stuff, embroidered with flowers. Fullskirted like a child's dress. Theo hated full skirts. Minnie bent forward to examine it.

"Imagine," she said, "a machine to put in all those flowers."

"How does it fit around the arms?"

Erica nodded.

"Good. 'Course it'll take a little time—"

"No hurry," snapped her mother.

"—since I lost my ripper. I told Mrs. Mahoney to pick me up one somewhere."

"Mahoney?" mused Minnie. "Not Jack Mahoney?"

"He's dead now, just tipped over quick," said Hannah.

"Seems like all the people I went with are dead now," said Minnie softly.

Erica edged herself carefully out of the white dress, trying not to prick herself with pins. Her mother had already put on a lace one. Hannah and Minnie eyed her critically.

"Lace," observed Hannah. "Looks like you're going to a wedding."

"No wedding," said her mother. "Make it an inch shorter, don't you think, in the front? I haven't got a bosom like this—"

She pulled the front out like a tent.

" 'Course, skirts is shorter now," said Hannah reluctantly.

"Even the choir wears 'em shorter. 'Course a thing goes across the front so it don't show their knees. I could put some darts in the front."

"The lace is torn, too. Do you mend lace?"

"Lace isn't good except for weddings," said Hannah, shaking her head.

He wouldn't like the dress, thought Erica. She scowled at it, hanging on the coat-rack. He wouldn't like it because her mother had picked the design, not for his marriage, but for marriage in general. Somehow the dress looked like her mother. She did not know why.

Late in the afternoon, Theo appeared at her house, dressed in a black suit with a bag of tools at his side.

"You coming with me to the undertaker's?"

She had not told her mother about this job. They took her bicycle, she sitting on the seat, he pumping in front, his haunches striking her in the stomach as they pitched uphill, past the park.

"I can get off, if you want to walk."

"No, you're light enough."

When they arrived at the funeral parlor, they were both damp with effort. They reached for the knocker, but a man in a moth-gray suit had already opened the door. Over his shoulder, Erica saw the rooms, with their high ceilings and French doors, opening into infinity, multiplying like a house of mirrors. She remembered this house from her grandmother's funeral: the parlors where the dead awaited visitors and the carpets that flowed from one room to another, gathering up all human sounds. Was it in this large room that they had laid her out and Erica had cried, not for grief, but because her mother was crying?

The man led them over to a small group of people huddled together on a sofa at the other end of the room: two men and two women, all middle-aged with pointed sallow faces. The women had covered their heads with black lace mantillas.

"This is the young student."

They rose and looked at him rather severely, then turned to Erica.

"My wife," said Theo. "She assists me."

The women removed their gloves and extended their hands to her. Then the taller of the two men inquired in an accent so pronounced that Erica wondered if it were real, "You have done this before? You know—"

"Of course," said Theo. "I have studied the trade in Germany."

"Well, then!"

They all looked immensely relieved. With a polite nod, the undertaker indicated that they might sit down and motioned Theo to follow him.

The body had been laid out, fully dressed, on a table and wheeled into a private room, empty save for a sink at one end. For a moment Erica caught her breath, but Theo gave her a look, and she said nothing. The undertaker lingered a bit.

"Won't take you very long, I suppose."

"No, not very long. You will excuse me—I prefer to do this work alone."

Blushing deeply, the other man muttered a little and bowed into the doorway.

"His face has already been shaved."

Pause.

"The family will be down in—say—half an hour?"

Theo nodded and waved him away. The door slammed, and his composure vanished.

"Open the tool case quick," he said. "Twenty minutes. Get out the plaster of paris. Can you mix plaster of paris?"

"I think so."

She rummaged through the little bag, pulled out a chisel and a towel, then a tin bowl and the bag of plaster, carefully averting her eyes from the body. Thinking only of what she must do with her hands, she carried everything to the sink, filled the bowl, turned on the water and began to stir.

"Stir faster," cried Theo.

"You never really were in Germany, were you?"

"Christ, no. Give me the plaster—quick, before it dries."

Now she stepped forward and watched, fascinated, breathing very lightly to avoid the real or imagined smell of formaldehyde in the room. Theo had spread the towel over the body, tucking it in at the collar like a napkin. The face looked much like those she had seen upstairs; about thirty, she thought, maybe older. It neither grieved nor frightened her, this thing. Theo loaded his trowel and spread plaster over the chin and nose, then lathered it over the eyes and stood up straight.

"Now we wait for it to dry." He was looking cheerful again. "Who knows, maybe he'll come out looking like William Blake."

A kind of chill touched her at that moment.

"Where do you think he is—really?"

"Right here, all there is of him." Theo was washing his hands at the sink. "Your aunt been working on you again? Listen"—he looked very fierce—"if you let her baptize you, it's all over between us. Christ, you're not marrying me, you're marrying your mother!"

"They can hear you upstairs," she hissed.

"Listen," he said, in a gentler voice, pointing to the body. "*This* isn't anything to be afraid of. I've got to get you out of that house of old women."

"I think it's dry."

He tested the mask with his finger.

"Not yet. We'll wait a few more minutes."

They slid down on the floor, leaning against the wall in ominous silence. Presently Theo got up, bent over the body and took the edges of the mask in both hands.

"A little cool, but it's dry enough."

He tugged, carefully at first, then more roughly.

"Give me a hand," he said urgently.

She stumbled to her feet and, suddenly nauseous, swallowed hard and touched the rough plaster edge over the ear.

"Push your fingers under it. You need leverage. Pull!"

"It's stuck!" she cried in terror. "Why is it stuck?"

"I think," said Theo, in an odd voice, "that I forgot to grease the face."

He had climbed up on the table by this time and was straddling the dead man's chest, clawing furiously at the mask.

"Chip it! Get the chisel! We'll chip it away!"

There was a muffled cry behind them, and turning, Erica saw that someone had opened the door. In the doorway stood the bereaved, their sallow faces livid with rage.

The tallest man made a leap for Theo but missed. Theo was already on the ground, and he plunged like a wild horse through the door. Erica followed him, running as if the dead man himself were after them.

They sat, shaking, in a cranny of rubber tires, at one end of Theo's city. The sun beat down on them, the hundred mirrors turned on their hooks and wires, and the springs, sleds, motors, rowboats, saws, clocks, flowerpots, and bedpans of humanity twirled past them. They sat in the shadow of a hundred furnaces.

"Best thing to do," said Theo at last, "is to forget the whole thing. A death mask, for Christ's sake!"

"If we were married and you died first, would you want to be buried?" she asked timidly, and realized, as she said it, that she was really asking something else.

"Ashes to ashes and dust to dust. No coffin for me. I want to go back to the earth."

A loneliness foamed up in her mouth when he said that. She had always assumed she would lie down with the rest of the family in one of the plots her father had bought years ago. Enough for the generations, he said. It wasn't a thing to take lightly. For when the trumpet sounded and everyone stood up in their graves, it was important, said her mother, to be among people you knew.

But by this time, lots of bodies must have scattered to dust.

The Lord knows his own, said her mother stoutly.

Erica saw them all very clearly, standing up in the graves and rubbing their eyes as after a long sleep, Hannah in the black dress she'd made for her funeral, her mother in the lace, Minnie, singing along with the heavenly host because she alone knew the words to the hymns, and herself in the white dress which would be her best dress forever.

"I took my French this morning," said Theo.

"You didn't tell me. How was it?"

"Awful. I flunked. I'm ready to pull out of this place." He touched her hair lightly. "And I want to take you with me. You got to trust me more, Erica. I'm not like your dad, but I'm all right."

"What are you going to do now?"

He shrugged.

"Go to some city, I guess. You can always find people in a city." Suddenly restless, he jerked himself up. "It's hot here. You want to rent a boat and go to the island for a swim?"

"I have to go home and get my suit."

"Jesus! Whoever swims near the island? Go in your underwear."

"A nice day," said the old man, sitting on a kitchen stool in front of the canoe shed. He looked past the open door toward the river, as if expecting someone to appear there. "Don't know why there aren't more folks out on the water."

The three of them went inside. Erica had yet to see a canoe in the canoe shed. Instead, it was full of nickelodeons, scrolled and flowered to resemble circus wagons, with the works decorously exposed. Behind little windows, the captive performers slept: drumsticks and cymbals, gears and piano rolls, perforated for the syntax of dead voices.

"Sign the book," said the old man, slipping behind a counter and handing Theo a pen. "You get number twenty-five. That really plays, Miss."

Erica was staring at the silver anatomy of a violin, spread open and joined to hundreds of tiny threads and wheels, as if awaiting a surgeon. She had not noticed it the last time. On the glass was a neatly typed label: JUDGED THE EIGHTH GREATEST INVENTION IN THE WORLD. CHICAGO WORLD'S FAIR. 1933.

"It sounds just like a real violin. Listen."

The old man took a nickel from his pocket and dropped it into the back of the machine. From deep inside she heard a sputter and a whirr. Theo bent closer to look; then all at once they heard a nervous spidery response, ping! ping! Wheels spun, silver pistons scraped the strings. The whole effect was oddly touching, as if they were watching a fading performer's comeback from senility. When its shrill and complicated heart fell silent, they all three burst into applause.

"You don't know that tune, I bet," said the old man, pleased and shy. "Go out that door to the docks and take the first boat on the end. The paddles are inside."

The island looked small, the way places always looked to Erica when she had known them as a child and then revisited them as an adult. Rocks scratched against the bottom of the boat, and she climbed out, bunching her skirt in her arm. Theo lifted the prow and together they pulled the boat over the thin strip of beach toward the trees.

"Come on," said Theo. "I'm going in."

He vanished into a bush. Erica waded along the edge of the water. The white skeleton of a crayfish surfaced as she dug her toes into the sand.

"Are you going swimming in your dress?"

She could not look at him.

"Somebody might come." But she knew there was nobody here but themselves.

"Good Christ," shouted the bush. "Since when is your own flesh a thing to be ashamed of?"

And when the voice spoke again, it was softer and more winning.

"Here I am."

Drawn by its strangeness, she turned. There he stood, very white and thin-legged, and oddly exotic in his nakedness, like a unicorn.

"Well, I'm going into the water."

He plunged forward with studied casualness, but his whole body grimaced when the water touched his waist. Then he stopped and carefully splashed his ribs and arms, humming quietly to himself. In the sunlight, his back was as round and white as a loaf of dough. Dazzled by the brightness of things, gazing about him at the mainland some distance away, he seemed to have sprung from the dark flesh of the water itself. Suddenly a whistle bleated so close to them that Erica started.

"Are you coming in?"

He was looking at her, over his shoulder, which prickled into gooseflesh as she watched him.

The whistle hooted again, louder this time, and they both turned in alarm. A steamer, covered with tiers and tiers of children, was chugging toward them, under the green banner of the Huron Park Day Line. As the whole side of the boat broke into shouting and waving, she opened her mouth to speak, but Theo was already lumbering toward the woods, the water weighing him down like a heavy garment.

"Jesus!"

Now it was passing them, slowly and steadily, but she could see the children jumping up and down, and she could hear the way they called her, *Hey lady, hey lady!* not because they knew her but because they did not know her. She shaded her eyes and waved, like one who has been working and glances up to see something amazing, a unicorn in the bush, a caravan of pilgrims on the road, a shipload of souls, rollicking and rolling into the new world.

Judgment City and Lonely Town

The first time I saw my love
She gave me chains of gold

Theo sings. It is like another person in him, this singing, it goes on spinning itself, and when he is happy he gives it a voice. He sings when Lotte Lockerson, manager of the Bow-Wow Boutique, sends him out to walk the dogs who live along Park Avenue. The six leashes converge to a point in his hand, and he strides along like Odin, calling the pack to order as it charges ahead of him, passing the sleek doormen again two hours later, who one by one take their dogs from the pack and send them gliding up in elevators into unimaginable suites. Unimaginable for Theo: he can get no further than gold fixtures on the bathtubs and sinks.

After the shop closes, he goes to the studio of Herr Graumann, teacher of voice and piano, on East Ninth Street. Graumann is an elderly Berliner who keeps an itinerant Russian painter busy painting murals in his kitchen. His studio is impressively classical; there are glassed-in bookcases full of Bach, two pianos—one upright and one grand—and any number of busts which sit on the pianos, bookcases, and mantelpiece like funereal sculpture. Herr Graumann carries a tiny bust of Bach in the secret pocket of the lining of his vest.

On Sundays, Theo rises at noon and eats an enormous dinner in the upper window of Pearlman's Furniture House on East Fifty-seventh Street. Mr. Pearlman—who saw Theo's picture in the *Daily News* walking a pack of dogs—furnishes him the dinner and a wife, a silky-haired blonde who won a Miss Clairol contest and wants to be in the movies. He also furnishes two children, courtesy of the Children's Studio, a boy seven and a girl nine, also blonde, but related neither to Miss Clairol nor to each other. And on the sidewalks below, the strollers gape up at this curious family, like sinners watching holy communion. For they don't see you, Theo Svenson, says Mr. Pearlman, they see themselves.

When Theo opens his eyes each morning, the Spring Street Pizza Parlor is already steaming below him. It is summer and there is no more school, and the pizza parlor is full of kids, dropping their pennies in the gum machines for the little prizes that show behind the glass but never fall into their hands: shrunken heads the size of their thumbs, skeletons that bob like spiders, combs, padlocks, and plastic medals that show the Virgin changing into Saint Joseph when you tip them in the light.

Theo stumbles out of bed and reaches for his trousers. Sleep rims his eyes so that they seem to be looking through somebody else's skin. Plodding downstairs he passes the tailor, Abe Hoffman, who rides his bicycle to the bakery every morning for breakfast and then, holding his bag of bagels in his teeth, seizes the bicycle by the frame, runs it up two flights of stairs to the safety of his shop, and calls out to Theo, "People will steal anything these days. Bicycles, doorknobs, parking meters, baby buggies, garbage pails—even full ones. And if the pails are too heavy, they'll take the lids. The lids! I have to tie 'em to the wall."

And when the hot winds of June blow down Spring Street, Theo hears hundreds of garbage lids clap and whistle. When he arrives at the shop, Lotte Lockerson has already let in the first customers, two Pomeranians, and a schnauzer. She is a little too thin, like her own overbred Afghans, whose honey-colored fur she has dyed her own hair to match. Theo has walked through this door a thousand times, yet he never loses the feeling that he has entered the inner sanctuary of a temple and touched the vestments and vessels of a forgotten god. The small boots, bathrobes, and rhinestone collars intimidate him, the chocolate-scented bones and wrist-watches for slim paws make him feel gross and uneasy. A single bark from a terrier in a dinner jacket or a poodle in a silver lamé cocktail coat fills him with shame and sends him inwardly howling with his tail between his legs. From hidden pipes, music pours into the shop, music so obsequious that you only miss it when it stops. All this helps Theo to rejoice in the perfect ceremonies of a peculiar kingdom: the weddings, litters, and funerals of the dogs.

Every morning Theo picks up a bag of dry kibblets behind the shop and lets himself into the shed where Lotte Lockerson keeps the shepherds. Already they have heard him coming, they are throwing themselves against their cages, snarling and yelping. Passing swiftly between them, feeling their eyes on his throat, Theo sings. Then they grow quiet, so that he can open the cages and fill their dishes with food.

"There's a big demand in shepherds this summer," Lotte Lockerson reminds him, "for there's no better protection. Don't forget to tell the customers we're the only handlers in town that cross-breed our dogs with wolves."

As Herold Nagy, the other dog-walker and a licensed poodle-clipper, waits in vain for the Trowbridge dog who has missed an appointment this morning, he practices a little shuffle step in the corner. Now Lotte Lockerson hands them the leashes and the two walkers start out, Herold with Lotte's two schnauzers and Theo with her shepherd. Slowly they collect their packs: two Great Danes and an Irish setter on Park Avenue, an Irish wolfhound, a Welsh corgi, a Pomeranian and two golden Pekes on Fifth Avenue, and the dachshund on Lexington, who always wears a batman cape and likes to nip at the heels of the bigger dogs. Herold handles the corgi, the two Pekes, the Pomeranian and the dachshund. He always wears a rust-colored silk turtleneck sweater because it matches the Pekes' glossy coats, and you can't help wondering if he would like to be in one of those collars, handed out by a doorman and exercised and handed in again. As they draw up together on the curb and wait for the light at Fifty-ninth, Herold turns to Theo and says very quickly, "You want to come to my place next week for dinner? I've got some splendid slides of the moon that I took through my telescope last winter. You hardly ever get a clear night in the city."

After work, on the way to Herr Graumann's, Theo wishes he had not agreed to come. For he can't forget the Herold he sees at noon, nibbling a cheese sandwich that he takes from a brown bag with deep grease stains on the side, and telling him that the world is going to end in fire, yes, the sun and all the stars. None shall escape.

But Herold, like every other creature on this planet, wishes in his own way to be immortal. To rise with glory on a sinking ship is better than not rising at all. Every day he carries his tapshoes to work, tied up with a black ribbon. If he swallows his lunch without chewing it, he has forty-five minutes left and he can make it to the Tip-Tap Dance Studio five blocks away, for his lesson. And such lessons! The only class offered at twelve-thirty is for the six- to eight-year olds who attend the elementary school nearby, but the teacher, impressed by Herold's earnest desire to learn, has made an exception in his case. The spinster piano player shakes her head as the pupils parade around for the Grand March, with Herold, tall as a postman, shuffling and tapping along in the middle. When they fall into line to practice the new steps, Herold and the teacher, looking gaunt and emancipated in her leotard and tights, stand eyeball to eyeball, knee to knee. The children help him learn the hard steps. The parents who sit on the sideline assume he is retarded, but Herold says he does not mind. He wishes, however, that the steps came easily to him, that he could be at least as good as the eight-year-old kid who according to his mother started putting bottle caps on the soles of his shoes at the age of two.

When Theo arrives at Herr Graumann's, he is ushered into the kitchen. The mural-maker has been living here all week, and Graumann assures Theo in a whisper that he would not have consented if the man had not played Bach's Violin Concerto No. 2 in E Minor for him almost perfectly, on Graumann's own violin.

"He's a Russian fellow, the brother of one of my students.

Calls himself a prophet, says he paints things before they happen! His English is a bit weak; see how you like him. You're a painter, too, aren't you?"

"Sculptor," says Theo, "without a studio."

A large shaggy man, mixing colors in Graumann's sink, acknowledges Theo with a nod. A Byzantine skyscraper rises over Graumann's stove and below it, faintly sketched, a procession of animals chases a man and a woman. Leading them all is a figure both fierce and holy, like an angel without wings.

"Hell, I expect," smiles Graumann. "Do you believe in hell, Mr. Svenson?"

"No, but I believe in heaven," says Theo. "My own version, of course."

"There's a Protestant for you!" shouts Graumann gleefully, sliding in at the piano. "Now, a few scales for me, Mr. Svenson."

Theo obliges. Graumann shakes his head.

"Theo," he says. "Do you practice?"

"I try," says Theo. "But you know, there's really no place when you live in a room like I do, with so many people around—"

"Theo," says Graumann, "I know a man who used to go to the zoo every morning and sing to the lions. You haven't seen him? Tell me, do you go to the public library? Have you heard the fellow there who stands under the trees to the right and sings for all he's worth? Theo, you must practice."

Theo hangs his head.

"If worst comes to worst, Mr. Svenson, sing to your dogs. Yes, sing them the Hallelujah Chorus. They will appreciate it. My mural-maker tells me there is a dog in heaven. He says there are eight animals in paradise: Jonah's whale, Solomon's ant, Ishmael's ram, Abraham's calf, Sheba's ass, Salech's camel, Moses' ox, and the dog of the Seven Sleepers of Ephesus. Therefore, Theo, go and sing to the animals."

On Sunday Theo sleeps late; he's barely able to make it to Pearlman's Furniture House by one. He carries his jacket, he can feel his shirt sticking to his back. The pinched, anxious look on Mr. Pearlman's face ripples away when he sees Theo coming. Locking the door behind them, he leads Theo through the air-conditioned salesroom, past overstuffed sofas and leather chairs, Danish consoles and lamps with wires concealed in the guts of marble horses. Already, as he climbs the stairs to the showroom, Theo feels the dust of the street drop from him.

"I've gone all Louis Fourteenth this week," says Mr. Pearlman. "How do you like it?"

Everything in the room is gold, except Miss Clairol's peppermint-striped hatbox of cosmetics and Mr. Pearlman, who is thin and dark, but even he looks almost golden in the light which the heavy drapes have sealed into the room. The walls are paneled in yellow brocade. Next to a yellow brocade love seat, a gold Mercury encircles the air with his arm, waiting to embrace an umbrella. The carpet is soft and yellow as butter.

Miss Clairol is already seated beside the blonde boy who is nobody's child, and who has been stuffed into a cream Nehru jacket and is now rolling the bamboo napkin-rings up and down the tablecloth.

"Quit it," says Miss Clairol.

Theo draws up a chair at one end of the table, opposite him.

"Where's the little girl?" he asks politely.

"She got hurt in a car," says the child. And then, as an afterthought: "She has to wear a lifesaver on her neck."

"My God," exclaims Theo, "she broke her neck?"

The boy shrugs.

"Told me she got a new head."

"If you're ready," says Mr. Pearlman, "I'll pull the curtain." Suddenly the shadows whisk away, and Mr. Pearlman disappears as if burnt to an ash by the sunlight as it blazes on the Meissen serving dishes and the golden skin of a roast duckling which Mr. Pearlman has had sent out from a restaurant two blocks away. Always in that first moment, Theo transcends himself, imagining that he partakes of a general perfection. Then he feels embarrassed, then he begins to eat. The child stares out of the window, sucking the end of his fork. Miss Clairol raises her knife, smiles radiantly, and impales a wing.

"Man," says the child, still staring out of the window. "I'd like to ride on that thing."

They all look. Directly across from them on a huge bill-board, they see a miniature ski lift full of people moving up and flashing over a white hill. KEEP KOOL WITH KOOLS, KEEP KOOL, KEEP KOOL, flashes the sign, and sure enough, every-one on the ski lift is lighting up a Kool, or lighting somebody else's and smiling out of sealskin parkas. One by one they disap-pear over the hill, then reappear at the bottom and start all over again.

"Do you ski?" asks Miss Clairol.

"No," says Theo. "Do you?"

"I used to," she sighs, "but it's so difficult these days. I mean, everyone's doing it now, and even the best places are full of beginners from the Bronx."

"Where are all those people going?" asks the child, still looking out the window.

"To that lodge," answers Theo.

"What lodge?"

"The man who made the sign forgot to put it in," says Theo.

Miss Clairol presses her lips into a hard line.

"Then how do you know it's there?" demands the boy.

"You sure talk a lot, don't you?" she says, staring him down. But the boy does not notice.

"My mother says when I grow up I'm going to be in the movies. I been on TV already. Did you see me?"

"I don't think so," says Theo.

"I was drinking lemonade."

Below them, the strollers watch indifferently. Only two women in Bermudas, pushing baby carriages, gape up at them.

"Think they'll buy anything?" inquires Theo.

Mr. Pearlman's voice makes the curtains quiver.

"Not those two. But it's good for them, a show like this. Gives them something to live for. Look down there, look at their eyes. They're saying to themselves, 'I can do that too, if I work hard, sit in a gold room and eat my dinner.'"

"You really believe they can?"

"Sure. My own father came over here with nothing, with less than nothing. Set up a little shoe shop on Ferry Street, made shoes to order. He had a form for every kind of foot, used to nail them on posts and keep them in the basement. You'd bring in the leather and he'd make you the shoe."

Theo can hear Mr. Pearlman breathing heavily. And then he adds, slowly and harshly. "Nothing makes me madder than all those people asking for handouts. And if they don't get what they want, they'll burn the place down."

Under his breath, Theo sings, for beyond the ski lift he sees a man step out on a rooftop and open the door of what appears to be a pigeon coop. The air around his head is suddenly filled with birds. And if Theo could look far enough, he knows he could see the old men playing bocchi on Spring Street, and beyond that the pawnshops glittering with harmonicas and guitars and knives, and beyond that the discount houses, as big as airplane hangars, full of plastic saints, decal bullet holes, balloons, clothing racks as endless as rows of corn, the Last Supper in marzipan and everything dipped in chocolate except for Christ, plates, socks, lamps, wigs, and picture frames, fingered, felt, coveted, and bought, pouring their way out of the store and breaking their way into the kitchens and bedrooms of the poor.

Theo knows for a fact that he sees better by night than by day. That's why he always wears shades during the day, to bring everything into focus. For it's only at night, when he becomes his own master, that Theo is truly awake. Now every evening he passes the library to hear the man who sings under the trees in Bryant Park.

"A true artist, isn't he?" says Herr Graumann. "He hides his face, he is nothing but song."

It is summer, and Theo is restless. When he walks the dogs at noon, he strides imperiously down the middle of the pavement. When he walks by himself at night, he moves as softly as a cat, avoiding open spaces.

And so it happened that one night, in the middle of Chinatown, as he turned into Pell Street, he saw a lanky black girl in an electric pink dress and a man's jacket, rolling before her the figure of an enormous saint. Rough-hewn, to be sure, and nearly eight feet tall, and standing on a skateboard, but what else could it be? Burlap was hacked and bunched around the face to suggest a beard. For the body, slats of all sizes were glued carelessly together and so roughly painted that Theo could see them as drapery and limbs only from a distance.

Waiters stood in the steamed-over windows of the Temple Garden and Fishy's Bar, waiting for their last customers to leave. At the feet of an enormous golden Buddha in the Gim Sua giftshop, someone had arranged an offering of ivory elephants, brocade slippers, and a bust of John F. Kennedy.

Theo stepped aside for the girl to pass, but the castors struck a grating in the sidewalk and the saint lurched forward as if enraged and hit Theo on the head. He grabbed its outstretched arm, stopped the fall, and found himself holding a sizable piece of the hand.

"Oh, my God," exclaimed the girl. "I'm terribly sorry."

Together they righted the figure on its base. Theo touched his head; there was no blood, and he immediately felt better. In the benign light of Buddha, her pink dress dazzled him. Her hair was short but so thick that the soft weight of it pushed her scarf up.

"His nose!" she cried. "You're stepping on his nose."

Theo bent down and picked up an angular slat of wood painted red and blue.

"How far do you have to push this thing?" he inquired.

She was mashing the hand back on the upraised stump.

"This fella, he going all the way to Chattanooga." She gave him a sly look and started to push the saint once more, and Theo, dropping the nose in his pocket, walked beside her.

"But how far are you going to take it tonight?"

There was a long silence.

"I got a sister who lives on Pearl Street," she said at last, "so I guess I can spend the night there."

They turned down Mott: HOT AND COLD HEROES, blinked a sign over their heads, speckling them with colors as if a shimmering net had fallen over them both.

"It's open," said Theo. "You want something to eat?"

She glanced up at the sign without slowing her pace.

"A cold hero is a dead hero," she observed flatly, "and I got no need of a hot one."

Now they took turns pushing, and the old saint wobbled as it hit the cracks. Feeling a twinge of joy rising inside him, Theo sang:

> *The first time I saw my love*
> *She gave me chains of gold,*

"That's nice," said the girl. "That's real nice."
"I take lessons," said Theo modestly.

> *The second time I saw my love*
> *She turned the summer cold.*

He sang to the end of the refrain, but her attention had made him self-conscious. Only the bars were still open. The strong bittersweet smell of gin breathed out of them, and the colored lights from juke boxes gleamed in the dark.

"Look there," exclaimed the girl suddenly, pointing ahead of her.

In the middle of the sidewalk, an old man was sitting on a battered suitcase, holding a small wheel and a pair of galoshes, swaying and humming to himself. He was quite bald but a broad pink scar, as trim and deliberate as a patch, stretched across his head. The girl went over to him.

"Hey, Mister, are you waiting to cross the street?"

The old man turned, peered crossly up at the saint as if its shadow had crossed his private sun, and made a hoarse sound in his throat.

"My God," exclaimed Theo, "an overcoat in this weather?"

"He can't walk," said the girl.

Theo bent down to the old man's ear; it smelled of whiskey and dead leaves.

"Where are you going?"

"He going no place," said the girl. "He going to sit here all night."

"Haven't you got some place to go?"

The old man brightened.

"I got a brother in Brooklyn," he said, as if he had forgotten his existence until this minute.

"He can't walk," said the girl.

"There's a phone-booth across the street," said Theo. "Listen, have you got your brother's phone number? I can call him and tell him you're coming."

"Trebby's the name," said the old man. "Ignatius Trebby." He rummaged through his pockets, pulled out a set of teeth and popped them into his mouth. Theo reached for his suitcase but he shook his head. In silence they walked down to the stoplight and crossed the street.

"Look there," said the girl suddenly. "A policeman."

The policeman, with studied nonchalance, was walking toward them, his hands behind his back.

"Any trouble?" he called.

Theo jolted the saint over the curb.

"No, Sir," he said. "No trouble."

"This old guy giving you trouble?"

"No, Sir, we're taking him to his brother's."

The policeman tapped the saint on the belly, looked him up and down, and turned his back on them all. Theo enclosed himself thankfully into the booth, dropped in a dime, and dialed the number from the little book in his hand. A loud buzzing sounded. Then a woman's voice broke through, low enough to be a man's, thought Theo, and checked the word "Ma'am" on his tongue.

"Yaaas?"

"Hello? Is this the Trebby residence?"

"Who? Jack Snell?"

"Trebby. Ignatius Trebby."

Through the glass he could see that the old man was trying to squeeze the wheel and the galoshes into his suitcase. The policeman looked as if he wished to eat him.

"Ain't no such fellow lives here."

"There is nobody here called Trebby?"

"That's right," said the voice, pleasantly, thought Theo, considering it was the middle of the night. "We got a Snell and a Doyle and a Glascock."

"Well, listen, do you live at thirty-two Haight Street?"

"Nope," said the voice. "But wait till I git the light on. I got the directory right here." The voice subsided to a mumble. "Samuel!" it shouted suddenly. "Is that the one?"

"On Haight Street?"

"Too bad," said the voice, as if Theo had just lost a bet. "There's no Trebbys on any Haight Street."

Outside he could hear shouting.

"Thanks very much for your trouble," said Theo. "I'm terribly sorry if I woke you up."

He pushed open the door. The policeman and the girl were arguing.

"He got so much liquor in him, Lady, he don't feel a thing. There's no use trying to help a guy when he gets like this. If he didn't want to live this way, he'd be doing something else."

"His name's Mr. Trebby," said the girl, "and we're going to put him on the subway to his brother's."

"Give them a dime, they'll just get more booze—"

Suddenly he broke off; there was the sound of rushing water, and they all turned toward Mr. Trebby, who was smiling and relieving himself against the wall. The policeman let out an inarticulate yell.

"Let's go," said the girl, nudging Theo.

"This man's not going on any subway," shouted the policeman, pulling a little book out of his pocket and flipping it open, as if he were going to pray over them. "Says right here, no intoxicated people in the subway. Lady, I'd be doing you a favor if I arrested him."

He began to prod Mr. Trebby with his nightstick; then he picked up the suitcase, and the old man hurried to take it from him and wedged himself in between Theo and the girl, and they started off.

"Don't look back," said the girl. "The cop's still watching."

"Let's find a flophouse," suggested Theo, looking sideways at Mr. Trebby.

The old man brightened.

"I often go to the movies," he said, happily. "A snug little seat in the balcony, air-conditioned."

"You sleep in the movies?" exclaimed Theo.

Mr. Trebby was still smiling, as if he had not heard.

"There's an all-night house up in the next block," said the girl. "Let's go."

Somewhere, beyond the rooftops of the hotels and office buildings, the turrets and marquees of the movie houses, morning broke. The sky was turning a watery blue, like thin milk.

The first time I saw my love
She gave me chains of gold.

"Lovely," chirped Mr. Trebby. "Just lovely." The singing and the thought of a movie had revived him. "Did you ever see *How to Stuff a Wild Bikini?*"

"Never heard of it," said Theo.

"It wasn't bad, but I thought *The Savage Seven* was better."

"You go to a lot of movies?" asked the girl.

"I go every day," he beamed. "Haven't missed one, except the time my appendix burst. Sometimes I stay all day, see 'em three or four times. I seen the Betty Grable pictures when they first come out, and now I see they're bringing 'em back again."

They passed a drugstore and stepped in front of the first marquee, which was flashing *Two for the Road.*

"I suppose you've seen this one," said Theo, reaching for his wallet.

"Doesn't matter," said the old man. "Hey, you ain't gonna pay the fare, are you? I'd never go to a movie if I had to pay. If the lady'll wait here—" he nodded at the girl—"I'll see if they left my door open."

"Will you wait here?" asked Theo. "I'll only be a minute."

"Maybe," said the girl. "Maybe not."

"Listen, I'll walk you to your sister's on Pearl Street. Then we can stop for coffee."

"Hope there's a seat in the balcony," said Mr. Trebby.

"Wait here," cried Theo, desperately. Mr. Trebby was suddenly a burden to him, he wanted to deposit him somewhere as efficiently as possible. But now the old man had found a crack between the theater and the drugstore, and like a cockroach in an overcoat he was already beckoning Theo to follow him. Theo eased himself between the walls, which pressed a clammy sweat against his cheek and smelled of urine. Looking back, he caught a last glimpse of the girl, standing under the arm of her saint as one might rejoice under a tree on the desert—two small silhouettes waiting motionless against the flashing lights of the marquees.

"It's a system," Mr. Trebby was saying. "In the winter when I go from one movie to another, I hardly need to go out of doors. Now if I was to come here from the other direction, I'd cut through four restaurants and two drugstores, and I'd be here."

They arrived at a large door marked EXIT.

"This one looks locked," said Theo.

Mr. Trebby opened it and vanished inside; it closed with a huff, like someone expelling a breath. Theo slipped in behind him. The darkness was total and overwhelming.

"Now I got to get down to where the seats are," whispered the old man.

Together they pushed a weight of curtains and tiptoed across the stage toward the dim light behind the screen. Suddenly there was a commotion out in front. Over the face of Audrey Hepburn, two enormous shadows had fallen like sin. Mr. Trebby vanished into the wings, and Theo, hearing footsteps, turned and fled out the door.

When he emerged into the dazzle of the street again, the girl and the saint were gone.

After that long walk to the theater, a strange ailment came over Theo: now he wakes with a burning in his throat, exhausted from the terrible exercise of his dream. For every night he stands before the ski lift which climbs, not to a ski lodge out of sight, but to an enormous movie palace. Inside, he remembers those yellow carpets, and those lamps with wires concealed in the guts of marble horses. And riding on the lift, transfixed against the zigzagging lights of the theater is a throng of people whom he doesn't know, blonde and black, old and young. They have broken the windows of Mr. Pearlman's furniture store and all the windows in the block, and now they are filling their arms full of clocks, knives, guitars, lamps, wigs, picture frames, and television sets. A boy is running down East Fifty-seventh Street with a bass fiddle and an armload of gladiolas. He drops the gladiolas. All the coffers of America have been opened. In the supermarkets, the managers are giving prizes to whoever can fill a shopping basket the quickest, and Theo is running from aisle to aisle with Mr. Trebby tugging at his sleeve:

"Faster! Faster!"

Whole walls of rice, canned soup, and frozen artichoke hearts come roaring down as if broken loose from a monstrous glacier. Their cart collides with that of a man as white as death; he is completely covered with flour. Their wheels have locked with his. The man begins kicking the wheels in an explosion of rage.

"Wait for me!" calls Theo. And now he is blubbering out loud. People on the ski lift are climbing away out of sight, he can hear them tap-dancing for joy. And there's the girl with her saint, telling them how it is in the Lodge, and how everyone lies around in the sun, singing praises to the Lord who has rewarded his servants with television sets and swimming pools and air conditioners and deep carpets and Cadillacs and acres of Coca-Cola that blossom in the pastures of America.

When Theo wakes up, his throat is burning.

"It's the city," says Abe Hoffman, the printer, running his bicycle past Theo in the morning. "It gets to you after awhile. The air's no good." As the hot winds of July blow along Spring Street, Theo sets out with the saint's nose in his pocket, as if he expects to meet the owner and be called to account. Perhaps it will happen some morning in the shed, when he goes out to feed the shepherds, or on Park Avenue, when he's out walking the dogs, or in front of the library, where he's stopped to hear the man singing in the darkness.

"Theo, don't strain so," says Herr Graumann gently. "This is *pianissimo*, yes!"

But when he sings *pianissimo*, he can hear the swish, swish of the mural painter's brush in the kitchen. Herr Graumann hears it too, as he lifts his hands from the keyboard.

"Ah, you should see what he's doing now! A Greek motif, the funeral of the satyrs, he calls it. I tell him he has to finish soon, he's running out of wall. And I didn't really want to drink my coffee in the morning with a funeral of satyrs."

So Theo is not surprised when Lotte Lockerson tells him that the Fisher dachshund has died, and Mrs. Fisher has asked for a burial and procession.

"We'll need six velvet coats for the poodles—they make the best pallbearers. Don't forget to polish the little coach where the coffin will go; somebody bit the upholstery last time, so we'll need that fixed before Mrs. F. comes in this morning to pick out a stone. I think she may buy one of our shepherds."

Herold stops clipping the Trowbridge poodle long enough to whisper into Theo's ear, "I wouldn't have a shepherd in the house. Just when you think you're friends, they'll turn on you."

But Theo knows it isn't the city, with its dogs and deaths that burns his throat and waits like a cancer in his mind, to blossom out in his dreams. Friday morning he makes up his mind to go down Pearl Street right after work and ask if anyone has seen a girl pushing a saint, bound for Chattanooga. It's not until he sees Herold, bouncing happily toward him with his tapshoes under his arm—as Lotte Lockerson is closing the shop —that he remembers his promise.

For Herold has been looking forward to this evening all week. Theo knows this the moment his friend opens the door for him. His hair is waved and fragrant, he has put on his best shirt, white with a great ruffled jabot, he has belted it like a tunic with a golden chain. Beyond him Theo sees a screen and a slide projector already set up, and two television-tables in front of the sofa.

"I thought we might eat while we watched the slides," says Herold, "since you're in a hurry. I'd love to let you look through the telescope, but I had to get rid of it. Too many people kept calling me up and wanting to bring their kids over to see it."

Theo steps inside. The room is full of clocks, china, and cats. Stray cats, tigers, calicos, and spotted cats, cats on the sofa, on the overstuffed chair, in the kitchen, and on the bed where Theo leaves his jacket. The clocks seem to squint like old men as they tick discreetly from bookcases and walls. They merge into a single sound, like a spring flowing under the floorboards.

Over the bed hangs a bamboo shelf of brass figurines in

medieval dress: on sideboards, on the mantelpiece, on brackets and shelves. Theo has never seen such a glitter of china; plates latticed with flowers, tureens, cups, teapots, and sugar bowls. Herold throws two cats off the sofa and motions Theo to sit, then rushes into the kitchen and back again.

"Soufflé," he says, setting before Theo a tray of covered dishes. "And peas. I hope you like peas."

Now they are sitting on the sofa with their television-tables against their knees. Theo chews mechanically. His throat is burning. He makes a great effort to swallow and stares at the screen. Herold drops in the first slide. The moon, Theo discovers, is as pebbled as the bottom of a stream.

"This one shows you a good view of the seas and craters," says Herold. "That's Mare Orientale to the left and the Jules Verne Ocean just beyond it."

Click. A shaded crescent, like a face turning toward the darkness.

"This was taken in the first quarter. It's mostly the dark side you get here."

Click. A heave of cracking asphalt, the cracks neatly labeled.

"I didn't take this one. A rocket took it. I sent away for it. Gives you a good view of the dark side of the moon. There's Mare Moscoviense and that one's Siokovsky."

Theo stops chewing.

"You mean those places have names?"

The idea dazzles him. A whole continent, as naked and simple as an egg.

"They say our earth looks like this from the moon. Sometimes it's full, sometimes it's crescent, and it has its dark side, too. Of course, when you consider there are millions of galaxies like ours in the universe, the earth doesn't seem so much."

He sighs, and the machine clicks to a planet encrusted with rings, like a fossilized top.

"You recognize Jupiter, of course. Oh, I enjoyed that telescope while I had it, and I enjoyed building it, but it just brought too many people. I think I'll do a harpsichord next. You can get almost anything in a kit these days."

Theo feels the cats creeping back to the sofa. One brushes his leg, makes several quick turns as if winding itself into a ball, then curls up against the instep of his foot.

Click. A landscape of coral: the full moon.

"There are just too many of us, and it's a problem we'll all have to face pretty soon. In twenty years there'll be standing room only and not enough air to go around. People just keep having kids without a thought for where we'll put everyone. Why, a man came by only last week to ask if I still had the telescope. He had one kid with him and two more at home!"

"We could colonize the moon," suggests Theo. "A new America."

"In ten billion years, the whole system will come together again, into one great fireball of matter, all the galaxies, the suns, everything. Then we can start over."

Herold's voice drops to a whisper. All around them, Theo hears the clocks running down and turning into water.

"With the world the way it is today, the only people you can trust are the animals."

On Pearl Street, to the left of the underpass stands a single apartment house. Everything else is knocked down or marked for demolition. And on the doorstep of this house sits a black woman shelling peas, shaking the pods from her skirt over and over, as if performing some test of patience set for her by the gods. Theo walks by once, twice, three times. He feels her eyes upon him, though she never stops snapping the peas into the bowl she holds in her lap.

"You lookin' for somebody?"

"I'm looking for the girl who makes saints," says Theo.

"Nobody like that livin' in this house."

"She—I—I helped her bring one of them, a big one, over to her sister's place. Her sister lives on Pearl Street."

Still the woman eyes him sullenly.

"What you want with that girl?"

"I want to give her the part that broke off." He pulls out the chunk of wood, rubbed paintless and smooth like a child's toy. "It's the nose."

He hears her chuckle a little. Then she says, without looking up, "She run off and got married a couple of nights ago. You're the fellow that sings, aren't you?"

"Yes," says Theo. His whole body is turning to stone.

"She told me how you sing so nice." Snap, snap go the peas, pinging into the bowl. "She broke that saint up when she left, said there wasn't no room for it, and she'd make another one when she got there. Is it true you can sing?"

Theo nods. The woman pushes the bowl from her lap, stands up and brushes herself off.

"Listen," she says. "My mother's inside. She's seventy-two today. You want to come in and sing to her? Ain't nobody else come by to wish her happy birthday."

In the corridor, littered with broken strollers, cartons, and bottles, somebody has ripped the mailboxes from the wall.

"Ain't nobody left but us now," observes the woman, pushing open the first door on the left.

Behind the door is a room so crowded with chiffoneers, bureaus, wardrobes, and beds that at first Theo does not see the old woman asleep in a wheelchair, nested among the legs of stacked tables.

"Mother," says her daughter in a loud voice, "here's a fellow come by to sing for you."

The old woman twitches like a bird walking, puts her hand over one eye, looks at Theo, uncovers the eye, and covers it again.

"She's got a cataract," explains the daughter. "The government's going to give her some money when she's blind. Stand right up close to her ear, so she can hear the words. You know 'The Old Rugged Cross'? That's her favorite."

"I don't know it," says Theo.

"Well, maybe you know 'Happy Birthday.' Don't matter much about the tune, just as long as she hears the words."

She draws up a stool next to the wheelchair, and now both women watch him expectantly. The long walk here and the burden of his anguish have drained him; his whole body seems inhabited by a cry. But how joyfully the old woman leans forward. His face hidden by the film over her eyes, Theo sings.

Going Blind

When the doctors wheeled his mother back into her room late that afternoon, Vincent was shocked. That morning she'd checked in and hung up all her nightgowns and her bathrobe in the closet, just as if she were in a hotel instead of a hospital. Now, with her teeth gone, her wedding ring taken away, and an identification bracelet sealed on her arm, she looked more dead than alive. The operated eye was covered by a perforated shield, a sort of miniature colander. But she was awake and it was his mother's familiar voice that introduced him to one of the doctors.

"You remember Doctor Herrgott," said his mother, as motionless as a stone speaking. "He gave you your first glasses."

The doctors lifted her from the table on a canvas stretcher. Her weight made the sides fold in around her, like a shroud for someone being buried at sea. They eased her onto the bed, both still wearing their green operating gowns. The taller of the two men smiled at Vincent.

"You look a lot like your brother," he said pleasantly. "Are you going to stay the night with your mother? We generally have a cot sent in for relatives."

"Oh, no," said Vincent. "I'm not going to sleep. I'm going to watch her to make sure she doesn't move her head."

He was an earnest young man, and after the doctors left he sat down and fixed his eyes on her face, as if he were waiting for Santa Claus. He was so boyish you couldn't help but like him, and he was always beset by calamity, so you had to pity him as well. He'd wanted to be a missionary in Africa but flunked Greek at college, so he tried selling vacuum cleaners, doing magic acts at children's parties, emptying bedpans at the Southern Michigan State Hospital, and ended up selling conservation films for an obscure company in Florida.

He made a little money and it went fast, for first he had one child, then another, and still one more. To make up for the early death of his father, his mother had given him all the advantages —boats, cars, electric typewriters—and advantages had become necessities. When he bought his wife a radio, it seemed necessary to get shortwave, the police, and the Detroit Tigers. And yet nothing in his house worked properly. The water pipes leaked, and the new dishwasher broke down, and the dryer burnt itself out the week after he bought it. His wife, Tania, worked hard and approved of everything. Her parents were actors, and her own childhood was so irregular that her marriage seemed both a continuation of it and an improvement, and as the children came, her fair hair grew darker and her face brighter. They had all the conveniences and no money and were content.

"Was it a good trip here?" asked his mother. "How'd the car hold up?" But caught in her own pain, she did not really sound interested in him.

"Pretty good. It broke down in Akron. But this guy let me park it on his lawn for fifty cents a day." He added the price by habit. Everyone in his family added the price except his brother, Theo.

"What time is it?"

"About eight."

He was going to remark how the dark came so much earlier now that fall was here, then remembered that she couldn't see the light.

"Well, you make yourself comfortable."

It wasn't as depressing a place as he had feared. Each room had its own desk, lamp, and television, and on every wall opposite the beds hung a crucifix. Vincent had a weakness for the visible symbols of faith. As a child he had been baptized a Methodist, then at fifteen he quit the Sunday School and attended

Greek Orthodox services in Greek for six months, and Lutheran services in German for two months, though he understood almost nothing of either language. He sojourned briefly with the Christian Scientists till he lost the hearing in his left ear the day after he went swimming with the mumps. Finally he joined the Pentecostal Bethel Church of God, because it promised him salvation through a life based solely on the teachings of Christ. He moved out of his room, with its clutter of hockey sticks and jigsaw puzzles and Monopoly sets, into the spare room, where he built a simple altar and a bookcase. The room held nothing else to distract him. He prayed, he read. He bought a paperback copy of the *Imitation of Christ*, but the language was not his language, so he gave it up and bought a copy of *The Cloud of Unknowing*, because someone told him it was good, and that was even worse. "When I say darkness, I mean thereby a lack of knowing," it said. "And for this reason it is not called a cloud of the air, but a cloud of unknowing." How could you love God if you couldn't know him? "He may well be loved, but not thought. By love may He be gotten and holden, but by thought never."

When Vincent was in high school, Theo came home at the end of his first year in college, and anyone could see he was a changed man. He'd left home, just as their sister Gertrude had left five years earlier, and he had never really come home again, just as Vincent himself had never really left it. Yet whenever he walked into what had been their room, he found Theo's old levis and sneakers in the closet and the Audubon records which Theo had prized, gathering dust in the bookcase, along with Steinbeck and fine editions of *Moby Dick* inscribed by librarian aunts who visited only on holidays. Theo knew the calls and colors of the birds; Vincent knew only that something had flown past him or was singing outside his window. When fall came, they lay awake at night listening to the wild geese flying south, and Theo told him everything.

It's very cold up in the air. They fly all night and all day. They feel magnetic currents in the earth and in the air, and that's how they know where to go. They have one mate all their lives and they never forget anything. Not one summer, not even the smallest blossom. It's all there.

Theo had left it all, like an outgrown shell. He had lived for a while in New York, but nobody knew how. His life was irregular, his political views unsettling (neither Vincent nor his mother asked about them directly), he called Castro "Fidel" and Guevara "Ché," and his mother, much against her will, sent him an encyclopedia of Russian history for his birthday. Without a photograph, Vincent could not remember his brother's face, except as it looked before he went away to school. And now he felt flattered that their mother had called him, not Theo, and he knew she depended on him as much as he did on her.

But now she was unaware of him as she considered the importance of her own pain, turning it over in her mind like a jewel.

"They used to put sandbags around your head so you wouldn't move," she said at last. "I thought about asking them to do that for me. But Ruth Tucker told me about a man who fell out of bed the day after his operation and could see fine afterward. Those are the kind of stories you hear that encourage you."

Vincent nodded eagerly, then realized she could not see him. Conscientiously, he kept his eyes on her face. His mother breathed so lightly she seemed to have fallen asleep, yet when Vincent stood up and went to pull the shade, she cried out, "Is somebody walking?"

"It's me," said Vincent, and hastily sat down again.

"Doctor Herrgott sang all the way through the operation. He's got a real nice voice, he sings in the Methodist choir. It said so in the paper when he got promoted. He covers you with a sheet, so just your eyeball shows; the nurses tie your hands down. I could see him stitching it, like he was crocheting."

Sitting in the dark, Vincent was restless. Always he surrounded himself with things that needed to be tinkered with, and now he had nothing to do. And he hated to waste time. He watched his mother's face and thought about money and how to make it. He could buy the land across from his house and build tourist cabins. Lots of tourists came to Florida. But that would take money. For a while he'd tried running a restaurant with Charles Ruddy, a man who once bought a vacuum cleaner from him, but the kitchen was too small and Tania had to make the salads at home. He'd come home and find hundreds of little jellos all over the house, on his desk, on the bed, on the dining-room table; there wasn't so much as a place to throw his coat down. And then people stopped coming and Charles Ruddy skipped out and left him with bills for a new stove, for two months' worth of food, for two dozen chairs and a dozen tables. Vincent carried the bills around in his wallet, took them out, studied them and put them back, till the print grew faint from being folded so often, and more bills came and he carried them all—as a rich man carries his valuables—to bed with him.

It was to get out of debt that he started selling conservation films. He wished Theo could see some of them. There was a very fine one about the survival of the whooping crane and another about parrots in South America, but in the meantime Vincent was spending money and the bills arrived each day and he tucked them, almost tenderly, in his wallet, as if he could re-deem them for a prize when he'd collected enough.

Across the hall, someone was coughing.

"That's Mr. Kinsky," said his mother. "He's got a monitor for his heart; he coughs all day. I think he's not as bad off as he sounds. He can always stop long enough to talk with the nurses when they come in. His heart was down to thirty-eight from seventy-two."

"Was it?" said Vincent. He could not get rid of those schemes for money; once they entered his mind they filled it, consumed him, lived with him like a legion of devils. His mother said nothing more for a while, and it hurt him to think she knew he was bored, so he got up and looked out of the window again, through a crack between the shade and the window frame. Highrise apartments, like giant headstones, were squatting all over in the park behind the hospital, which had been a graveyard when he was a kid. The municipal au-thorities had dug up the bodies and moved them, but only a year ago, workmen digging a carport for one of the apartment buildings found a mummified professor and immediately went on strike. Lights twinkled from all the windows, and that dark stream running between them, that was the river with the willows sinking along the banks where fifteen years ago he and Theo walked together and later he and Tania. But he could not see that time clearly anymore, try as he might; it always had the vague colors of a vivid tale told by someone else.

His mother was moving restlessly.

"I think I'd better ring for a pain pill. Doctor Herrgott said I could have up to three if I needed them. You know, it's so hard to get a nurse to come. I saw a TV program about death. It said that nurses hate to answer the bell when they know someone is dying."

And then her voice dropped to a whisper: "Grandmother made the most awful smells in the room when she died."

"What did she die of?"

"A stroke. Strokes and cataracts run in our family. Let's see, my mother had them on both eyes, my grandmother had them, and of course Velda got hers before she was forty, and then on your father's side I think there were some."

"I'll probably have them," said Vincent. His eyes were not good. He was nearsighted and his left eye veered out unless he kept it in check.

"Don't say that," urged his mother. "Where does it say in the Bible, 'The thing he greatly feared came upon him'?"

"Well, if I'm going to have them, I'm going to have them."

"I don't know. You give it importance by saying it."

He reached up and felt his eyes. He had been forcing them open to stare at his mother's face so long that his eyeballs felt chapped. Worse, he was beginning to grow sleepy. He felt in his shirt pocket for the candy bar he'd brought and tried to unwrap it quietly, so the cellophane wouldn't crunkle. The old man across the hall was whispering to himself: *one two four, one two three, one two four.* His mother heard nothing. The railing on the side of her bed looked like the white fencing around a pasture for horses. The sheets looked so white and the upper part of the bed had been cranked so high that she seemed to be riding through the dark on the back of a huge white dog, leaning against his neck. Vincent threw the wrapper on the floor and bit hard into the toffee.

"I smell oatmeal cookies," exclaimed his mother.

"It's me. I'm eating a toffee bar. Do you want a bite?"

"Oh, I couldn't. I'm full as a tick. What time is it?"

He peered at the traveling clock on her night table.

"A little after eight."

"Does that clock glow in the dark?"

"A little."

"Velda and Jack said they were going to drop by and see how I felt. When you go home in the morning, be sure to check my desk for the deeds to those cemetery lots."

"What cemetery lots?"

"I'm giving them to you. I'd have had to pay a nurse if you hadn't come, and I don't want you to feel you've wasted your time."

"What lots are you talking about?" he cried.

"Your father bought a bunch of them in Fair Haven on Gates Road when you were born, and put some in your name, some in Gertrude's, and some in Theo's. You've got at least thirty of them. You can sell them for six hundred dollars a pair."

He felt utterly astonished. He had not told his mother how much money he owed, only sometimes he asked her for a little money to make ends meet at the end of the month. She always sent him whatever he asked for.

"When Posey Tuttle's husband died, she had to get a pair way behind the mausoleum. We have ours right in front. Grandmother used up two of them. They buried her sideways. I remember they asked us if we wanted them to dig her up again, but we said no. They could do anything and we'd never know. In Clayton County, around my grandfather's farm, people used to bury their dead in their front yards. I always thought the water tasted funny."

And then she added, out of fairness, "I gave Theo the deeds to *his* lots for a wedding present, but he never did much about them. We've got enough lots for everybody—you and Tania, and Theo. And Velda and her husband, though if we start with Velda's family, they'll go pretty fast. Sometimes I don't know what to do, everybody wants to be buried in our lots. You can hardly refuse them."

Her voice sounded more and more agitated.

"I was telling Velda that the old Walled Lake Cemetery would be nice. It's close to where your grandmother's house used to be, and there's a lot of very educated people in it. We brought Great Aunt Harriet there so she could be near her mother. Ah, Vincent, she was a saint! She used to give all the tramps who came to her door a good meal and throw out the dishes afterward. She'd die if she knew we didn't get Perpetual Care when we buried her. It's gone up from two to three hundred dollars."

Exhausted by these worries, she lapsed into silence, while Vincent luxuriated in plans: he would advertise, or get someone to sell the lots, and how much would that bring? Enough to pay off the bills. Or he could invest the profit in those cabins and the money would come in steadily after that, and he would never have to worry about bills again. Yet he both worried and did not worry; he knew he could not pay them. He would take them out of his wallet, study them, and having punished his extravagance with fear, put them back in his wallet and out of his mind, and he would feel better immediately. But now his mind was wandering away toward sleep. He saw himself leading it on a tether, letting it go just so far, then jerking it back. He must not let himself go to sleep, on any account. He changed his position and stared at his mother's face but found to his surprise that he could not keep it in view. In the dark it kept changing, it was infinitely plastic and terrifying. He saw the flesh from her chin to her throat shining like a beard on a Spanish peasant. Then even as he named what he saw, the whole apparition flowed into something else, metallic, like the imagined monstrous face of a car, sexless and strange, and then again, when he tipped his head, it showed him once more his mother's face. As a child, he had done that with objects in his room at night. The whole world could twinkle into monsters at the flicker of an eyeball. He had trouble not believing in ghosts. His father had believed in them, and he remembered coming upon some of his sister's books which his mother had hidden, and he remembered how his mother burned them, so that not even the dogs would find them in the garbage can and maybe carry them to where the neighbors might see them. What books? Testimonies of the living about the return of the dead. Sitting in the dark, unable to read,

Vincent felt dead himself. He heard his mother sigh and it roused him awake.

"Mother?"

"My mouth is all chapped. Rub one of those suppositories on my mouth."

"Where are they?"

"In my purse. I hid it in the closet. You aren't supposed to have any medicine except what they give you here."

He rummaged around in the closet, found the purse and a little bottle of suppositories inside, took one out and rubbed her lips with it. In the light from the hallway, her forehead shone like the new skin on a child, whereas the skin on her cheeks looked coarse-grained and blotchy.

"When your grandmother died, I remember I had to swab her lips, they were so dry."

"You skin is real smooth, Mother," he said, and she knew he was not flattering her, for he did not know how.

"They gave it a good scrubbing. I thought the nurse was going to take my eyebrows off."

The voice across the hall began counting again, and his mother stiffened. "Is that Mr. Kinsky? He makes me so nervous. He lies there counting by the hour."

"What's he counting?"

"I heard him tell the nurse he's counting the beats of his heart."

Vincent caught his breath. Oh, how was it that in the darkness he could see his life so clearly? Here was the sweetish smell of cough medicine and the scoured untidiness of his grandmother's house, long since pulled down to make way for the new Walled Lake Post Office. His grandmother was so clean that she hired a girl to help her scrub the cooking pots and together they scrubbed holes through three of them. For what you paid her, said Grandfather, you could've bought new pots. He was tidy, but not overly clean. Grandmother made a fetish of cleanliness but she was not tidy. She was always cluttering up the rooms that they did not rent out, so that she could find things better, because she could only find things if she had a lot of places to look. She quickly cluttered her husband out of the house. He had a round table in the storm-cellar where he kept his books and ate apple butter and then, late every afternoon, walked a block uptown to bring back a pie or half a dozen sausages for dinner. Grandmother could make bread and preserves and codfish pudding, but she hated to cook, and after her two daughters left home, she would not touch the stove except to boil water for coffee.

As a child in her yard, Vincent felt very small—and it was always *her* yard, *her* house, for everything in the world, as far as he could see, was run by women. Grandmother took in the rents and Grandfather, who had the gift of healing in his hands, gave infrequent osteopathic treatments and raised radishes in a tiny plot at the back of the yard. When bumblebees lit on his hands, he showed Vincent how to rub their backs, and they stayed on his knuckles, transfixed with contentment, like purring cats. Behind the shed, plums dropped from the trees into a patch of wild asparagus, as frantically bright and delicate as green fire.

Grandmother gave Vincent a bunch of old keys whenever he came to visit her; she never gave them to Theo. The keys made him feel important, in charge. She told him that you could stop time if you stopped the giant cylinders in the window of the newspaper office two doors down because they were making time in there, lots and lots of it. The cylinders were long and fat and shining brass, like the inside of his music box at home.

Behind the room where Grandfather gave his treatments, she let him play in her bedroom. It was so crowded with things you could hardly find the bed. On more bureaus and tables than he could count, she kept bowls of buttons, photographs, underwear, and the broken heart of an old chandelier. Its glass pendants kept turning up everywhere, like fancy tears: in the silverware drawer, behind books and sofa pillows, all over the house. He wanted to take some of them home, but Grandmother would not part with them; someday, she told him, the chandelier would all be put back together again.

He was afraid to touch things for fear they would all come down on him. Half a dozen chairs stood on their heads, tied in a tower with paper-wrapped legs sticking into the air. A piano keyboard showed between the two giant blue urns that once stood on his grandmother's front porch. But in the middle of the room stood an old osteopathic table that his grandfather had used when this was the treatment room. That alone was permanently screwed in place, and the boy used it for his horse.

You can have anything you want in this room, said his grandmother, taking him by the hand.

He stood there, dazzled by the quantity of chairs, books, and drawers spilling out of nowhere.

Except, she added, this Royal Dalton lady.

She reached behind the urns and pulled out a plaster statue of a woman in a red dress. Her nose had broken off, and it gave her a bewildered expression.

I got it at Christiansen's. Isn't it nice? You can't have that one.

He looked around wildly, for fear she would change her mind about the other things, too. He knew that his mother would not like to find him here, choosing a present for himself when it wasn't even his birthday.

Can I have that record?

Where? Where?

Over on that bureau.

Which bureau?

THERE!

He pointed to a small black victrola record with a big hole in the middle.

Somebody sent that to your grandfather, she said, and handed it to him.

He put the hole on his thumb and spun the record around and wondered what it sounded like. Grandmother did not have a victrola. So Vincent went to see Mr. Harris, who lived in the other half of the house, and asked him to play it. Vincent sat on the horsehair sofa, embarrassed and excited, while Mr. Harris raised the lid on the machine and dropped the needle. The machine was as tall as a table. Through the ornate meshwork in front came a series of thumps, beating in pairs at all different speeds, one after the other. Mr. Harris, smart in his vest but so thin that Grandmother complained she could hardly see him, lifted the needle and squinted down at the label.

DIAGNOSIS OF CARDIAC DISORDERS, he read. That's a hell of a present to give a child.

Mr. Harris was a magician. Shall I find a key on your person? he would say when he came to visit. I know you have the key to our quarters.

Vincent knew he didn't.

I know it's here, persisted Mr. Harris, and began lifting up all the pillows on the sofa.

Lots of dust here. Your grandmother needs to clean up.

He rattled the glass bookcases and pulled out a book and shook it.

Not there, he said. Why don't you hand it over? I know you have it.

The boy was stammering out a denial when Mr. Harris reached over and deftly pulled the key out from behind his ear.

Even now, sitting by his mother's bed, though Mr. Harris had long ago turned to dust, Vincent felt behind his ears to check for the key.

"You have visitors, Mrs. Svenson. Shall I let them in?"

A nurse was standing in the doorway.

"Who are they?" asked Vincent.

"Mr. and Mrs. Tiedemann."

"Tell them to wait a few minutes," said his mother.

The nurse disappeared.

"Was she black or white, Vincent?"

"I didn't notice."

"She sounded black to me. Help me on with my robe and slippers."

"You're not going anywhere."

"I know, but I'll look more dressed up. They're in the closet."

He found her slippers in the suitcase, small furry beaded ones, with turned-up toes; terribly gay, he thought. He lifted the sheet and slid her feet into them. They felt small and dry, like parchment.

"Where'd you get these slippers, Mother?"

"Ordered them from the catalogue. Just lay the robe over me."

The robe was new, too, purple silk, printed with pagodas, and as it fluttered over her, she pinched a corner of the fabric between her fingers.

"The bridge club gave me that when I went in the hospital for my gall bladder. It's real silk. Mrs. Thorn picked it out; it cost twenty-five dollars. Nobody else ever got that much. I didn't tell anyone when I was going in this time. Thought they might feel they had to get me another one. My radio, where is it?"

He took it out of the suitcase and put it beside the clock.

"Ever since I dropped it, all I can get are sermons. I wonder, if I had it fixed, could I get shortwave? You remember how Theo always liked to tinker with radios? Sometimes I think I'll turn it on and it'll be him saying, 'Hello, Mother, how are you?' just like those tapes he sent us the summer he worked at the radio station."

And then, without any warning, Velda and Jack walked into the room. Hastily, Vincent stood up. Jack seemed to have been born a retired high-school principal; he always looked exactly the same. But Velda's hair was gold now, to cover the gray, and she had grown a little stout, though her arms and legs were slender, almost delicate.

"You look real good, Maggie," said Velda. "Doesn't she, Jack?"

"I saw pretty good when the doctor finished, except for spots."

"Spots?" asked Vincent. His mother had not spoken of spots before.

"Sort of like black lace."

"Oh, I saw black lace for weeks after I had my cataract off," said Velda. "Black lace is such an impediment to vision. Does the TV bother you? There's a talking dog coming on at nine Jack hates to miss."

She fiddled with the dials and Jack drew Vincent's chair over to watch. Both Vincent and Velda stood awkwardly at the foot of the bed.

"Go ahead," said his mother. " 'Course I can't watch anything myself."

"I'll give you some of my vitamins. They say you can combat blindness with vitamins. I broke my bottle of vitamin C in the car, but the pills are big, you can still swallow them. I didn't think the nurse was going to let us in, but I kept saying, 'I'm her sister, her only sister, she's expecting me, and I got to know how she is.' "

"Turn up the TV," said Jack. "I can't hear."

"Who is it?" asked Vincent's mother.

"Marv Clifford."

"Oh, I like him," exclaimed Velda. "Did you see him the time he had on that Canadian faith healer? Oh, he was grand. Marv Clifford had sinus trouble and he told the faith healer to cure him. So the faith healer put his hands over Marv Clifford's eyes and started to pray. " 'O, Lord,' he said, 'if it be thy will, take away this man's sinus trouble.' "

"And did it work?" asked Vincent eagerly.

"Not a bit," said Velda. "But I like Marv Clifford, don't you? I always think he looks like Theo." She turned to her sister. "You heard from Theo lately?"

"Not a thing since he wrote he was married. I was glad to see him leave New York."

"We missed the talking dog," growled Jack. "The show's been going on for half an hour. We missed the dog."

"I sent a silver bowl," said Velda. "The price of silver on the market is going up, did you know that?"

"Did you get a thank-you note yet?"

"Not a word."

His mother bit her lip.

"She had no humor at all. She was Dutch. I told Theo, you aren't marrying her so she'll put you through school forever, are you? But when he gave her that real expensive book, I saw it had gone too far. He never did that for any other girl."

"I've seen him with other girls. They always had such a lot of spirit," said Velda.

"Remember that rich Janet Wills who sang in the choir and

did everything in church?" said his mother. "She had embroidered shoes."

Vincent shook his head.

"He never liked her, Mother."

Velda smiled at him.

"How's Tania? She's such a sweet girl."

"Fine," said Vincent, and realized he had hardly given her a thought.

"And you, you're working hard as usual?"

"Oh, sure."

"Hard work will get you places in this world. Remember Robert Grouts? He's a doctor now, makes a lot of money. He wore out a chair studying."

"Ah, damn it," cried Jack. "The sound went off."

"You broke it?" Velda looked at him accusingly.

"I was trying to get another channel."

Suddenly Velda gave a shriek of joy.

"Look! It's the King Sisters!"

"What? What?" said Vincent's mother.

"There are three old women in formals and three young girls," said Vincent. "They're singing together, Mother."

"I can't hear a thing," she complained.

"Punch it," said Jack. "That's what I do when mine goes bad on me."

"What are they doing now, Vincent?"

"Now there's a whole stage full of pianos and a whole lot of people all playing together."

"Oh, they're a remarkable family," said Velda.

"Now the lights are going up behind them and there are a whole lot of people playing guitars. My God, the place is full of them!"

It was an extravaganza for the deaf. The mothers were singing, the daughters clapping their hands, the husbands rushed at a dozen pianos as if they were charging a school of whales, the boy cousins in tight pants thwanged away at electric guitars, and as Vincent stared, they increased, and multiplied before his eyes. Jack gave the set a gentle kick, which jiggled them all into fragments, like a broken mirror, yet the next minute they were back together again, glittering and whole, as if the lost pendants of a chandelier had reassembled themselves, so that all their playing and fiddling and singing, their secret griefs and expectations of joy gave forth a fantastic spectacle, an inimitable harmony.

Suddenly they all disappeared behind a lady holding a box of bleach.

"That's bad stuff," said Velda. "I lost a nightgown in the laundromat with that once, when my washer broke down. Melted clean away in the dryer."

They watched the lady set down the soap and pick up an alarm clock.

"Nice clock," said Vincent.

Velda smiled at him.

"I got one like that. You get one each time you make a five-hundred-dollar deposit in the First National Bank. I got about six clocks now; I'll give you one, Vincent. I gave one to my cleaning lady and she says it runs fine."

"Six!" exclaimed Vincent. "You make a lot of deposits."

Velda shook her head.

"No, I take out five hundred and put it back in a few days later."

How was it that everybody won things except him? Aunt Velda was always winning things. She had a real knack for contests. One Christmas the whole family ate out in a restaurant because Velda forgot she'd invited them and had bought forty cases of olives and there was no room for anything else in the kitchen. She and Jack had been eating out every night and nibbling olives in between. She sent in eight hundred slogans about why she liked Melbourne's olives, written on labels, and as Jack said, with that many, she should know. Two months later, the company sent her a free case of olives and a toaster.

She was lucky; how did you get to be lucky? When drawings were held, for anything, she always won the doorprize. She was good at cards, she knew what ball teams would do well and what horses would win, and she had an eye for bargains: a rotisserie free, with two hundred coupons from Deli-Quik banana cake

---

mix, a bedroom set free, for picking up her telephone and identifying a song.

When they were gone, Vincent found himself hoping he had pleased her. She had no enthusiasm but rather a peculiar charm —you were flattered if she liked you because you felt yourself chosen, through no virtue of your own, and lifted above the groundlings where you had stood but a moment before. After high school she had worked in a real estate office, got together a small fortune and married, at the age of thirty-two, a man nearly twenty years older than herself. Ten years later she found herself burdened with the hereditary blindness that touched so many in their family. Her husband kept her cataracts in a silver phial and said they looked like pearls, and they did, in a way, gray and curled up into beads, but Theo had offended Jack by saying they looked like slugs.

So it was Vincent, not Theo, that Velda invited to play bridge, and shuffle the deck for solitaire whenever the two families visited each other. He stayed with her once when Uncle Jack was away overnight on business. She did not like being alone, and a ten-year-old child in the house was proper, and better than no one at all. She let him play with the mirrors and combs on her dressing table while she made a little bed for him on the sofa. The brushes had little knots of her long red hair in the bristles. There was a comb with diamonds on the handle that he especially liked and she let him take it to bed with him.

In the middle of the night he woke up, still clutching the comb, and smelled bacon. Staggering into the kitchen, he found his aunt cooking. The stove was covered with pots, all boiling away, and the grill hissed and sizzled as his aunt turned an enormous omelet.

You hungry? she asked.

She cut the omelet in two. It was more than he could eat, but he was determined to get it down, for he wanted his aunt to like him. She smiled, seeing him eat.

And then she whispered—was it to him or herself?

I'm always afraid of finding someone dead in bed.

And then she smiled again and their eyes met.

You want to play a game of hearts before you go back to bed?

The next morning, her face was as closed and strange to him as if he were a child again. She sent him home on the bus. But never again did he ask his mother why Uncle Jack kept her cataracts in a silver phial. And when he opened his suitcase, he found the diamond comb.

Now, sitting in the dark by his mother's bed, he took out his wallet, pulled out all his bills and dropped his debts, one by one, into the wastebasket. And then he began to dream. Vincent had a dream that used to come to him whenever he had a stomach-ache, or when the bills he carried in his wallet began to chafe at him:

He is sitting with Velda and Jack in a television studio. Velda sits on one side of him and a young girl with black gloves on the other. They are sitting in the dark, looking across hundreds of other people to the stage, with its huge placard, THE HONEYMOONERS, and its tiers of prizes: toasters, irons, boats, sofas, hedge clippers, ice boxes, fur coats, tastefully arranged between Doric columns, like a votive offering left for a god. There is a young couple on stage with the Master of Ceremonies, who claps his hands and says:

Now if the husband will step backstage—

General laughter. A girl in a long black gown leads the husband offstage. The Master of Ceremonies offers the young wife a chair and takes one himself.

Now, I'm going to ask you a few questions. And if you can tell me how your husband would answer all of them, you'll both win a free trip to Honolulu and our little Starcraft Cruiser. If half your answers match his—

Vincent looks at the boat and sees himself at the wheel and a violent desire to possess it makes him break out into a sweat.

But now the Master of Ceremonies has begun the questioning.

What is the most babyish thing your husband does?

The young wife looks as nervous as if she were on the witness stand.

He sleeps curled up at night and chews his thumb.

Chews his thumb! cries the Master of Ceremonies. And what part of your legs does he like best?

My legs?

What part of your legs does he like best?

The—the knee, she says. I think the knee.

And now, what color is the inside of your house?

Why, it's white. We just had it painted.

Let's bring her husband out here and see how well she knows him! Shouts the Master of Ceremonies. And he turns to the stocky blonde young man who is running his finger along the edge of the boat just as Vincent is feeling it with his mind, and says:

What is the most babyish thing you do?

I don't know, exclaims the husband. Sometimes I leave my shirts on the floor.

General laughter from the audience.

Your wife says you curl up at night and chew your thumb.

She told you that! He turns to his wife, chagrined. I didn't think you'd tell anyone that.

And now, tell us, what part of your wife's legs do you like the best?

The ankle, says the young man. Without a doubt, the ankle.

Oh, I thought it was my knees! Cries the young woman.

You said knees? The young man pounds the back of her chair in a burst of rage. Don't you remember we talked about it only a couple of nights ago?

And now what color is the inside of your house? Asks the Master of Ceremonies, grinning and winking at the audience.

I don't know! I don't know!

But we just had it painted! Cries his wife. You picked the color out yourself!

Somebody, somewhere, starts playing the organ, and the Master of Ceremonies joins their hands.

Well, I'm afraid you haven't won our Starcraft Cruiser. But for being on our show and being such good sports, we're giving you a Sunbeam Egg-cooker.

The girl in the long black dress comes out carrying the egg-cooker on a satin pillow, and leads the couple into the wings.

And now, ladies and gentlemen of the studio audience, the moment you have all been waiting for. Our own Willie the Wizard will walk through the audience and pick out the happiest couple here. And to that couple we will give the Starcraft Cruiser.

A little man in a red sequined union suit and a fez is walking down the aisle, pointing a forked stick ahead of him.

He's coming over to us, whispers Velda.

The rod quivers over their heads; the Wizard closes his eyes.

He's stopping in front of Vincent, says Uncle Jack.

Vincent's heart sinks. But the Master of Ceremonies is already calling him to the stage.

You and your wife have won the grand prize, sir. Congratulations!

The girl in the black gloves smiles happily.

Congratulations, says the Wizard.

She's not my wife, says Vincent softly.

Hush, whispers Velda. Pretend she is.

Not your wife? says the Wizard, and everything grows silent.

The girl says nothing.

O, pretend she is! says someone two rows back, and now the whole audience takes up the chant.

Pretend she is! Pretend she is!

And just as he is about to win the Starcraft Cruiser, Vincent jumps up from his seat, runs down the aisle, and bolts out the door.

His mother was asleep. Vincent, his back aching, stood up and tiptoed into the hall to find a men's room.

"Nice weather for hunting, isn't it?" said a voice from the opposite room. "My son's up in Northern Michigan right now, hunting deer."

In the dark, Vincent could make out the shape of a man sitting up in bed and he could hear the occasional beeps from the monitor that ran his heart.

"Nice weather," said Vincent politely.

"My son has a license to hunt deer with a bow and arrow,"

said the voice, sorrowfully. "Sometimes I ask myself, Why should a nice Jewish boy want to hunt deer with a bow and arrow?"

When Vincent came back into his mother's room, he found someone had turned on the night light over her head.

"Mother, are you awake?"

There was something strange about her face.

"The nurse picked these up off the floor, asked me if I wanted them. 'What are they?' I said."

She uncrumpled her hand, and he saw that she was holding the bills.

"Five hundred dollars for gas! Two hundred dollars for a new stove!"

Vincent felt himself growing cold all over; he had never heard anyone say the sums aloud.

"The stove was for the restaurant. Mr. Ruddy hasn't paid me yet."

"He'll never pay you," his mother cried out. "You could sell the stove and make a little money on it."

"Mr. Ruddy took the stove with him."

"And five hundred for gas. How could you run up a bill for five hundred for gas?"

"I have to drive a lot when I sell my bird films, I use a credit card. My manager says I'll get it all back."

"You'll never get it back," said his mother.

Vincent sat down; his hands felt huge. He blew his nose until it hurt.

"Don't blow so hard, you'll blow it off," said his mother. "At least try to hang onto something. Listen, Vincent, we'll sell the lots right away. I think I can borrow a little money to pay off the biggest bills. Do you need anything at home? Clothes for Tania? The children?"

"No," said Vincent.

"I got some dresses on sale for the girls. 'Course half of 'em aren't the right size, but they'll grow into them. Lizzie wrote a note on my birthday card that she wants me to send her an electric fan. I don't know what a girl just starting school wants with an electric fan in the middle of winter. And a bill for pizzas, a fifty-dollar bill for pizzas! You buy so many pizzas."

"Tania likes pizzas, Mother."

"Couldn't you sell the radio?"

"I got to have music, Mother. And you know, if anything happens to Tania when I'm away, she can call the police; we get the police on our radio."

"But how are you going to pay for all this?"

Vincent said nothing. He wanted to weep. When his mother spoke again, her voice was gentler.

"Did you pray about it?"

But still he could say nothing.

"Well, well. I know it upsets you. Let's save it till the morning. Open the window a little. It's so stuffy in here."

A crisp breeze chilled the room.

"I twitch and sweat so much," she remarked. "I don't know why I should be sweating. Isn't it wonderful I can move my legs?"

"Mr. Kinsky told me his son hunts deer with a bow and arrow," said Vincent.

"Ah, I knew a boy who used to do that in Wisconsin, on the farm where your grandmother grew up. When Velda and I were kids, we used to spend every summer there."

Her voice dropped. It sounded so dreamy that Vincent leaned forward to see if she were falling asleep.

"When I was fifteen and Velda was eighteen, we served dinner to the harvesters. 'Put on your best clothes,' Mother told us. 'You're from the city and people expect more of us than other people.' So we put on our blue taffeta dresses and Mother wound our curls on her finger, and Grandmother got a huge meal ready for when the men should come in at noon. They went from farm to farm, and all the women outdid themselves laying on a fine spread. 'Well, they didn't have two beautiful girls to wait on them in anybody else's house,' said Grandmother."

Outside, it seemed to Vincent the sky was getting light, and he could smell the sunlit fields and the steamy comfort of his great-grandmother's kitchen, and he could see his mother in her blue taffeta dress, and Velda, high-spirited and entirely beautiful, the way he knew she really looked if he'd had eyes to see her.

"And at last they came, all the young men from the fields, one by one into the house, so shy when they saw Velda and me that they wouldn't speak two words to us, but only smiled a little. Grandmother had a pitcher and basin by the door for them to wash in. I remember how they rolled up their sleeves and poured out the water and splashed their arms in it and rubbed their faces, and then they sat, all wet and red-faced, while Velda and I brought on the chicken and the best preserves. You can't imagine how beautiful we were, Vincent! Each day they went to a different farm till the corn was standing in shocks over every field, but they never forgot that meal at our house."

Morning was at his back. He could feel the sky growing light behind him and he could hear the wild geese, far out of sight, flying south. *They never forget anything, not one summer, not even the smallest blossom.* The sound passed over him and he felt their shadows, as if his own blindness had already started and a thing too dazzling to be remembered had grazed his heart from the lost world of sight.

Children Passing

The telephone was ringing. Clutching the *Sunday Times*, Erica ran the three flights upstairs, unlocked the door, flew into the kitchen, and grabbed the receiver off the wall. Her head spun and she sat down quickly, a little frightened, for she almost never felt ill.

"Hello," she panted.

"This is Gertrude. Is Theo around?"

"He's not here."

"Is this Erica? I don't believe we've met. When my brother comes back—will he be back soon?"

"Pretty soon," said Erica, leaning her head against the cool porcelain of the sink.

A long silence answered her.

"Well, when you see him, tell him I called from Rumpus Mitchell's Hot Spot diner, crushed into a telephone booth with my conjure woman. The telephone booth is adjacent to the magazine rack. My conjure woman and I are surrounded by dirty old men. The apple-pickers of Travers City proving unpleasant, we set out for the raspberry farms of Saugatuck————"

"They took us for trollops," came a second voice, presumably the conjure woman's.

"We set out," resumed Gertrude, "following the lady with the geese. Truly, I didn't think there was any countryside left in

America, but it is not so. Not so. New York is not America. It is only the dirtiest city in America."

The sound of coins tinkled like hail over the words; then all at once the operator's voice broke in, rapid and fuzzy, from a great way off, and then the dial tone erased everything. What of the lady with the geese? On Gertrude's tongue she sounded as hermetic as a sign in a forgotten zodiac. Disappointed, Erica hung up the receiver, splashed cold water on her face, and ran downstairs to check the mail. The rusty box in the front hall held a postcard from her parents who lived about a mile away. The handwriting was her mother's. Reading, Erica walked slowly toward the diner where perhaps Theo was having one of the secret breakfasts he sometimes ate after he'd eaten one of hers. Though she'd caught him at it twice, he admitted to nothing.

Her mother wrote:

Your phone has been busy for a week. Is it out of order?
When are you moving?
      (Don't know, whispered Erica.)
Has Theo got a job in New York?   *
      (Not a job. Something else. He fell in love with some
      streets and some smells and some people. He can't
      remember their names.)
Are you sick? need money?
Come soon about important business.

Somebody nudged her rudely and she glanced up.

"A letter from your mother?" inquired Theo pleasantly, his arms full of empty cartons.

"Your sister called. She's here with a—a conjure woman."

"Lordy, Lordy! Did you leave the door open for them?"

"No," said Erica seriously.

"That's okay," smiled Theo.

"What is a conjure woman? A lady magician?"

"No," said Theo. "A conjure woman is more powerful. She doesn't do any tricks. She just knows, man."

Laughter and the smell of bacon filled the hallway as they climbed the last flight of stairs to their rooms. A deep voice—it might have been a man's, yet it sounded like a woman's—was singing:

Wild goose nest, wild goose nest.
Is all yo' eggs white, sister?
One egg black, go back, go back.

A tall red-haired girl in chinos, a navy T-shirt and a railroad cap darted out on the landing. She looked, thought Erica, both ragged and luminous, like a vaudeville Joan of Arc, and she spoke rapidly, as if she were afraid of losing her listeners.

"We cooked everything in the house. The bacon, the beans, two pork chops, three glasses, a pile of well-seasoned books—oh, I said to Wanda, 'We might have eaten before we came, so as not to appear ravenous.' 'Have you forgotten,' said Wanda, 'that I was carrying our combined resources in my stocking when we were robbed, rolled and what-all in the orchards of Traverse City?"

"Traverse City?" repeated Theo.

"We went to make our fortune picking cherries."

Gertrude embraced her brother and smiled at Erica, whose way of standing did not invite an embrace, and who looked round the tiny living room with dismay. Humming like an icebox, an enormous black woman in an orange dress with gold pineapple earrings was unpacking—or perhaps packing—a suitcase, as if she intended to stay, or to repossess what was hers. The tree of heaven outside the open window rose like a stately palm over the bright green scarf on her head.

"I suppose you're on your way to Wynadotte to see Mother," said Theo.

Gertrude had taken all Theo's books off his desk and piled them on the floor, and was now setting out Erica's best linen napkins—how, thought Erica, did she find them?—and folding them into little papal crowns.

"Now how can I go see Mother if I have not yet made my fortune? Perhaps a great fortune lies even now in the foundations of this building."

"I don't smell no fortune," said the conjure lady.

"Theo, this is Wanda," explained Gertrude. "Wanda, this is Erica."

Theo was looking at his desk.

"Gertrude, you know I don't like anyone messing with my stuff."

"My hands have never touched a thing of yours," said Gertrude. "What does fortune smell like, Wanda? Erica wants to know."

"Cooked brass," said the conjure woman. She opened the back door and sat down in the overstuffed chair on the fire escape. "Nice chair," she remarked. "Bet you paid something for this, honey."

"Theo found it in front of somebody's house on clean-up day," said Erica uneasily. "People throw all sorts of stuff away."

She felt a queer sick feeling rise in her stomach as she followed the conjure woman outside. A pile of fenders Theo had saved on that day glittered in the pit of gravel and weeds below them; behind the mortuary directly across the way, a thin dark man was sitting under a yellow beach umbrella, engraving a stone, white as a tooth. Suddenly the light left the sky as if someone had blown it out, and thunder rolled faintly but clearly.

"What's that shining down there?" called the conjure woman.

They all came out to look.

"That's old car parts," said Theo. "Thought I'd see what I could make out of them."

"Last time I was here you were making a whole city out of junk," said Gertrude.

"The Presbyterians bulldozed it. They're going to make a parking lot down there."

"Are the ponies running at Northville Downs?" asked the conjure woman, squinting off into the distance. Rain was beginning to fall. "My first husband won five thousand dollars on a horse called 'The Wounds of Jesus.' "

"Lordy, Lordy," said Theo. "I wouldn't bet two cents on 'The Wounds of Jesus.' "

Erica went inside, pushed aside her bookbag and a pile of

her clothes on the bed, and lay down. Over her head, the light bulb that snaked out of the ceiling was spinning wildly.

"You look poorly, girl," said the conjure woman.

"It's the heat," said Erica. Something in the air warned her not to admit weakness; something else made her want to lay her head in the conjure woman's lap and beg for a cure.

"Take yo'self a little molasses and some Jockey Club cologne—you got any Jockey Club cologne?"

"No," said Erica.

The conjure woman was laying hands on the lamp, the chair, the napkins, as if blessing them.

"Well, I expect you gettin' ready to travel. First time the Lord called me to travel I was living on Pearl Street. Ate me some bad hog's eyes—I do love hog's eyes—and I looked up and saw the Lord in his airplane, and it was all made of air, air motor, air brakes, air wings. 'I'm the doctor, sister,' says the Lord, 'and there ain't nothin' I can't cure.'"

Erica watched the woman's hand sweep some change off the bookcase into her pocket with a flourish, as if she were going to turn it into doves.

"And the Lord told me, 'Sister, y'all are come to the end of the road and to my twelve gates of jasper and sapphire and topaz and emerald—I won't name 'em all.' 'Scuse me, Lord,' I says, 'but I don't see no city yet, I don't see nothin' but grass.' 'Sister,' says the Lord, 'you see that wild-goose nest in the grass yonder? Look into the nest and tell me if all the eggs is white.'"

From the conjure woman's dress gleamed a hint of great riches; its folds swayed under the weight of them, and a fork sprang out of her pocket.

"And I look in and say, 'No, Lord, they's all white but one.' And the Lord says, 'Sister Wanda, turn round 'cause there ain't no rest for sinners.'" The conjure woman stopped swaying around the room and broke off her story. "You still feelin' poorly?"

"No," Erica lied. "I'm fine."

"You ain't pregnant, are you?"

"I don't know."

Behind the conjure woman, Theo and Gertrude were talking on the fire escape with their heads bent together like two stalks of wheat against the dark sky.

When Erica woke up the next morning, she heard Theo dropping things in the kitchen. Gertrude lay motionless on the sofa, wrapped in a huge paisley shawl. The conjure lady had disappeared.

Erica stumbled out of bed, opened the bottom bookcase and counted the silver demitasse spoons nestled beside her mother's tea service. Twelve.

Sniffing hungrily, she closed the door to the bookcase and tiptoed into the kitchen.

"Your mother called," said Theo. "She wants you to sign something."

"Where's the conjure woman?"

"Gone."

"She took all the change on the bookcase."

"I think," said Theo, "that Gertrude gave it to her. She loves to give presents, and she doesn't have anything of her own. How do you feel this morning, my lady?"

"I'm okay," said Erica. "I'm going downstairs to do the laundry."

Later, riding the bus to her parents' house, she felt herself healed as the outlines of the conjure woman's visit faded into the afternoon sunlight. The stores and office buildings grew sparse and gave way to arching elms and maples.

As Erica crossed the front lawn, she saw her mother vanish from the kitchen window and reappear in the doorway.

"I was just frying some hamburgers. Come on in."

At the dining-room table, her father was spearing tomatoes and snapping them up like the grim reaper. Bowls of green beans and yoghurt rose out of a clutter of papers.

"Our lawyer called," said Mother, sitting down at the papers as if they were a salad, "and told us we better get everything in order, or you'll have to pay 28,000 dollars inheritance tax. Now, Erica, if I die—are you listening?"

"Yes," said Erica, cutting herself a piece of cheese.

"If I die first, Daddy gets ten thousand dollars. If we both die together, you get ten thousand dollars. And if you die, your children get ten thousand dollars." She hesitated. "That is, if you have any children. The lawyer said to put the money in trust. I didn't want to do it at first. Mabel Fowler put her money in trust, and when she got sick her son wouldn't give her a cent." She arranged the papers into little piles. "But I know you wouldn't do that. How's Theo?"

"He's okay."

"Well, that's nice."

And then her mother added, as if she hardly knew she was saying it,

"I saw Donald Fox in church the other day. He's the district attorney now. Remember how he pulled the fire alarm in high school and nearly got expelled? He just married a millionairess."

Her father was chewing, with his eyes closed. How old he looked to her all at once! She could not help staring at him; he was quieter now than ever. And when had his hair turned so white?

"Donald used to take you to such nice places," said her mother wistfully. "You'd never have gotten to see *My Fair Lady* if he hadn't stood in line five hours for the tickets."

But they were the same places everyone else went, thought Erica bravely. She hadn't seen the inside of a theater for six months. Sometimes Theo took her to the free flicks.

"I saved you the clipping about the wedding," said her mother. "His wife is as ugly as homemade sin. Minnie says she has a glass eye and she takes it out every night to wash it. They say she's real nice to him, though."

"I'd never marry anyone with a glass eye," said Erica. It was dangerous to think about him; thinking of people you'd forgotten sometimes made them appear. She tried to put Donald out of her mind.

Her mother shrugged.

"Why, I suppose it's dark when they get into bed."

A scraping and rumbling startled them; Erica turned to see her father pushing his chair away from the table as he got unsteadily to his feet.

"Don't want to miss the news," he said.

"Erica," said her mother, "come and see the President on TV. They've done something to make his face look longer. And his color is wonderful. Sit in my chair—I'll be right back."

Erica sat down beside her father. Presently her mother reappeared, bearing an armful of clothes.

"Erica, do you think Theo could use Daddy's old coat? It's brand new and he won't wear it. He says it's too warm." She unfolded it to show the silken label on the neck. "A hundred percent cashmere. I don't believe I've ever seen Theo in a winter coat."

"Save it for him," said Erica. It was an old man's coat, and she knew Theo would never wear it, but she let her mother tuck it into a shopping bag.

"And here's a nice hat. Somebody picked up Al's in church and left him this one. It must have belonged to a man with a very big head." She set it carefully on top of the coat. "How do you think Daddy looks?"

"A little older. He's so quiet."

"Mel Shepley told Minnie, isn't it too bad how Al's slowing down? And just last week Mel died of a heart attack while he was blowing his nose. I saved you the clipping."

Far away, the bell from Theo's truck called her. She jumped like a child. Her mother followed her to the front door.

"Minnie's picking us up tomorrow for church. Don't wear your sandals."

That night, at the bottom of the universe called sleep, Erica walked into a windowless room full of skeletons and found Wanda, sitting under a mastodon, sewing and singing:

> My baby needs shoes, come on, seven,
> She can't get 'em if I lose, come on, seven.
> Roll them bones the whole night long.
> O, roll them bones.

She was stitching together the neckbones of a salmon. All around her lay bones, fins, scales, and hooves. A dozen leg-bones, white as chalk, stood poised for flight in the corner.

"Did you pluck me a goose for my supper?" asked Wanda.

"Yes," said Erica.

"Did you throw away the feathers?"

"I threw away the feathers."

And far away on earth, she heard children shouting as they opened their mouths to catch the first snow.

"Then I'll make your child. Only I can't hurry it. Can't hurry it. Go out and fetch me some pebbles for its teeth."

Erica opened her eyes. The late morning light mottled the curtains overhead as the tree of heaven, rank and indestructible, nosed the window. She glanced at the clock—a quarter of seven. She had forgotten to set the alarm. Moving softly, so as not to wake Theo who lay on his back with his arm thrown over his eyes, she pulled on her clothes.

But as she was buckling her sandals, he called to her,

"Are you going to church?"

"Mother's coming for me."

"Well, that's a good thing to do on Sunday."

She couldn't smell Sunday here the way she could at home as a child. In the window of the laundromat, a girl wearing a leotard sat, eyes closed, under the hair dryer recently installed by the management. Erica walked past her slowly, calculating minutely the sensations of her own body, trying to locate the exact place where she did not feel well. Never mind, she thought; when I'm in church I won't notice.

And she tried to see herself easing her way past knees and pocketbooks toward an aisle seat. The windows of Saint John's Lutheran glittered with lilies and sheaves and lambs, brilliant and relentless as the Ten Commandments.

Suddenly her body lurched forward and she threw up. A black car, monumental and immaculate, drew up to the curb beside her, and a man reached over and opened the door.

"Erica, can I give you a ride to church?"

She peered with astonishment into the face of Donald Fox. Once, years ago, he'd chosen her for himself. He was a law student then, four years older than she was. She was eighteen. Four years seemed forty.

"No, thanks."

"I didn't know you lived around here?" he said, in a voice which told her that he did.

He had grown stout, and his opulence appalled her. His Lincoln was sleek as a hearse and its white leather upholstery smelled like a woman's glove. Vomit was sticking between her toes, and she tucked one foot behind the other. His mouth was moving. We can talk on the way to church, said his mouth, and he gestured again to the seat beside him. Erica shook her head, no, no, and started walking, and the car glided slowly along beside her, the door hanging open like a broken wing. Ahead of them, over Rumpus Mitchell's diner, a window opened and an old man in an undershirt stuck his head out.

"She's from the circus, mister," he bawled. "I seen her on TV last week, a-hanging by her knees fifty feet up in the air. Take it from me, you'll never catch her!"

Sinner, Don't You Waste That Sunday

Through the open door of the emergency room, she watched the nurse, a small black woman, caught like a moth in the light that dangled over her desk. Far down the dingy corridor, a man was singing:

We are poor little lambs that have lost our way.
Baaa, baaa, baaa!

Erica lay motionless on the stretcher, longing for the fresh air of the summer night, and as she listened, she saw the sheep wandering among the huge pipes in the boiler room—every basement had a boiler room—and a surge of pity for all lost creatures brought tears to her eyes. Who was the last person to lie on this stretcher? Cupboards hung open above the dirty towels heaped on the floor; bottles of rosy fluid peopled the table and the sink.

The singing stopped; the singer came into the room. He was a small man with dark graying hair and a pointed beard. In spite of his green gown and surgeon's cap, he still looked to Erica like a magician, and when he laid his hands across her swollen belly he seemed about to counter her fear with a runic spell.

"I should say the child weighs close to five pounds. If you woke up at three, you've probably lost about two cups of blood. Where's your husband?"

"Theo's parking the car."

"I'm sending you to the labor room. The nurse will tell him where you've gone."

A young woman in green carrying a clipboard pushed the stretcher, creaky as a baggage cart, to the elevator. The doors hushed themselves closed, trapping them both in the harsh light. Overhead, in hundreds of rooms, the sick were sleeping or tossing or crying out for pain in limbs that weren't there and nerves that were.

"When are you due?"

"Not for six weeks yet."

The girl said nothing more, but when the elevator lurched and stopped, she guided the stretcher through the doors, and turned into a small room, monastically white, furnished with a wall clock, a bed, and a nightstand which held a kidney basin. Handing Erica a shapeless white gown, she began flipping briskly through the papers on the clipboard.

"Let's see—you're Doctor Sloane's patient, and he doesn't believe in prepping." She reached into the top drawer of the nightstand, pulled out a razor and a syringe, and dropped them into her pocket.

"Age?"

"Twenty-one and a half."

Erica pulled off her dress, slipped the gown around herself and groped for the ties, but found none.

"Insurance?"

"I don't know. My father has some."

"Husband's occupation?"

Erica thought about that one, for there were any number of appropriate responses, all of them true. On Monday, Wednesday, and Friday, Theo cleans fossils for the owner of the Fur 'n Feather Pet Shop. On Tuesday and Thursday he sweeps out the cages for a nation of gerbils and myna birds. On Saturdays he makes frames at the New World Gallery for other people's paintings.

"Sculpt-or," she said, very clearly. "He's studying to be a sculptor."

"Student," murmured the nurse, writing it down.

Erica was just settling down among the sheets, when her

stomach sucked into a hard knot. The intensity of the pain astonished her. She grabbed for the kidney basin, held it cool against her cheek, and threw up. How they anticipated everything here, she thought. Knowing that she would grope for such a pan, they curved it to fit her cheek. Her teeth chattered as if they had muscles of their own, and her whole body quaked.

Hands urged her body to turn; she felt a faint chill as the back of her gown fell open, but the needle came and went, sly as a thief. And suddenly there was no more pain, only a change of light, like a palpable anticipation of something not yet known.

> *Where is the way where light dwelleth? And as for*
> *darkness, where is the place thereof?*
> *Hath the rain a father? Or who hath begotten the*
> *drops of the dew?*

She repeated it like a charm; it was a gift from Theo. Asking the right questions, he said, was a way of keeping your balance. The first time she came to his place he was asking questions; he'd flunked his geology midterm and was making up an exam to send Professor Leech.

> *Out of whose womb came the ice? And the hoary*
> *frost of heaven, who hath engendered it?*

> Circle one: Mother Leech
> Mother Courage.
> Jack Frost.
> Admiral Byrd.
> YAWEH

"What's YAWEH?" asked Erica.

"The secret name of the living God."

"If it's secret, how come you know it?"

"Because I am a student of the divine alphabet."

He had waved conspicuously but casually at the books that cluttered his desk. Erica had never seen so many library books in one place, except in the library. She fingered the biggest one, bound in disintegrating leather. *The All-Wise Doorkeeper, Exhibiting to all who enter, the Science of Things Above and Things Below.* A postcard fell out, typed with frightening accuracy:

You have three hundred and two books charged to your name. Please return or renew them before the end of the term. Books must be brought in to be renewed.

"There's a lovely sunset going on," said Theo, "for anyone sitting on the holy mountain."

Sitting on the fire escape, they could hear the bells of Saint Stanislaus and look across the vacant lot into the kitchen of Rumpus Mitchell's Hot Spot, and watch the greenhorn busboys sneaking out for a smoke among the garbage pails. Sometimes, huge, fiery-haired Rumpus Mitchell would come out to meet his wife, who was always just arriving from California with Rumpus Mitchell's little boy at her side, and a little girl of uncertain origin still in her arms. The boy would lean against his father's great belly and the little girl would lie with her cheek on his shoulder while he sang,

> Sinner, don't you waste that Sunday.
> Sinner, don't you waste that Sunday.
> The people keep comin' and the train done gone.

When he was not outside he was inside, harassing the customers. To shy boys who brought their girls for coffee after a movie, he would say solemnly, "Who was that wild-looking chick I saw you with last night?" Erica had once seen him cut a man's necktie off with the breadknife, because he complained that the chili was too hot. The smell of chili flavored the whole block.

"I suppose you're hungry," said Theo.

The kitchen was cluttered with sketches of nudes and cats, and bishops turning themselves into flames. Erica was about to say yes, when she realized he was speaking to the battered orange cat that rubbed up against her legs.

"See if there's some milk in the icebox for Saint Orange Guy."

She opened the door and a slab of ice crashed from the freezer to the floor. On the bottom shelf, an ancient pork chop lay all alone, like a peculiar island.

"There's no milk."

"I wonder if Rumpus Mitchell will give me some fried liver on credit. It builds strong teeth and claws ten different ways."

He opened all the cupboards and peered inside. "All the dishes are dirty. I'll have to eat out."

"You could eat at our house. Mother made a meatloaf."

"No, thanks. I'll run out and get a pecan ring."

"A pecan ring! All you ever eat is pecan rings."

"So? If I get a fresh one, it'll last all day."

He walked her home. All over the city, spring touched the maples with lime-colored blossoms.

"I'll pick you up at nine for the free flicks."

"No, you won't. I have to finish reading *Rasselas* by Monday for my eighteenth-century class."

"So what's *Rasselas?*"

"A novel. Rasselas is the prince of Abyssinia."

"Jesus! What a name!"

"My dad thinks *your* name is funny."

"Oh, no," said Theo. "Mine's a lovely name. It means 'the son of silk and music, the immortal one, the heavenly music-maker.' "

"You told me you couldn't carry a tune."

Theo shook his head.

"I used to play the flute in third grade during arithmetic. It was invisible. The teacher told my parents I was mad."

They stood on her doorstep, unwilling to leave each other. Out of the corner of her eye, Erica saw her father walking up and down the yard, tapping the pear trees that sprayed jets of white flowers into the air. Every fall the pears caught in the lawn mower; one year he had the trees injected to stop the harvest, and the next fall they bore twice as many. He hates anything that bears fruit, said her mother, who loved the trees and the overgrown forsythia and honeysuckle that ran wild in the backyard. Her father had taught chemistry and, according to legend, wrote caustic remarks on freshman bluebooks. At seventy-four, he walked slowly, like a mechanical toy about to run down.

"I'll call you," said Theo.

Her mother came out of the kitchen when she saw him go.

"You could have asked him for dinner. He doesn't have much money, and I don't think he eats very well."

"I did ask him," said Erica.

In the twilight of the dining room, crystal decanters and silver candlesticks gleamed along the sideboard. As a child Erica had laid out whole cities with them when they arrived, along with a grand piano, soon after the death of an aunt whom she had never seen. Most of her father's family she had never seen, and the little daguerreotypes didn't help much, for mildew had eaten away the image of a nose here and a shoulder there, and all the people in them were either children or brides.

"I've hidden the silver under the bookcase in the attic. You won't be afraid to stay alone for a week?"

"I'll be okay."

"Daddy would hate to miss the train trip and the banquet. He's the oldest living graduate of Grand River High School. And the valedictorian."

Her father glanced up from his ear of corn; kernels hung like tears on his cheeks.

"How many in your class?" asked Erica.

"Four," said her father, and sank behind the corn again.

"You can always sleep over at Mrs. Elderfield's place, like you did last year, if you're scared," said her mother.

It was always "Mrs. Elderfield's place," though Mr. Elderfield lived there, too. Mrs. Elderfield had a parakeet which she fed from her own lips at breakfast, holding grains of seed between her teeth. Mr. Elderfield had insomnia and wandered about the house at night in a red plaid bathrobe. At two in the morning he would go out and work on his driveway, which he was paving with bricks; the old widow who lived behind the Elderfield's told everyone he was digging a grave.

"I'll be okay alone."

Her mother lowered her voice.

"Don't forget to lock the door. We have all those Oriental rugs in the living room; someone could just roll them up as easy as pie. Then they could walk out with the color TV; I'm sure it would fit through the back window. I stuck your diamond ring over the curtain rod. They'll never think of looking there, though it would be a whole lot safer if you wore it."

"Oh, Mother, I can't. It looks like an engagement ring."

How quaint! Theo had told her when she wore it with him once to a movie. Engaged to your mother!

"It's a dinner ring. Everyone should have a dinner ring. I had mine made out of Grandma Schautz's diamond earrings."

A comfortable silence settled over the house as the taxi pulled away. Erica went to the kitchen and squeezed herself some orange juice, drummed on the piano for awhile and tried to play a few pieces from her mother's *College Favorites*, the only music in sight. Then, unable to postpone it any longer, she picked up her battered copy of *Rasselas* and curled herself in front of the dark television set to read.

I cannot forbear to flatter myself, that prudence and benevolence will make marriage happy. The general folly of mankind is the cause of general complaint. What can be expected but disappointment and repentance from a choice made in the immaturity of youth, in the ardor of desire, without judgment, without foresight, without inquiry after conformity of opinions, similarity of manners, rectitude of judgment, or purity of sentiment?

Someone had written in the margin: *up yours*. Erica quit reading the text and read the comments. There were two voices: that of the first owner, whose comments ran to obscenities, and that of the second owner, who had underlined all the speeches in red and crossed out the most offensive opinions of the first owner. Far away, the campus carillon chimed eight; she gave a guilty start and brought herself back to the text again.

Such is the common process of marriage. A youth and maiden, meeting by chance or brought together by artifice, exchange glances, reciprocate civilities, go home, and dream of one another. Having little to divert attention or diversify thought, they find themselves uneasy when they are apart and therefore conclude that they shall be happy. They marry, and discover what nothing but voluntary blindness before had concealed; they wear out life in altercations and charge nature with cruelty.

Her mind wandered; ten minutes on half a page! She

thumbed the pages yet to come and felt panicked. By the time
Theo called, she had read five more.

"I'm coming to pick you up for the nine o'clock show."

"I can't go," she moaned. "I have a hundred pages left."

"What have you been doing for the last two hours?"

"Reading."

A sigh breathed lightly through the receiver.

"We might as well have gone to the flicks. Do you want me
to come over?"

She read on, listening for him, yet he did not come. At
midnight, much disappointed, she locked the door, marched upstairs, kicked off her sandals and her skirt, and climbed into her
mother's bed, because it was the only bed in the house with a
soft decadent mattress and two purple eiderdowns. Finding her
mother's book of Bible readings under the pillow, Erica pulled it
out and lay there, listening to the dark till it blossomed into
small cries.

Then she sat up and looked out of the window.

What green birds were these that pressed their masked faces
against the pane? How cold we are! they pleaded, and fluttered
their pale wings. Behind them, the pear blossoms were turning
to snow. Kneeling on the bed, Erica unlocked the window.

I told you, said her mother's voice, not to let anyone in.

But suddenly the bedroom was filled with them, chirping
feverishly, and already they looked larger than they had outside,
and now they were flying up and down the stairs.

Out! Shouted Erica, clapping her hands.

How had she failed to notice their fine claws and the tiny
whips they wore under their wings? They poured past her and
flew into the living room, caught the edges of the Oriental rugs in
their beaks, rolled them up smartly, and carried them out of the
window on their backs. The teapots and silver spoons under the
bookcase in the attic began to rattle and hum, and the birds
hustled them gaily out of the front door, which burst open at
their coming. As the last birds passed her, bearing the color tele-
vision-set like a sedan chair between them, Erica latched the
screen.

That inflamed them; the whips under their wings quivered;

they rushed at the door with fierce faces, some hooded in black feathers like executioners, others masked in scarlet as for a dance. Hastily, she ran to the cellar, slammed the door, and turned the key. Crouched on the top step with her hands over ears, she heard—in spite of herself—vases overturning and drawers spilling to the floor.

Give some folks an inch and they'll take a mile, said her father's voice in her ear.

A pale green wing slipped under the door, groping. Erica backed down the stairs and clambered up on the big laundry tubs.

"Erica!"

A handful of pebbles hit the window by the bed. Pulling her skirt on, she ran downstairs to let him in. Drops of rain gleamed on his hair; his face was shining.

"So how are you, Ice-Maiden?"

She opened her mouth to protest and burst into tears.

"I thought you weren't coming."

"I had to arbitrate in a domestic quarrel. Rumpus Mitchell's wife blew up and wrecked his guitar. He cut her new poncho into shreds." Theo waited for her to stop crying, then he asked, "So what happened?"

"I had a bad dream."

"Why, didn't I promise to come over and guard you?"

She trudged upstairs with Theo behind her, rummaged through the big bureau in her mother's room, pulled out a torn sheet, and handed it to him.

"Some layout!" he observed. "Purple curtains, purple bed, purple rugs—it's a regular brothel!" He thumped the bed like a buyer. "Do you want to be tucked in?"

"Yes," she said.

He tucked the blankets into the mattress so tightly that Erica felt as if she were being swaddled; then he sat down on the edge of the bed.

"If you give me a couple of minutes, I can think of a story."

Once, when she had the flu, her father had come in to tell her a story. *Once there was a little girl who took a walk through a city where everything was falling asleep. The trees curled up their leaves and slept, the dogs dropped down on the sidewalk, and soon the little girl herself fell asleep.* He never came to tell another. That night she had dreamed curious dreams and forgotten them. In the morning, she felt she'd traveled all night in that land.

Now, years later, morning amazed her all over again as sunlight broke over Theo's back. She lifted her head; she could not remember where she was.

The doctor was greasing her stomach and smiling at her astonishment.

"We're going to hear from the unborn," he explained, holding—for her inspection—a microphone which was attached to an amplifier on the nightstand.

Under the sheet she thrashed her legs. Pain ran beside her, as inseparable from her as her shadow. Ah, now she was pulling ahead, but she knew it would cut through the forest and meet her at the next bend in the road.

"Give me something to make me stop hurting."

"You want a spinal injection after all? It will numb you from the chest down, and you won't be able to push the baby out. Fix your eyes on one point. No, not the clock; that only makes time go slower. Forget about time."

He pressed the microphone to her belly and adjusted the dials on the amplifier. Suddenly she heard a loud beating, a rhythmic thudding as from an invisible drummer, that seemed to fill the entire room and rose over the clatter of approaching wheels in the corridor.

"You see, he's still alive," said the doctor quietly.

She clawed her way onto the stretcher and felt herself borne down the hall with the slow majesty of a barge. Brass plaques on the walls passed her at eye level, with the discomforting solemnity of tombstones:

THE GIFT OF MR. AND MRS. LEANDER RICH
IN MEMORY OF HIS FATHER

IN MEMORY OF
DOCTOR JOSEPH O'BRIEN

A GIFT OF THE FAMILY OF
MR. AND MRS. JUDD CARUSO

The stretcher scraped against a small plastic box, quite empty, studded with lights and dials like an electronic reliquary. The legend passed her at eye level:

THIS INCUBATOR WAS DONATED———

Her feet touched bottom. The heavy metal doors swung open and she entered the cool air of the delivery room, where sunlight glanced off metal and glass.

"I'm giving you a shot in case I have to cut," said the doctor. "You won't feel it. If you watch in the mirror, you can see everything for yourself."

A plump woman in green scrubs lifted her onto the table, set her legs into stirrups, and covered her with sheets, as if arming her for a long journey. High in front of her shone the mirror, without reflection, like a child's dream of the sun. The nurse tipped it this way and that. Suddenly it caught someone: a man holding a syringe in one hand and an oxygen mask in the other. So strong a fear gripped Erica that she twisted her head back to see him.

"That's Doctor Wong, our anesthetist," said the nurse pleasantly. "We're required to have him here for emergencies."

"My glasses," called Erica. "Where are they?"

"Right here. I'll put them on your nose."

As the blur of equipment splintered into bewildering and exact detail, the masks and gowns warned her of sinister disguises. Nothing showed her an honest face. The anesthetist waited just out of sight; she could hear him padding about behind her.

"Push," urged the doctor. "One long push is worth ten short ones. Round your shoulders. Put your chin down."

Closing her eyes, she gathered her strength into a noose around the pain that had so long tormented her and pulled it tight. In the silence, the doctor's scissors snipped away at her flesh as if he were fashioning her from paper.

She gasped, and the nurse caught her head, and in that instant she felt something leave her and heard a faint watery cry.

He lay on her stomach, warm, wet, and crowned with blood. His skin flushed purple, white curds smeared the creases of his arms and legs, his eyes were cat-slits, his enormous mouth slobbered mucus.

"Into the world we come, pissing and crying," sang the doctor.

A wild joy filled her; her arms moved restlessly under the sheets, trying to find their way out, but already he was clamping and cutting the cord that joined her to this secret she had carried so long, and the nurse was lifting the child up and carrying him away.

"The bassinets used to be made of wood," she observed. "I like the clear plastic ones better. You can see through the sides." And then, after a pause, "I think he favors his dad."

Oh, when did he happen? In her mother's bed, among the Bible verses and the purple eiderdowns? Or that night they'd walked back from the library and stopped at the park to play in the sandbox—was he created to the comfortable creak of the merry-go-round, emptied of children at that hour, pushed slowly around by the wind? Or that Sunday morning, when they rode the river curled together in the ribbed body of a canoe, while the wild flags snapped and sank under them, but rose again in their wake—did he happen then? Far off, the bells of Saint Stanislaus rang the faithful to worship. It was eleven o'clock. Her mother and father, tired from the train-ride home, were nudging into their pew at Saint John's Lutheran, and waiting for the opening prayer, which her mother knew by heart. Erica could not remember when she stopped saying her prayers. She used to pray before exams, and occasionally for advice, but she never expected an answer. During services, she ticked off the hymns and responses in her head, but came alive during the music and wondered what it would be like to meet God face to face. *All flesh is grass*, murmured the minister darkly. *The Lord have mercy on us.*

Let's get married next Sunday. In the middle of a forest, said Theo.

Erica rolled up her eyes.

You haven't got a job.

So? Behold the lilies of the field. They neither toil nor spin. We'll get jobs on a ship. We'll make love in every hotel in Europe. Then on to Asia. To Australia. There won't be a tree on this planet that doesn't know us, a stone we haven't baptized.

In the shallows before them, a school of carp lifted their finned backs above the water, splashing and leaping. Though the canoe caught them in its shadow, they heard and saw nothing but their own dance.

"Here's your son. Isn't he beautiful?" exclaimed the nurse. "He's a real peewee."

The head poking out of the swaddling blanket was that of a tiny old man.

"How much does he weigh?"

"Five pounds, two ounces. He's big for a preemie. I shouldn't think he'd need the incubator."

Through fear, through the craft of time and the cunning of pain she had almost lost him. The doctor, sewing her up like a turkey, had stopped singing. She saw herself leaving her inheritance for thieves to thrive on and setting out with the baby curled like a flower against her heart.

"Now we must get up," buzzed a voice in her ear. "Hang on to me. Don't look at the floor."

What time was it? She looked for the clock, but it was gone. The room was new; the sun stained everything in it with the rich glaze of twilight.

Clinging to the nurse, she allowed herself to be eased out of bed, and the new seams in her flesh stretched and seared her. The nurse was short, with thick glasses and a little sign on her breast that read *Miss Trout* like a nameplate on a desk. Over her shoulder, Erica saw a girl sitting up in bed, cradling a telephone receiver under her chin, and arranging a vast collection of cosmetic jars on the tray that swung from a stand across her bed.

"I'm little," said the nurse, setting Erica on a chair, "but I'm strong. You got some flowers while you were asleep."

She pointed: on the nightstand, between the bedpan and the kidney basin, stood a fat ceramic lamb rolling its eyes and spraying blue daisies from its head. The nurse picked up the card propped at the base, and read, "For that very special baby boy. Love, Mother."

"Did Ron tell you? He has blond lashes and eyebrows," cooed the girl in a singsong voice, pinching a clamp the size of a tooth extractor on her left eyelashes. "His nose is straightening out today. It looked so smashed. There was a little problem with his shoulder. It got stuck."

"Come," said the nurse. "I've made your bed."

How smooth and cool the sheets felt! When the nurse bustled out of the room, Erica felt herself becoming invisible, as if she were returning from the dead and had lost her foothold among the living. The girl's conversation seemed of immense importance, a token of the awful innocence of being alive.

"Today I had someone else's menu. It was lousy. Tomorrow I choose my own. Bring me a milkshake, love. A lemon one."

She hung up, and the eyelash curler clattered to the floor. Only when she climbed out of bed to pick it up, did Erica notice how tiny she was, no taller than a twelve-year-old child, with a round face and a large stomach that hung over her black bikini pajama bottoms. Erica moved her legs restlessly and the girl smiled.

"I'm Tina. You had the baby that came a month early, right?"

"Six weeks," corrected Erica.

"Six weeks! Well, better six weeks early than six weeks late. Two days over your due date, and you feel like you've been pregnant forever."

She worked her way into bed again and gave a curious little sigh.

"I got flowers with my first one, too. Yellow roses in a musical pram. We can't have anymore; we only have two bedrooms in the trailer. Does the smell of nail polish bother you?"

"No," lied Erica. "I like it."

"Thank Heaven! My mother used to send my brother and me outside when she did her nails. In the winter it was awful, sitting out on the patio in our snowsuits."

Outside in the parking lot, doors slammed and voices drifted up through the window. Only later when the telephone woke her, did she discover that she'd slept through the visiting hours, and Theo had come, waited outside in the hall, and gone home again.

The line buzzed ominously. Her mother's voice sounded stretched and faint, as if she were speaking under water.

"How's the baby?"

"All right, I guess. He weighed five, two."

Her mother clucked.

"My first one came two months early. I even heard him cry. I suppose nowadays they could have saved him. For heaven's sake, don't forget to boil everything. I used to boil all your toys till they warped right up. What did the flowers look like?"

"Blue daisies."

"I told them roses. I've found a woman to help you. A trained nurse, so I'm pretty sure she's sterile." And then, a little hesitantly, "I've ordered you a sterilizer from Penney's. You didn't say anything about having one. You can't be too clean around a new baby. Minnie read in the paper that lots of people have parasites in their eyebrows. She's been washing hers every day. Just a minute. Daddy's coming."

"How is he?"

"About the same. He fell down again while I was going to the bathroom. One minute he's watching 'What's my line?' and the next minute he's on the floor. I wasn't gone more than sixty seconds. 'Al,' I tell him, 'When you want to get out of your chair, call me,' but he always forgets. Sometimes I tie him in with the clothesline. Mrs. Elderfield offered to watch him while I'm in church. Last night I put the chest of drawers against his bed, and even then he got out. But when he tries to move everything, I hear him and I get up."

The phone went silent, except for the sound of scraping and breathing. Then a high voice whisked over the line.

"Hello."

"Hello, Daddy? How does it feel to have a new grandson?"

"What?"

"I said you have a new grandson."

"I can't hear you."

"A baby!" She shouted.

"What?"

She gripped the receiver in despair; she could hear him listening eagerly.

"I can't hear you." He sounded genuinely sad. "I'm so sorry. I just can't hear you."

"Erica, how are you feeling?" exclaimed her mother's voice.

"Better now."

"That's nice. Oh, isn't it wonderful how once you see the baby you forget all the pain?"

As Erica hung up, the nurse appeared with a tray of paper cups.

"This is your sleeping pill. If your stitches bother you, you may have a pain pill also."

What time was it?

Someone was drilling a hole in her sleep.

In the darkness she raised her head off the pillow. Far away, she heard the shrill cries of the babies, like tree-frogs on a summer night. Steps drew near and a policeman strolled past the doorway, his gun gleaming on his hip.

Now the cries mingled with the clatter of wheels. Tina stirred in the next bed. The nurses swept by, pushing trains of bassinets in front of them. The whole floor was a wailing corridor peopled with angels harvesting the newborn.

"Anapolous?" asked the young nurse in the doorway.

"Right here!" said Tina eagerly.

"Svenson?"

Erica raised her hand as if she were going to recite. The nurse snapped on the nightlight, rolled a bassinet against the bed, and lifted the baby into Erica's arms. His swaddling blanket held him stiff, like upholstery.

"Here's his bottle. You'll be feeding him glucose and water till your milk comes in. Don't worry if he spits up. You're trying to clear the mucus out of him."

Silence settled itself like a wing over the corridor. Erica took the bottle and touched it to the baby's lips, which sucked once, twice, and stopped. Behind the cat-slit eyelids, his pupils lay hidden, like agates at the mouth of a cave.

Who are you?

For his face was as blank as a fine plaster mask, without lines, without eyebrows, without eyelashes. Veins laid their complex waterways just under the skin on the top of his head, where the soft spot pulsed in the star-shaped absence of bone.

She pushed the bottle against his lips, but he slept on, his fine breath brushing her hand, and she pushed him up against her shoulder the way she had seen other women do. His head lopped forward and struck her collarbone, and he let out a quick cry, and Erica propped him in her arms and gave herself up to admiring him, till the nurse returned.

"How are you coming?"

"He fell asleep."

"You mustn't let him fall asleep. Snap his feet. Like this." As she unbound the swaddlings, his thin legs drew away like the amorphous flesh of a sea anemone. He cracked open his eyes and his arms stroked the air slowly and tenderly, as if he were feeling for the tides that had long since pulled out, trying to find the current that would take him home.

"I'll be back. See if you can get him to drink something."

"Five fingers, five toes. You beautiful little thing," sang Tina, and added, glancing at Erica, "My husband was born with six toes on his left foot. A club foot it was. So that's the first thing I asked: How many fingers? How many toes? Isn't it funny, all the boys I dated were six feet tall, and I married a guy five foot six with a club foot. It was a blind date. He came for me on his motorcycle."

Thunder muttered on the horizon. Outside, in hundreds of trees, squirrels were scurrying for shelter, foxes and moles were burrowing into their holes, and fawns were folding their matchstick legs under them. Erica shivered. Tina's voice was as warm as a lullaby.

"My little boy asks me, Where do the birds go when it rains? Why does Daddy have to go to work? All day long, it's why, why, why."

When the nurse returned, Erica put the baby in her outstretched hands and watched her tuck him back into the bassinet, where he lay like merchandise under the label above his head.

Baby Svenson. Five pounds two.

And then, in scrolled letters below,

This is God's gift to you.

At nine the next morning, Theo peered into the room, holding a tumbler of wild honeysuckle.

"I tried to come earlier, but you were asleep. And last night the corridor was chained off. The nurse said it was feeding time. Jesus, I told her, what is this, a zoo?"

"Did you hand out candy hearts on Main Street?"

"I tried. Nobody cares any more these days. I did all your crazy errands."

He sat down on the edge of the bed, searched his pockets, and brought forth a handful of cornflakes and a crumpled list. Erica recognized her own handwriting, but it looked strange to her, like a letter coming back because of an incomplete address.

"I got the undershirts, the diapers, the fruit juice, and the Borax. Also some loose catnip so Saint Orange Guy can roll his own mice. And I brought your watch."

As he slipped it on her wrist over the plastic bracelet which the hospital had put on her, she stared, fascinated, at the items and tasks she herself had numbered; they seemed steps in the irrelevant ritual of a dead faith. And the watch, ticking fast and small, so that not one hour should escape—what were those hours but a purpose laid upon things which run their course untouched by numbers and twenty-four-karat hands?

The hands tell her it is eleven o'clock. Her mother is nudging into her pew. *Sinner, don't you waste that Sunday!* Her father is home, tied to his chair, dozing in front of the television under the watchful eye of Mrs. Elderfield. In the hospital, visitors are arriving; the new mothers have put on their best nightgowns and their brightest robes, and leaning proudly on their husbands, they take their first painful, uncertain steps down the hall to the nursery, where they stand in front of the glass window and search the rows of bassinets for their child.

Here is the big blonde woman who wanted a boy and just had her sixth daughter, and the black girl who had a boy and walks about in a black satin robe that fits so tightly over her protruding stomach that she seems to be carrying him still, and when Erica meets them in front of the window, they chatter like old friends about the length of labor and whether the milk is coming in, and the husbands listen, bewildered both at the intimacy and the new concerns.

Theo presses his face to the glass.

"What if he grew wings?"

Erica looks at him, puzzled.

"What do you mean, wings?"

"He could be the first man on earth to be born with wings. We'd have to learn how to take care of them. We couldn't get them wet, or they'd lose their natural oils. Of course he couldn't fly right away, but we'd teach him to zip around. And we'd fold them up for him at night. 'Oh, Doctor Spock, my little boy has broken his wing, what should I do?' We'll walk him on a string, like a balloon."

And then he said, very seriously,

"When we're pushing eighty, he can fly us around on his back."

She nods, she is beginning to understand. Distance from the world has fallen across her, as if she breathed a different air and moved in a different space; the distance that separates those who sleep at night from those who are most alive during those hours and hear the first birds calling each other awake while the sky is still dark.

She sleeps with her feet curled against her belly, the way the child slept all the months she carried him, and she feels her body becoming his body, her face becoming open and small like his face. The folds in the sheet show her grotesque mouths, dwarfs playing invisible flutes, the running of foxes and the folded wings of birds flying through that forest she has not visited since her own childhood, lying awake in her crib, watching the shadows from the cars outside unleash wings and mouths and paws.

And now, heavy-eyed with sleeplessness, she sees them keep watch around her bed; kindly rabbits and comfy bears, offering her their backs to ride as in the old days, before she learned to tell time.

By the end of the second day, her hearing has grown sharper and her sight keener. Before the babies are rolled out of the nursery, she feels their crying like an ache in her back. Every bird, every door cries with a child's cry, and she can pick out of all those sounds under the stars the one cry which she alone can answer. Outside, plans for the rape and salvation of the earth are going forward; factories rise up, and whole cities crumble away on command. Theo is performing all those tasks she laid on him before she realized that nothing is ever finished. With the baby resting against her shoulder, she is moving backward, away from the sun. Green birds turn their masked faces east and fly ahead of her, *this way! this way! Make way for the son of silk and music, the immortal one, the heavenly music maker.*

Behind the letters of the divine alphabet there is one face, just as behind every child's face lies the face of its father. How then, can she tell her loss to the young nurse who that evening wheels in only one bassinet and says, "Doctor Sloane has your little boy in the incubator so he can keep a close watch on his breathing. He'll be in to speak with you tonight."

Before the nurse can stop her, she is running down the corridor in her nightgown. The incubator has been moved into the nursery. How many times have she and Theo remarked with mild interest on that delicate machine, sitting empty in the corridor? Pressing her face against the window, she sees the child's belly heaving up and down inside. He lies in the intestines of an electronic bogeyman surrounded by more tubes than she can imagine uses for. One tube is taped to his nose, another to his arm, and they alone connect him to the cold air and harsh water of the new world. His belly flutters and grows still, heaves hard and grows still, like the body of a wounded bird.

So she arrives at last, and stands at the foot of the holy mountain, crying out to the Living God of Whom she has heard all her life.

"What's it all worth, Lord? Our bodies tear and our hearts

break. You think anybody would choose this life if they could avoid it?"

But there in front of her the babies are wailing to be fed and even now, in millions of men and women all over the planet, blood is gathering and preparing once again to shape those frail bodies. The sun is crossing the sky and calling all green things to come forth, the pear trees drop their fruit, and the field sends up sumac and wild honeysuckle. All flesh is grass, cry the birds, and all flesh is beautiful. And breaking free from the flesh of their parents come the children, who have already forgiven them.

The Life of a Famous Man

Holding her suitcase very tightly, she stood on her toes and kissed Theo's ear and let him lift their son into her arms, then turned around and realized everyone else had already boarded long ago. A long long time ago. She turned and ran past the empty check-out desk and the unguarded passenger door, and skimmed across the dark airfield to the plane, which blinked and hummed, a huge comic animal, striped black down one side like a skunk's dream of flight. How cold, how dark the air was turning! She climbed up the steps, ducked her head, and hugging the child against her, stepped into the body of the plane, somewhere near its eyes. A stewardess, in a camel's hair mini-dress, slammed the door behind her.

Inside, men and women were reading, adjusting their seats, squeezing their coats into the overhead racks. Erica worked her way down the aisle to a window seat over the wing. Nestling her suitcase under her, she buckled her safety belt, settled the sleeping child on her lap, and pressed her face to the pane of glass, very small, one vertebra among a hundred. Far away, behind a huge plate-glass window, the land people waved like observers at an aquarium.

The motor rumbled alive; there was a smell of shoepolish and gasoline as the plane turned, gathered its bulk, and headed for the broad road to heaven. Ahead of them, the airstrip was lit with tiny blue lights like cornflowers, bright on the bare field.

Out of the corner of her eye Erica noticed a woman tenderly fluffing her hair. That, and the curve of Anatole's cheek against her shoulder, and the hands waving on the far side of the darkness crystallized and crushed her, as suddenly the earth seemed to split in two and she felt herself torn from him, tossed high, and snuffed out, over the fiery body of the plane that carried her. She did not know what sky or what field received them.

With a cry she awoke. Or was it the child who cried out? Beside her, Theo slept on. Groping for her glasses, she squinted at the clock. The hands pointed to seven; the plane left Albany at nine. The drive to the airport took two hours.

"Get up!" she shouted, jumping out of bed. A heap of books crashed to the floor. Already she saw her mother's disappointed face in the lobby of the air terminal in Detroit. And her father—would he be disappointed?

Theo opened one eye.

"The plane will be twenty minutes late," he said, as if he had learned this in his sleep.

Anatole was lying on his stomach in his crib, head up like a turtle, leaning on his elbows, babbling at the tulips she'd cut from the seed catalogues and pasted on his crib. His thin blonde hair lay in distinct lines across his scalp, like sea grass combed flat by the water. Not a hair out of place, she told Theo. Hair that only a mother could see, Theo told Erica.

She laid the child on the rug and wrestled him into his new blue overalls while the cold air mottled his skin, making all the veins prickle alive underneath. Would he take care of her when she got as old as her father? She could not imagine herself as old as her father, or this child coming to see her on her eightieth birthday—a finely carved edifice toppled by a stroke.

"My boon companion," said Theo, standing in the doorway, hands slouched over the waist of his levis, "Are you almost ready?"

Now she found herself once more at the passenger gate, kissing Theo's lean bristly cheek and taking Anatole from him, yet not exactly as she had dreamed it. In the dream—in all her dreams—she was younger and smaller and always alone, wearing the brown knee socks and red tam she still wore, and the green wool cape she'd lost long ago in the Cleveland bus station. And everything was dead quiet, as if someone had forgotten to turn on the sound.

"Am I crazy? I never came home for his birthday before. He has to have a stroke to get me home."

Theo pulled the sleeve of his army jacket out of Anatole's mouth.

"He's an old man. You don't need any other reason to go."

"Maybe," she whispered, "he won't even know who I am."

She found a seat next to a portly man with white hair who was gazing earnestly out of the window. The stewardess bobbed down the aisle with an armful of telephone books in kodak-yellow plastic covers.

"Would you like a magazine, sir?"

He closed his beat-up paperback copy of *How to Sell Yourself* but kept one finger at his place.

"What have you got?"

"We have *International Business, Business Week, International Travel*—"

Erica laughed. Cuddled on her lap, Anatole cracked open his eyes and sucked his thumb hard; there was egg, she noticed, on the cuff of his new sweater. The man looked at them both, puzzled.

"I don't believe I'll take any, thank you," he said, and opened his book to a chapter near the end: Failure is Death.

"How old is he?" cooed the stewardess.

"A year and a half" said Erica. "Going home for his grandpa's eightieth birthday," she added, feeling it was expected of her, and as she said it her father sounded oddly like a legend, not merely old, but ancient. He was fifty-five when Erica was born, yet when she was five and going to school that first fall day, he walked so fast that she could not keep up with him. Every morning, after the news, her father turned up the radio in his room so that Erica could hear Uncle Buster, who at eight-thirty turned his magic eye on boys and girls, hurrying to dress for school all over America. *This morning it looks like the boys might win! I see a little girl in Oklahoma who isn't even out of bed. Now the girls are ahead: I see a boy in Illinois who can't even tie his shoes!* Erica did not like the magic eye and always got dressed in the closet.

Several years later she thought she heard that voice when she lifted her head to look at the clock during a spelling test. *I see a little girl in Detroit who can only spell half the words.* Who, though Erica, could that be? She herself studied every afternoon for the sheer joy of it, walking over to the chemistry building and clutching her books as she climbed the dingy stairs to her father's office. Her father sat at a desk strewn with letters, calendars, photographs, and fossils, and she breathed in the strong clean smell from the adjoining lab. On the bookcase which reached nearly to the ceiling sat a white owl, the pet of a graduate student.

"Daddy, it's me."

He swiveled around and smiled.

Well, you can sit here if you want to study. I was just going to finish up some work in the lab. What's this—a book on bees?"

He flipped through it curiously.

"I'm earning the beekeeper's badge in Girl Scouts."

"But you've never kept any bees."

"I don't have to. I only have to give a report."

"I didn't know you were interested in bees."

She unloaded the rest of her books and pushed his papers aside.

"It's the first badge in the book. I want to earn them all, alphabetically."

As she read, munching on the sesame bars he kept for her in the top drawer, the radio in the lab buzzed the news. German troops were retreating across Poland. Outside, the maple leaves bobbed and washed and scattered the clear October sky. The sound of her father's footsteps was as comforting as a heartbeat. Now her mother said that he could not even stand up without a walker.

What was a walker?

When Erica called home, her mother would tie Daddy to the chair by the downstairs telephone, then run upstairs to the bedroom extension. He loved to listen in, though he never spoke much, and he couldn't hear well at all.

"How's Minnie?"

"Nutty as always. Ever since she moved in with us, she wants to take us to that health resort in Miami."

"That would be nice."

"But she wants to go by taxi, so we won't meet any hijackers. Did I tell you about her retirement dinner? The other teachers got together and gave her a bicycle."

They would chatter about Anatole and about Theo's new job as a monkey-nurse for the Zoology Department and how somebody had promised to come from a big gallery and look at his new piece—a galaxy of one hundred moons cut from old fenders—and hadn't shown up, and sometimes Erica could hear Daddy breathing, and then she remembered she wanted to talk about *him*. So after awhile her mother would say loudly,

"Nice talking to you, Erica. Good*bye*."

Adding in a low whisper, "It's not a real goodbye. Don't hang up, Erica."

Then in a loud voice again, "Good*bye*. You can hang up now, Daddy."

Sometimes he wouldn't hang up but would linger on, hoping to hear a little more, till Aunt Minnie came and helped him to his chair in front of the television.

The plane rolled forward, creaking softly, as if someone were pulling it by a string. Globes of light bubbled across Anatole's closed eyes. For an instant the machine hung back, then it gave a roar and charged. The child awoke with a cry and Erica lurched forward and grabbed him and clenched the armrest. All at once they were leaving the earth, it was angling away under them, and already the trees looked small and new. The man put away his book.

"Punkins down there," he observed, wagging his head at Anatole, who stopped crying and leaned toward the window to look. Below them lay the gold tarnish of the maples and the monopoly board of human ambition, each field as straight as if plotted there at the beginning of time.

"Will you look at those trees!" he exclaimed.

"Where are you from?" asked Erica curiously.

"I was born in Buffalo. Ever ride the old Wolverine that

run from Buffalo to Detroit? I'm sorry to see 'em take that train off."

Sun burnished the hair that shone gold on his wrists, beyond the white cuffs. Had her father looked like this when he traveled to give lectures? She always gave him socks and handkerchiefs for his birthday, and he always left them in expensive hotels all over America. And when he came home at night—it was always night when he came home—she would stand by his suitcase, which lay open on his bed, and wait to plunder the silken pockets for the miniature bars of soap stamped with Statler or Ritz. Sometimes he remembered to ask the desk clerk for matchbooks, from which he removed the matches, for he did not smoke. She had, at the height of her collection, over a hundred matchcovers and forty bars of soap which she could never bring herself to use, because having forty of them was more important than being clean.

And later he would bring out his slides, mostly of banquet tables where other chemistry teachers sat before water glasses and chrysanthemums. What was chemistry? She did not know. Not till she was sixteen did she understand that her father was well known to many who would never meet him. That summer, when her mother left for Coronna to see Grandfather through the last months of his life, Erica kept house for her father. She cooked great pots of squash and corn, tomatoes and Brussels sprouts, as she had seen her mother do, for he ate no meat, and she learned to shop at small expensive stores for the delicacies she knew would please him—pomegranates, mangos, and avacados. Evenings she sat at his desk in the sun parlor and typed his letters, mostly to young men in India and Japan who wrote— Honorable Professor!—begging the honor of studying with him. He stood behind her chair, leafing through the day's mail and dictating replies.

Sirs, I enclose two dollars. Please renew my subscription to the letters of Nostradamus.

She ended the sentence, but he did not bend over to sign.

"Erica, have you ever read the letters of Nostradamus?"

"Never heard of him," said Erica. "Who is he?"

"A prophet. Born in the sixteenth century. There's a medium in California who gets prophecies from him. Your mother doesn't believe a word, but maybe you'd like to read through them."

From the desk drawer he pulled out a package of mimeographed sheets and put them into her hand. She took them cautiously, as if they might burn her.

"What does he say will happen?"

"He predicts a great explosion on the West Coast, possibly an invasion."

After he had turned off the lights and she lay in bed waiting for sleep, she heard the loud whisperings of his prayers from the next room, and listening hard, she caught the sound of her own name.

A man's voice filled the cabin with the information that they were flying at thirty thousand feet. Yet it seemed to Erica that they were standing still, that nothing in this country was moving and nothing would ever change. Far across the shining pasture of clouds stood a farmhouse in an orchard, bleached white as in a negative, for all that showed her a dark face on earth gave her a light one here.

Fasten your seatbelts, please, flashed the sign over the aisle, and she tightened her grasp on Anatole, who was beginning to squirm on her lap.

"There will be a twenty-minute delay," crackled the pilot's voice, "due to fog in Buffalo."

But beyond the window, the sky dazzled her and hurt her eyes: a floor of clouds, inflated with light, stretched for miles in every direction.

"Why is it so nice up here and so bad down there?" asked a child's voice behind her.

"The weather," said a woman's voice, "is on *earth.*"

Two hours later they plunged into a gray rain and touched down in Detroit.

From the passenger's entrance, she could see her mother standing behind the lobby railing. In her bulky plaid coat and babushka, she looked like a peasant woman around whom chic young girls eddied and vanished. How round her face looked under the pincurl bangs springing from under her scarf. Erica had worn scarves as a child, and curls—wetted every morning and spun around her mother's fingers. In the winter they always froze on the way to school and wept down the back of her dress all morning.

"I'm here!" called Erica.

"*Aw*," cooed her mother, reaching out to kiss Anatole's sweetly indifferent cheek, "what a little skeezix!"

They all three collided in an awkward embrace.

"You're too thin," said her mother, pulling back. "Have you been dieting again? Where's your suitcase?"

"I'm carrying it. This—here."

She pointed to the flightbag over her shoulder. Her mother shook her head, the way she'd shaken it the last time Erica came home, with her best taffeta dress mashed into her bookbag.

"How's Daddy?"

"Very quiet," said her mother. They walked toward the main exit across acres of light, that filled the terminal—for all its traffic—with a luminous emptiness. "I don't believe he's said three words today. I had to call off the party. Thought it might be too much for him. But he wanted to come to the airport."

"You mean he's in the car?"

"With Minnie. I could hardly get her to drive out here, she's so afraid of getting polluted."

The cars glittered row upon row, like a vast audience waiting for the curtain to rise. What color was her father's Buick? Erica could not remember, though he had driven her in it often. He had even won a certificate from the Buick Dealer for being the oldest man in the city to have driven nothing but Buicks for the last thirty years, ever since the day he stepped into his La-Salle, braked with the accelerator and flew clean through the garage, bringing down the clothesline in Mrs. Treblecock's yard. Like superman, he walked away whole, attended by little puffs of smoke.

Suddenly she recognized his slouched tweed cap and ran to open the door.

"Daddy! It's me! Happy birthday!"

His face looked furrowed and brown as a walnut and his white hair lay thicker than she had ever seen it. His eyebrows were so black that she drew back with a start. Always he had enjoyed the attentions of the barber, and the ritual of lathering and shaving each morning, of plucking stray hairs from his nose, and annointing his head with oil, so that Erica had never seen any part of him growing wild. She kissed his cheek, freckled and sunken while Anatole bobbed up and down in her arms and reached for the planes that roared overhead.

"He looks pretty foxy, doesn't he?" said Aunt Minnie. She had put on her wig for this expedition, and Erica felt oddly touched. She knelt so that her son was eyeball to eyeball with her father.

"This is Grandpa. Can you say Grandpa?"

"Pa," said the child and stared at him.

"He knows you, Daddy. He carries your picture around at home."

Sitting in the backseat with Anatole on her lap, she touched his lips with her finger, but when she took it away, he went on making airplane noises and pushing his fist through the air over her father's head.

"Remember Sammy Elderfield?" her mother asked suddenly. "They have a new baby. You remember Sammy from second grade?"

"Not very well." She remembered a figure in a blue corduroy jacket but could not make out the face.

"They had a boy. It's a shame about his ears."

"What's wrong with his ears?"

"He has one of Mona's and one of Sammy's. Sammy always had lovely ears. Such awful things can happen—it's a wonder people have children at all."

Anatole leaned his chin on the back of the seat and his fist came to rest behind her father's collar.

"Can you say Minnie?" asked Erica.

"Minnie," said Anatole, peering into her purse and pulling out a blank check scribbled with wilting letters.

"Can you say A?"

He looked at his feet and said nothing.

"Oh, Mother, I taught him through G last night, and he's forgotten everything."

But when the car turned into the driveway, he said in a voice so small that Erica alone heard it:

"A."

At lunch, Erica could not take her eyes off her father, except to watch Anatole. Her father ate at one end of the table, silently spooning up puréed peas, and Anatole ate at the other end in Erica's old highchair, steering with a doughnut. Through the French doors she could see Aunt Minnie on the back porch in slacks and trenchcoat, rummaging among boxes and bags lined up on the sofa.

Her mother shook her head.

"She never sits down anymore, since she got so healthy. She eats only one meal a day, a protein drink."

"A what?"

"A protein drink. I'll make you one, if you like."

Aunt Minnie burst through the back door, clutching half a dozen vitamins to her bosom.

"I got some organic spinach at the market this morning, if anyone wants to try it."

"No thanks. You got to boil up half a pound to get a tablespoon."

"Where do you get all this stuff?" asked Erica.

"Why, there's a health-food salesman who comes around once a week," said her mother. "A young fellow. Isn't he nice, Al?"

The old man nodded, pushed aside the empty dish in front of him and reached for the stewed prunes.

"His hair was beautiful," remarked Minnie. "He told us about a program, guaranteed to help you or your money back. You eat one banana mashed in protein powder for breakfast, six lecithin tablets at each meal, and kelp flakes for dinner. En-Er-Gee Proy-to power. Very spluzy stuff, seven dollars a jar." She held up a small can, labeled with Atlas fully flexed, and glanced at Erica's father, who was leaning forward and straining his arms against the edge of the table. "Think that program is making him any better, Erica?"

"Daddy, stay with us for awhile," pleaded her mother. "You haven't seen Erica for a year."

"I'll miss the kick-off," he said sadly.

Mother sighed.

"Erica, you take one arm. Al, push yourself up."

Though her mother helped to support him, Erica had never before raised such a dead weight. Yet it was he who taught her how to float when she was five, and his hands that let her lie on the surface of the water. *Now just let go. Don't kick.* Later, digging in the sand, she looked up and saw his belly rising far off like an island in the deep water where he floated for hours, as if he were napping in his own bed. Dragonflies paused there and flew on. In the water he took care never to disturb them; on land he took a net and caught them, and the butterflies too, so that Erica could study them and learn their names.

The three of them shuffled toward the television room. Not until she had to guide him did she realize how cluttered her mother's house was. Here in the living room stood Minnie's electric organ with its earphones dangling down the side, and there by the door were the two loveseats upholstered in horse-hair, dreadful to the naked thigh. And her father so hated clut-ter: at the reception after Minnie's first wedding, he had gone round as happily busy as a child, folding up the chairs after each guest who went for a second drink of punch.

As she eased her father into his big leather chair she felt the muscles of her arms tremble. Orange light beamed through the plastic embers in the fireplace and played across her father's shoes. Her mother turned on the television and sat down be-side him.

"We just had the downstairs painted, to the tune of a thou-sand dollars. Looks nice, doesn't it?"

In the old days, when Erica was at home, they didn't bother to repaint anything. When the blue paint started to chip off the bathroom floor, her mother said, "Paint me some flowers to cover it up." So Erica painted white roses around the gray patches on the stone tile, and went on to paint roses around the toilet seat as well. She'll paint on your coffin, warned Minnie. Mother had seen a flowered toilet seat—very posh, said Minnie—for twenty-four dollars, in one of the catalogues she read every evening. She had hundreds of catalogues heaped on the window ledge with her old piano music, back issues of *Fate, Time,* and the *National Geographic,* and some beautifully bound books on the history of witchcraft, which came after her dad started tearing out coupons for free offers. No salesman called—still, you have to watch him, Mother said.

"Who's playing?" asked Erica.

"I don't know," said her father.

It was the half-time of somebody's game. Out poured the band. Ta ra! A man in an absurd fur hat strutted out on the field, silver baton in hand, gold buttons gleaming. Behind him, the whole band was spelling out something very clever, but Erica couldn't read it. Then the camera cruelly discovered five men in business suits, puffing and twirling and squinting under their tasseled beanies.

"We bring you the a-*lum*-ni" shouted the announcer, as static from a storm far off blurred and flattened the five men into a single ruled line, zap zap into rainbow noodles, and back again. "Aren't they *won*-der-ful?"

Her father's head sank onto his chest and his eyes closed. Her mother jumped to her feet.

"Al!" she shouted. "Al!"

He stirred, opened his eyes, and gazed up at her.

"What's the matter?"

The fear slipped out of her face.

"Would you like a glass of cider?"

In the kitchen, her mother was calm again as she hauled the big jug out of the icebox.

"I always find him like that when I go to call him for lunch. He looks sort of pathetic, doesn't he? That's a clean glass on the sink."

What was dirty and what was clean? The telephone on the wall was gray with dust, and grease glazed the stovetop grill. Erica held her father's glass, while her mother poured.

And as the glass filled up and chilled her hand, she saw herself at all the suppertimes of her childhood. *This is WXYZ. It is time for the six o'clock news. It is time for the weather. Fair*

and cloudy tomorrow. Small-craft warnings for Lake Michigan.
Her father's little portable sat beside his plate and opened like a clamshell, to show the crystals lying exquisitely under a sheet of clear amber, like the works of a watch.

Over her father's silence, Erica and her mother chattered, interrupting him for only the most urgent requests.

Pass the to-*ma*-toes, Al, pass the to-*ma*-toes.

Because if you didn't ask, he forgot to pass, and all the dishes stopped at his end of the table, and slowly, absent-mindedly, he finished them all. He would stare at guests as they helped themselves to seconds. There's plenty more in the kitchen, Mother would say. We have a whole bushel of tomatoes. And he would glance round with an innocent smile, and only then would they realize he had not been watching them at all. His eyes were bright as a rabbit's and very sharp, yet he did not see well, and that was why last Christmas, he tripped over Anatole playing on the floor and nearly knocked him into the fire. It was a real fire that year.

When she was little, he carried a pince-nez for reading, and in the evening she watched it inch down the bridge of his nose toward the newspaper—plop!—and waited for him to jam it on again, and to fold up the newspaper and take out his pocket diary.

"Erica, what did I do yesterday?"

"It rained," said Erica, seating herself on the arm of his chair. "And it was hot."

Rain, he wrote, and frowned.

"Did I do anything else?"

"We went downtown to get your new reading glasses."

Looking down his nose he wrote *new glasses*. He was pleased that he did not need glasses for driving. The voice on the car radio that warmed the dark mornings when he drove her to school—how it sparkled with news of the cold weather as she climbed out of the car one morning, knew she was late, and slammed the door on her own coat. And as the car sped into traffic, how small her fists sounded, beating on the closed windows *stop! stop!* But her father was listening to the news and heard nothing; the light turned red and he stopped at the end of the block.

Later he sat on the edge of her bed with a wooden box on his lap and lifted out dark panes of glass which came to life as he held them to the light for her. How could that be? To stay so dark in his hand and to show her nothing, yet when held to the light, to show her a table of ripe melons, dew gleaming on the rinds, and behind them, a bough covered with white blossoms.

What are they? she asked.

Autochrome plates. They'll never fade, he said proudly. He put the box back on the closet shelf. She never tried to take it down herself, for fear she would drop it. Fifteen years later, as she went upstairs, she knew she wouldn't drop it now.

She stood on a chair and peered at the clutter while her hands pushed aside old lampshades, broken cameras, small flowered hats, and velvet-lined boxes shaped to fit brooches long since lost; a gold pocket-watch without face or works, a pair of copperized baby shoes, an American flag, her father's bathing suit.

And here was the Adam's hat he'd bought after ten years of listening to Lowell Thomas—or was it Drew Pearson? He bought it because it could be rolled up, would travel well, and would probably last forever. It came in a plastic tube and looked as shapeless as a gangster's fedora, and her mother hid it in the attic, though he sighed over it for a year.

Behind a half-crocheted blanket, she found the box, as heavy as if it held stones.

Downstairs, she found Anatole hugging the lid of a valentine candy-box between his knees and her father slumped down in his chair, and she could hear her mother stacking the plates in the kitchen.

"Daddy!"

She grabbed his shoulders and shook him, and he opened his eyes, and a huge sense of relief ran through her.

"See what I found, Daddy," she said.

And sitting down beside him, she pulled out a square of glass and held it up to the lamp over his chair. Between her thumb and forefinger stood a dark-haired woman in a salmon-colored Chinese robe turning her back on the camera, to show the dragon embroidered there. She was massive as a caryatid, yet she seemed to hang in empty space.

"Daddy, who is this?"

He squinted at the image in her hand and leaned his head so close to hers that she could hear his breathing, light as a cat's; could very nearly hear his heart.

"I don't know."

"Well, it's a lovely picture."

Suddenly Anatole scrambled up beside them.

"Look, sweetpea."

She pulled out another slide, held it up, and lo, ripe melons swelled deep yellow on a scarlet cloth under a bough covered with dogwood blossoms, and all were charged with the far-off presence of things in a dream.

"Daddy, do you remember when you showed me that one?"

He watched anxiously as she put the glass in its dark slot and it jammed against a postcard which pulled loose and fluttered to the floor. Erica bent and picked it up. Here was a house, but none that she knew. The upper window, diamond-paned, set in half-timbers, stood open to let out a queer procession of figures who seemed to be moving on a potter's wheel: the knight, the emperor, the priest, the angel, the fool; their course as fixed as the hands on the clock-face above them. She turned the card over but there was no message, only the name of the town: *Rothenburg ob der Tauber.*

"What year were you there, Daddy?"

"Twilight," he answered.

"But what year?"

"Why, the porter met us at the dock and put our suitcases on his bicycle and took us to the east gate. A wall runs around the city. There are two gates."

He paused, she reached for the card but he held it firmly.

"We stayed at the Golden Hirsch. They gave us the bridal suite. From the window you could see the orchards. Everything was in blossom."

Erica had not heard her father speak so much in years.

Maybe never. Not to her, anyhow. And even now he seemed to be talking to himself. Anatole began to bounce the heart-lid on the floor, and her father's eyes followed it, up down, up down, like an aged hawk.

"Don't throw that," he whispered.

The child dropped it at once and turned stumbling out of the room.

Not until she went to bed that night did Erica remember she was leaving tomorrow morning. Anatole had pushed his head into her armpit and curled up against her, sucking his thumb. How warm he felt, and how little space he took in her bed! It was the same bed she'd slept in since her fourth birthday, and the familiar skyline of clutter still rose from the top of the bureau, loaded with books, drawings, unmatching knee socks, and velvet headbands. Overhead shone the paper stars that her father had bought; they glowed in the dark. The painter worked half a day with the dictionary propped on the stepladder, open to *constellations—northern hemisphere*, because her father wanted all the stars in their proper positions. Guests who used the room complained the stars kept them awake, but Erica loved them, and Anatole stared quiet and astonished at Orion, the Big Dipper, and the Little Bear, before he fell asleep.

Now the glue was turning brittle and one by one the stars were falling. The first one fell on Theo's head the night he'd walked her home so late after a party that her mother said he might as well sleep in the spare room and go back in the morning. She heard him moving about—clothes dropping to the floor, change rolling under the bed, she closed her eyes, and all at once he was standing before her, as white and naked as a fish.

"I'm Adam," he'd said, and would have said more if they had not both heard the door to her parents' bedroom opening. He vanished with a bound into the closet, and Erica, going to shut her door, found her father, naked and hairy as an ape, eyes tightly shut, shuffling down the dark hall toward the bathroom. The next morning, at breakfast, she saw a tiny star tangled in Theo's hair like a sign of grace.

Anatole's breath moved her hair, and holding him close she

opened her eyes wide. All those accidents, those chance meetings and matings! Extraordinary that out of each generation one had grown up and sent forth his seed, and that this seed should come forth at this time to create *this* child and no other. And then, that each child should survive the difficult journey from the immortal darkness of its beginnings to the cold weather of the world.

Someone was piling another eiderdown over them.

"Mother, what time is it?"

"It's two o'clock. I had to get up for Daddy. He wants to play the radio."

By the time she knew she was awake, her mother was gone. Muffled voices came from her parents' bedroom, and as she listened she felt the sheet under her turn warm and damp. Lifting Anatole in her arms she stumbled out of bed. The bathroom light cut a thin swathe down the hall. Somebody had fed her, nursed her, and changed her for more nights than she could imagine. And when she was as old as her father, maybe somebody would again? She propped the sleeping child on the john, struggled to unfasten the back of his pajamas, and feeling something jab her side, she saw—for the first time—the lid to the valentine box he had smuggled into bed with him.

The sky was white; downstairs, Captain Kangaroo was singing to Anatole who had already escaped his bed. Erica jumped up and ran down the hall shouting,

"Get up! My plane leaves at ten o'clock."

Then she caught sight of her father, dressed in his best suit, perched on the edge of the bathtub, with a silver mirror in one hand and his electric razor in the other. ZZ-ZZZ-ZZ. Her mother was holding him up by his belt and reading the Sunday paper.

"Look, Al, Doctor Drake died. Now you'll be the oldest living alum. With him around you didn't have a chance. He was a hundred and two."

"Mother, my plane leaves—"

"Go downstairs. I got breakfast all ready."

Her father ate alone at the dining-room table—which was set as for a wedding breakfast with cut-glass goblets, brocade napkins, and the best silver—while the waffile iron steamed in the kitchen and her mother heated the maple syrup.

"Mother, I don't have time for breakfast."

"You can't take Anatole on the plane without breakfast. He can eat in front of the TV."

"He won't eat waffles, Mother. All he'll eat are hotdogs and bananas. Where's Minnie?"

"Upstairs, mixing her protein drink."

"I got to pack, Mother. Don't make anything for me."

Her mother pulled out the plug of the waffle iron.

"Erica, let me get you that little rocking chair of yours I saved for Anatole. I got lots of stuff saved for you."

"Oh, Mother, we don't need anymore furniture."

"I got to get rid of things." Over the hiss of water gushing into the dishpan, her voice flowed without interruption. "Minnie brought all her furniture when she moved in, and it gets so we can hardly move. That's her umbrella on the front doorknob. I read in the papers how burglars break the glass and open it from the inside. So we'll hear them knock down the umbrella. The other night I was sure I heard a man in the attic. I went right up and turned the key in the lock, and I haven't opened it since."

Every leavetaking was like this, thought Erica, as she crammed her dirty underwear into the flightbag and rummaged the bedclothes for Anatole's undershirt. Her mother followed her from one task to the next.

"You want a glass of cider, Erica? You want to take that silver candelabrum back with you this time? I can put it in a big box and you can check it on the plane."

Standing in the front hall, ready to go: *how did I get all this stuff? I only brought one small bag.* There was a shoebox of sterling napkin rings, a shopping bag full of towels, and the candelabrum which didn't fit in any box. Her mother had powdered her face so fast that the powder lay in thick pools on her cheeks.

"Al, are you still eating? Hurry up, Erica has to catch a plane. Where's Minnie?"

A general sadness wrinkled across his face. How odd that she was traveling away from him instead of he from her! Always it was she who stood on the platform, holding her mother's hand—goodbye! goodbye! Bring me a present!—while steam frosted the windows, and porters pushed carts on great spoked wheels, loaded with mail bags and suitcases. Standing onstage at her high-school graduation and waiting for her name to be called, she could see her father in the very back row of the auditorium, and she could see the clock on the wall, and now he was putting on his jacket and moving toward the door, hurrying to catch the taxi that would take him to the train. "Wait!" she wanted to shout. "Come back! It'll only be a moment longer! Four more names and it'll be my turn!"

And then, just before she heard her own name, she saw the door close behind him.

"I believe I'll stay here," he said, and his voice was frail as a husk.

Erica leaned over and kissed him, then picked up Anatole. "Wave bye-bye."

But Anatole buried his face in her neck.

"He's forgotten. I'll come home again soon, Daddy." She realized as she said it that he hadn't asked. How dark his face looked, as if a light had burned out somewhere behind his eyes.

"Erica," said her mother, "Minnie is waiting in the car."

The backseat was suddenly full of packages.

"How do you think your dad looks?" asked Minnie, pulling on her gloves.

"About the way Mother described him."

"Thank heaven he eats okay. Anything you put on the table, it just goes. I left a quart of organic prune juice and a cheese-cake on the table yesterday, and he finished them both."

"My God," said Erica.

"You know he never used to eat cheesecake."

The plane was not crowded, and she found a seat for Anatole by the window; they had a whole row to themselves. The smell of the vinyl upholstery made her feel queasy, and when she had fastened Anatole into his seat, she sat back and closed her eyes.

Opening them, she discovered she had come back to the

little house in the orchard in the shining pasture that billowed like endless acres of fresh bread. Suddenly she wanted to walk there so much that indeed she was there, and here before her was a little station-house, weathered to pearl, and there sat her father on the platform, waiting for the train.

"I brought you a present," he said.

In the kindly light of this country he looked younger as he opened his briefcase and shook into her hands a dozen tiny bars of Ivory, Palmolive, and Camay, stamped with *El Camino Real*.

She tucked them carefully into her purse and sat down beside him, for there was no hint of a train. No bell sounded, no leaf stirred.

"When are you coming home?"

"I don't know. They've taken off the train," he said and shook his head sorrowfully. "Also the tracks."

"Oh Daddy, what a shame!"

"I'm real sorry they took off the train. There's no way to get back home."

"What station is this, Daddy? Where are we?"

He looked at her, puzzled.

"You mean you don't know either?"

Together they rose and looked up and down for a sign. There was none. But from the east, a little man on a bicycle was pedaling toward them.

"Your suitcase, Sir?"

"Right here," said her father, and watched anxiously as he strapped it on the handlebars.

She raised her hand to shade her eyes; far off she could see the walls of the city.

"Have a good trip, Daddy."

"I do miss the weather," he said. "I mean, not having any." And then he added, "When are you coming back?"

But before she could answer him, the plane sank into darkness, and she saw the airport twinkling beyond the window. Anatole had fallen asleep with his head on her shoulder. Hoisting him up carefully, so as not to wake him, she grabbed the candelabrum and her flightbag and eased herself into the aisle.

As she walked to the passengers' entrance under the sullen

sky, a fine rain was beginning to fall. She slipped her glasses into her purse, stepped through the last gate, and waited to be known.

"What," cried Theo, "is that thing in your hand?"

"A candleholder. My mother gave me some stuff. I checked the rest of it."

"Can't you go home just once without bringing something back? Wait right here!"

He started to lift Anatole from her, but she shook her head, set the candelabrum at her feet and wrapped her arms around the sleeping child as if he were a life-preserver, kissing his eyes, his nose, his hair, till she realized the men at the ticket-desk were all staring at her. Nobody around her was kissing anyone; they were all scrambling for suitcases. How good he smelled! tasted!

"Look, sweetpea!"

And she held him up to the window as their plane turned solemnly and glided down the runway, faster and faster, then tucked up its wheels and somewhere out of sight changed into a bird and broke through the heavy clouds into morning.